The Ghost Shipment

Geoffrey Robert

First published in 2024 by Geoffrey Robert,
an imprint of Red Piano Limited

This book is dedicated to my parents, Joy and Merv.

ISBN 978-0-473-69228-5 (Paperback)
ISBN 978-0-473-69230-8 (Kindle)
ISBN 978-0-473-69229-2 (Epub)
ISBN 978-0-473-69231-5 (Apple Books)

www.geoffreyrobert.com

About the author

Geoffrey Robert is a New Zealand novelist who writes as he has lived – choosing adventure over security, challenge over routine, David over Goliath. His novels propel readers into thrilling adventures to exotic and unfamiliar places, with everyday characters pitted against powerful vested interests. Each story seasoned with values Aotearoa New Zealand and Kiwis are renowned for: independent, ethical, authentic, edgy. And fun.

Through travel and work as a journalist, political press secretary, communications director and volunteer, Geoffrey has witnessed first-hand the swelling disparities in wealth and influence at the root of many of the world's problems. His books explore some of the big issues of our time.

Also by Geoffrey Robert

The Alo Release
Finding Fabi

'No great mind has ever existed without a touch of madness.'

Aristotle

Prologue: The Barrel

He looked around the room. They'd all crashed.

He tipped the contents of the packet onto the table, used his credit card to divide it into two lines, rolled the one-hundred-dollar bill into a tight cylinder.

Poking the makeshift straw up one nostril, closing off the other with his finger, he breathed in gently, moving evenly along the line.

It burned.

He exhaled, slow, steady, then sniffed again to pull it higher.

His eyes watered, his top teeth went numb.

He swapped nostrils, sniffed the other line.

His heart began racing. His breath quickened to keep up as his skin flushed warm and the tingling spread outward from his chest to his fingertips, toes.

The room appeared brighter, sharper.

The breeze through the open doors magnified the crows of a rooster and swept the rush of the river from way down in the valley up, up, up into the room, swirling through the metal fish on the wall until the light blue one out front, leader of the pack, pulsated, shouted to the world, *after me you losers*, let's *do* this.

The keys to the Harley were on the sideboard, beside the GoPro.

The security guard at the Nyalahutan resort would later tell police the young American took both helmets off the handlebars, threw them over the wall, rode off south towards Ubud without turning on the lights.

At Simpang Tohpati, he swung onto the bypass road,

cranked the throttle, tilting and weaving through the light pre-dawn traffic with the wind caressing his face, the *potato-potato-potato-potato* of the engine streaming with nodding palms and the black-white-black-white-black-white curbing into a mesmeric haze.

A CCTV camera mounted near the entrance to the underpass on the edge of Ngurah Rai Airport recorded the Harley bellowing through the tunnel. Another on the second floor of the BNI building captured the American saluting at the statue of a surfer.

He turned off the bypass at Jimbaran, slowing only slightly as the road got bumpier and tree trunks pinched in on both sides. After the roundabout with the archer statue, he started climbing, the Harley emitting harsh, even rasps. He caught glimpses of the massive floodlit Visnu riding a garuda on the hill to his left, before the *crack-crack* glide down to the coast.

A woman dusting inside the Rip Curl store at Padang Padang would later tell police she saw the young American ride up onto the sidewalk beside the gateway to the temple. Another woman cleaning the windows of the ticket booth – closed that time of the morning – said the young tourist greeted her with a polite *salamat pagi* before shuffling down the steps and taking a small plastic bag from his pocket.

He tipped the powder onto the stone, knelt, snorted the lot in one go. Felt it trickle down the back of his throat.

Teeth flared from the smiling gargoyles guarding the entranceway, like embossed words on a book cover. The strokes of a woman sweeping the floor of the small temple rasped full noise.

His chest started pounding as he skipped down the gap in the limestone cliff, keeping his head down so the GoPro wouldn't hit the overhang. The beach was deserted, except for a guy setting up a t-shirt stall under an umbrella.

The vendor would later describe to police how the American stole a surfboard from one of the rental racks and stripped naked before entering the water wearing only the strange *benda* on his head.

He paddled directly out from the beach, cruising through a gnarly rip current, the chill water caressing his balls and the numbness rising to his neck, his chin, teeth. As he approached the takeoff zone, he shut out the thundering of the surf, visualized the epic peak, paddled like fury and dropped into the perfect green barrel.

A photographer trialing a new rectangular fisheye inside the bowl where the tube opened up would later tell police a badass swell from the south-west was hurling eight-foot offshore barrels onto the shallow coral reef. He had a bad feeling the moment the naked dude stood up on the board.

1. Vein for a vein

This was it. The moment that could swing the debate, hand Ped Garland victory in the winner-take-all Florida primary, crack the race for the Republican nomination wide open like a ripe pecan.

Or, if the kid – the Ciph – had screwed up one line of data, harvested the wrong cohort, Lawd have mercy.

The question was: *What was he was going to do – specifically – about drug traffickers?*

He'd gotten this far with his stump lines about the war on drugs failing America's kids. How the careerists in Washington had tried locking people up left and right, then flipped the script and started talking about reducing harm. All the fancy talk made not a lick of difference. Surveys kept showing one in four young adults using illicit drugs. One in four! It was downright outrageous you could line up four young folks against a wall, and only three would be clean. Or lying. The whole drug situation was like a never-ending billboard of what was wrong with America.

The contest for the Republican nomination started with five candidates. Two dropped out after failing to take any delegates in Iowa or New Hampshire. A third bailed after Super Tuesday, leaving Ped sole challenger to the clear frontrunner, Kate Hunter. But despite throwing everything into the cluster of primaries the following week, he'd fallen further behind and was already being written off by some muck slinging journalists.

The question was repeated: *'If you become President, Mr. Garland, what will you do about the traffickers?'*

He took in the wall-to-wall faces, the red and blue of the

CNN banners flanking the auditorium. The spectacles perched on the bridge of his nose glinted in the probing white heat of the spotlights. After a quarter-century of planning, he was about to put everything on the line on the advice of a pimply adolescent with no knowledge of – or interest in – politics.

He adjusted his glasses, pinching the thin metal frames, looked smack-dab at the camera.

'Lethal injection. A vein for a vein.'

*****

Most people had them. Special places in time, nirvana moments stored away in the memory to be dusted off when needed, wanted, or triggered by some random flashback.

Bec Corelli had fewer than most, but this break in Varkala on the south-western coast of India was definitely a candidate. The main beach and the shacks and stores and eateries and bars lining the path above the dramatic cliffs, the bohemian vibe, all-day warmth, heavenly food and sublime sunsets practically ordained relaxation. Rejuvenation.

And anonymity. No-one in this stress-free oblivion knew, or probably cared, that one of the journalists responsible for uncovering the truth about the Cabo virus was sharing their stretch of sand, haggling over the price of a prayer wheel at the Tibetan market, laughing over the names of cocktails at God's Own Country Kitchen.

Varkala had been a welcome tonic for Bec's mental health – an emotional oasis after the turbulence of recent months. Aristotle – the name she used for the color risk scale that helped her self-manage her borderline personality – was behaving.

Green signified the lowest risk of a meltdown. Blue was guarded but manageable. Yellow meant elevated risk. Orange was high, AKA freaking out. Red was bouncing off the walls. Flipped. Unhinged.

Since arriving in Varkala, Bec's vision, her days, her worldview had been drenched by the swaying greens of the palms above the cliffs, the sweeping blues of the Arabian ocean and unbroken Kerala sky.

Part of Bec could stay here forever. But, as the Walrus famously said in *Alice in Wonderland*, *the time had come to talk of many things…*

2. Thousands of hands

'They've given us the five-minute warning sir. Time to get the family out there and seated.'

Ped kissed Patricia on the forehead, squeezed her elbow, hugged their daughter Sophie. As they went through the door, the rumbling from the auditorium rose another notch.

He reached for his jacket, had a last look at the monitors on the wall. It was being called a rout, landslide, shellacking, depending which network you preferred.

Ped had gone into the day trailing by 223 delegates. Victories in the winner-take-all states of Florida and Arizona, plus dominant showings in Illinois and Wyoming gave him 222 of the 255 delegates on offer. More importantly, he'd closed within 28 points of Hunter.

Analysts were crediting his *vein for a vein* line for the turnaround, surprised how much it resonated with voters. What the analysts didn't realize was that Ped had asked the Ciph to dig deep into her data for a game-changer, and she'd identified a latent desire for the death penalty. And that within minutes of him uttering the line in the Florida debate, social media feeds and email accounts of tens of thousands of carefully selected voters had been targeted with messages tailored to trigger a positive reaction with each individual.

Followed in the days since the debate with even more subtle peer-to-peer text messages to hairdressers, teachers, cab drivers, brothers, drinking buddies, priests and others identified through their social media activity as likely to influence the core targets.

'Good to go sir?'

Ped adjusted his tie.

'Let's do it.'

The floor shuddered as he approached the steps to the stage, the announcer struggling to make herself heard.

'Ladies and gentlemen… Thanks to your support, and the support of well over two million Americans in Arizona, Illinois, Wyoming and this great state of Florida, it gives me great pleasure to welcome…'

His name was overwhelmed by a tsunami of screaming and waving that morphed into cries of *Ped, Ped, Ped, Ped* as he swashed through the explosion of red, white, and blue confetti to the podium.

He waited for the volume to subside, then slowly raised his right hand until his index finger was pointing to the ceiling. Thousands of hands rose in unison.

He repeated the gesture with his left, then started pumping both hands as the crowd chanted his campaign slogan: *Straight Up, Straight Up, Straight Up, Straight Up…*

*****

Bec had on a hippie-cut cotton dress with floral print in green and blue, though her anxiety over whether two of the most important guys in her life would hit it off called for something in yellow.

Jay Duggan and Mike Bullard. The man of the moment and the lifelong soulmate. The rough and the diamond. The off-grid nomad and click freak.

Before meeting Jay, the only person on the planet who *got* Bec – other than her father – was Mike. Had done since they'd met as teenagers at Thomas Jefferson Academy in North Carolina. While the fair weathers distanced themselves from the freak, Mike researched borderline personality, encouraging Bec to find ways to self-manage the condition rather than go down the medication route. To *accentuate the positive, eliminate the negative.* Which led Bec to Aristotle.

Through their university days at Chapel Hill, the year travelling together in South-East Asia before their first steps into journalism, Mike treated her as normal, didn't try to heal or rescue her. Just quietly, calmly stuck by her, like a real brother. Through love and hate, attachment and rejection, through blue, yellow, orange, red. And dreams of green.

Jay also ticked most of Bec's boxes. In the short months she'd known the New Zealander, he'd proven himself through the fire, witnessing her in the red and not bailing. Most men reacted to even her nutshell explanation of borderline personality by running for the hills. Jay had simply shrugged his shoulders, said *we're all on the spectrum.* Only fellow travelers could truly understand how much that meant to a person constantly forced to mask her condition, presenting a façade of normality often to the point of exhaustion.

Or how important it was to Bec that these two men in her life got along.

After bumming around Kerala for days that drifted lazily into weeks, Bec and Jay had come down to Trivandrum Airport to meet Mike and take him back to the beach house in Varkala to decide on their next project.

Jay, hanging loose in a tattered Kingfisher singlet, frayed denim shorts and jandals – as New Zealanders liked to call flip flops – had no inhibitions or male ego issues ahead of his first face-to-face with Mike.

The electronic board had noted the arrival of the Emirates flight from JFK and Dubai thirty minutes earlier, which should have given Mike plenty of time to clear customs, immigration and collect his luggage.

Flashes of yellow – the flight information logo, a passing sari, gold bling, duty free bags on the backs of trolleys – were starting to intrude into Bec's vision, before Mike emerged. Dressed for March in Manhattan. Dark woolen coat, dress jeans, leather boots, a smile that beamed as soon as their eyes met.

Once Bec peeled herself from his bear hug, Jay and Mike pre-empted her awkward introduction with a friendly handshake.

'Good to finally meet you in person Mike. Brace yourself for some tropical heat, mate. I'd lose that jacket before the door if I were you.'

The taxi had hardly left the parking lot before Mike was glued to the screen of his phone.

'Can't that wait till we get to the beach?'

'Come on Bec. We've been offline more than four hours.'

'We?'

'The Aristotle channel's getting an average fifty subscribers an hour, guys. Plenty of people are ticking the poll. One in ten putting money where their mouths are. We're talking serious moolah.'

'Thanks to your social media following.'

'That definitely helps. But it's only half the story here Bec. You've still got to have a product people are willing to support, and the reaction to our exposé has been, well, out of this world. There's talk of a Pulitzer.'

The cab turned onto the bypass road, and they headed north-west, parallel to the coast.

Feedback to the virus story, which they'd published under the Aristotle byline, had given Mike and Bec the idea – and confidence – to quit their journalism gigs in New York, go freelance. Mike had spent the last few weeks setting up a YouTube channel that gave subscribers the opportunity to vote for one of ten proposed investigations, and the option to pledge money towards the journalism.

'So what projects are getting the most support?'

'Votes are spread pretty evenly across three or four of our proposals. We can go into that in more detail later. Pledges for specific projects are also evenly spread. The big surprise is the generic pledges.'

Jay turned his head from the front seat.

'Meaning?'

'From people who just want to support us and our journalism – and are happy for us to decide what to investigate.'

Which was cool, Bec thought. One potential downside to letting the public call the shots was the possibility of conflict with funders. All the proposed investigations were international in scope, most with formidable, vested interests.

She gave Mike a gentle nudge.

'So, you think this scheme's gonna work?'

'It better. I've quit the job at Wooster.'

After lunch of red snapper cooked in banana leaves, they walked back to the beach house to make their decision.

They'd narrowed it down to three potential projects: human trafficking, drug trafficking or child labor. All three received strong support from the voting and pledging.

What tipped the balance was an email from Neil Scott, billionaire founder and CEO of a company based in New York that developed software for hospitals. A Google search showed the company was a pioneer in the use of artificial intelligence in healthcare, and one of the principal investors in a new privately-owned supercomputer.

Mr. Scott's son Charlie had died surfing in Bali, while high on cocaine.

For Bec, the clincher was the moving plea by Mr. Scott to uncover the people *ultimately* responsible for his son's death. He wasn't interested in the bottom-feeder who sold the coke to

Charlie; he wanted the Aristotle team to trace the drug back to its source.

Jay indicated he'd be happy tackling any of the shortlisted projects but was attracted by the scale and challenge of Mr. Scott's suggestion. He also 'admired a guy prepared to put his money where his mouth is'. The businessman had pledged $100,000 up front, and a further $500,000 if the Aristotle team could complete the assignment.

The tipping point for Mike, other than the money and exotic appeal of Bali, was the video. Mr. Scott's email came with a police report and witness statements from Denpasar, and a video shot from a Go-Pro attached to Charlie's head. From a journalistic point of view, it was pure gold.

They decided to split up. Mike would return to the States to interview Neil Scott; Bec and Jay would head to Bali.

3. Cathedral Square

'And how do we spell that ma'am?'

'With a Y and two Ss. A L Y S S A.'

Ped was signing campaign t-shirts, hats, yard signs, foreheads, copies of his book – at a volunteers' party in Madison, Wisconsin.

After continuing his momentum with wins in Alaska and Hawaii, he'd ended the day with another resounding victory in Wisconsin, overtaking Hunter as the frontrunner.

His press secretary, Amanda Rosenthal, appeared at his side.

'We need to leave sir, to make it for the interview.'

On the fifteen-minute drive to the Fox affiliate, his campaign manager gave him an update. Volunteers were signing up faster than work could be allocated, speaking requests were flooding in – enough to keep him tongue-tied at breakfast, lunch, and dinner until Christmas.

'More than two-thirds of the invites are from women's groups. They seem smitten.'

Patricia gripped his hand a little tighter, leaned into his shoulder.

'How you gonna keep all these women at bay when you're President, Ped?'

'I think adoring women will be the least of our worries for the next few weeks, sir.'

Amanda had an irritating habit of snuffing out light-hearted moments with cold reality or nagging reminders to *stay on message*.

'Now you're the frontrunner, you can count on being one of

the most scrutinized politicians on the planet. Journalists, bloggers, consultants, Hunter's team, the Dems, they're gonna hunt down every family member, old friend, enemy, cellmate, playmate, college roommate, locker room buddy, old flame you ever…'

'Thanks for the…'

'Not to mention political analysts and armchair shrinks. Those suckers are gonna toothpick over every word in every line of every speech or interview you give.'

'I get the pic…'

'Pick your nose, scratch your ass in public, it'll be on YouTube, WhatsApp, Insta before you can…'

'Thanks Amanda. That's good to know. But what's the lowdown on the interview I've got in about five minutes?'

The press secretary groaned.

'They'll likely go you over *a vein for a vein*. Had this mom on the show this afternoon, wanted to know if her son caught selling weed to his friends in school would get the lethal injection under a Garland presidency.'

'So I'll hem and haw again.'

'You're gonna have to start giving detail on…'

'Didn't appear to ruffle any feathers with the fine folks of this state at the voting booths today, Amanda. Or in Florida or Arizona last week. Any other last nuggets of wisdom you'd like to share?'

'That you're a damn fool wasting time on a local station when you could've had your pick of the networks after today's result.'

Ped had his reason, and *she* was emerging from the entrance to the building as they pulled into the parking lot.

The singer-songwriter known as NatZ grew up in Milwaukee as Natalie Zhang and was already being tipped to add to her bulging trophy cabinet of Grammy awards at the next ceremony still months away. She had 150 million followers on social media, was in the middle of a 20-city tour, and called out as their entourages crossed.

'Congratulations Mr. Garland.'

He turned, feigning surprise.

'Thank you… Natalie.'

Her eyes popped. 'Seriously? Like, you got my real name?'

'Sure thing, Natalie Zhang. I'm a big fan. I often play the chord pattern to *Cathedral Square* when I'm kickin' back, unwinding.'

'The next prez of the United States rocks the keys? That's wicked cool.'

'A baby grand. Some folks would say I *hit* rather than *play* the keys.'

'Awesome. Hey Mr. Garland…'

'Call me Ped.'

'I dig what you're sayin'. Comin' down on the pushers.'

She pointed a thumb back to the studio.

'I just wrapped up this interview with a friend I used to roll with back at Tenor High. She OD'd.'

'That's truly terrible news. I'm so sorry to hear that.'

Natalie sniffed, wiped her nose on her sleeve.

'Yeah. It's seriously messed up. Her folks are totally crushed. Like I said, you're spot on comin' down hard on the pushers.'

'We're late sir.'

Amanda's timing could be unbelievable.

Natalie reached out a hand, resting it on his shoulder.

'I'd like to help Mr… Ped.'

'Well, I appreciate that, Natalie. Look I've gotta go. I'll have Vanessa here, my manager, reach out to your team. See if we can't get together sometime.'

*****

There weren't too many scenarios – outside being shot at and sex – that caused Jay's heart to skip a beat. Queueing in line for immigration was one of them, particularly when the country he was entering had the death penalty. Even if you got to choose to stand or sit in front of the firing squad.

Jay smiled at the *No Corruption* signs on screens above the desks. Consoled himself that the Indonesian officials at Bali's Ngurah Rai International Airport would be preoccupied looking for the sweaty brows and shifty eyes of drug mules and jihadists.

Still, given his history and attitude to laws that deserved to be broken, Jay was relieved when he and Bec cleared customs to reach the furnace of the open-air arrival hall.

The young man smiling above the handwritten *Little Banana Guesthouse* sign introduced himself as Komang.

Jay had spent a few weeks recuperating in Bali after a mission in West Papua several years ago, but it was Bec's first visit to the *Island of the Gods*. She gushed – about the decorated bamboo Penjor poles arching across the roads, the scale and color of the Titi Banda statue of Rama and his band of monkeys, passing glimpses into temple compounds – most of the way to Ubud.

The town was busier than Jay remembered. Komang had raised his eyebrows when Jay asked him to drive through the center to introduce Bec to the island's cultural capital. They soon learnt why. The streets were nose-to-tail SUVs with tinted windows, and motorbikes – helmets optional. Narrow sidewalks pulsed with iPhones, fanny bags, body ink. Boy-men lifted rocks the size of watermelons into bamboo baskets on the back of scooters. A European woman with botox lips and silicon breasts like some ageing porn star jogged past touts wearing traditional udeng headgear shoving pamphlets for dance performances into the hands of tourists outside Puri Saren Agung Palace.

A cultural mishmash. Satay and Starbucks, sambal and selfie

sticks. Jay blamed Julia Roberts, whose movie *Eat, Pray, Love* lured tourists by the busloads to an Ubud already on the downslope of the idyllic curve.

The Little Banana Guesthouse was a couple of miles from the center of town. Komang, a son of the owner, led them through the intricately carved paduraksa gate, explaining how the stone Dwarapala statues on either side welcomed visitors with good intentions, scared away those with bad.

A path with white pebbles inlaid in the shapes of flowers led through the family compound with water trickling over stone fountains and shrines dedicated to various Balinese Hindu gods.

One of Komang's sons steered a remote-controlled plastic car into Bec's leg. Another, wearing a costume that looked like a cross between a frog and a llama, jumped out from behind a statue. Laughter spilled from the kitchen. This was Jay's sort of place.

The guest rooms were at the rear of the property, with views over rice paddies.

At least its clean summed up Bec's impression of their room, which to Jay was decadent compared to some of the dives he'd grown accustomed to in his former life.

'The palm trees are clever. Look at the way the light plays through the green fronds.'

She was looking at an abstract painting on the wall above the bed. All Jay could see was a muddle of colored triangles.

After shedding the clothes they'd worn since India, showering, and enjoying a complimentary tea on the balcony, they picked up the keys to the Honda Megapro Jay had arranged to hire off Komang and went to work.

The resort where Charlie Scott spent the last night of his short life roosted in the jungle overlooking the Ayung River. The entrance was impossible to miss – NYALAHUTAN belted out in ten gold letters beside a life-size stone mural depicting a scene from the Ramayana. Fountains pretending to be waterfalls, marble pathways, lawns clipped like golf greens. Jay felt as out of place as he obviously looked, from the undisguised contempt in the face of the guy behind the desk in the lobby.

Then Bec opened her mouth, reminding Jay of the unlocking power of an American accent.

'We're looking for a place to stay when we come back to Bali next year, and you've been recommended to us.'

'Of course.'

A woman floated into the lobby carrying a silver tray with iced rose waters. Another staffer materialized the moment Bec put her glass down, and guided them beside a crescent-shaped infinity pool wrapped round a restaurant and bar. Paths led down to secluded villas set into the hillside. They recognized the large four-room villa Charlie stayed in from the school of metallic fish flowing over a wall.

The open-air bathroom was three times the size of their entire unit back at the Little Banana. Jay lingered in there with the staffer long enough for Bec to shoot footage on her iPhone of the living area, private pool, and view from the veranda down to the river.

Back in the lobby, Bec made a show of interest in pamphlets for spa treatments – Jay's cue. He leaned towards the front desk clerk.

'Can I have a word in private?' he whispered, pointing his thumb towards Bec, 'so my girlfriend won't hear.'

The man smiled, nodded, and led Jay through a side door.

'The thing is, I'm going to propose to my girlfriend tonight. Do you by any chance make special arrangements for...'

'A wedding?'

'I was thinking honeymoon.'

'Indeed, we do sir. Our honeymoon package includes a relaxing full body massage, aloe vera scrubs, rose petal bath...'

*****

Staff of the *New York Times* may not *pose as anyone else when they are working as journalists*. Nor, according to the Handbook of Values and Practices for the News and Editorial Departments, may they *invade computer files*.

Bec, a multiple prize-winning reporter, had left the *Times* after reaching the conclusion such rules were written to defend the status quo, protect privileged elites. Blind adherence to the law invariably disadvantaged the little guys and kept the bad guys in business. It was time to trust her own judgment, take control, play to the court of public opinion.

As soon as Jay and the desk clerk left the room, she returned the pamphlet on singing bowl therapy to the stand and slipped behind the desk. Yellow marigolds in a dish beside the monitor had Aristotle creeping into her vision as she examined the screen, relieved it was in English. There were tabs for room status, staff, maintenance, security... She chose *central reservations system*, then navigated to the date Charlie Scott checked in. They knew the names of his three American friends, but there was a fourth name listed as sharing the villa: Gusti Suardika.

4. A hard bargain

Finding Chase Morton had been a priority for the media and political enemies from the day Ped announced he was seeking the nomination, and the hunt took on rabid dimensions after the Florida primary.

Morton's sweet-as-molasses face beamed from the front page of the *Atlanta Journal-Constitution,* which had tracked him down to a duplex in Peace River, a town in the north-west of Alberta, Canada.

The double murderer who served twelve years at Hays State was now gainfully – though not lucratively – employed weeding the flower beds and herb patch at a miniature golf course. He was also a regular at evening prayers at the Alliance Church on 106th Ave.

Chase Morton had shared a cell with Ped for most of the eight years Garland was incarcerated at Hays State, and the newspaper devoted half the front and a double page spread inside to the outcome of their *global manhunt.*

Patricia floated into the room with a coffee pot.

'Thank you Sugah.'

They were in the kitchen of their home in Atlanta taking a break from the campaign during the two-week gap between the Wisconsin and New York primaries.

Cutting to the Chase, as the article was headed, would have been political dynamite if virtually all the *revelations* hadn't already been documented in Ped's book, *Straight Up.*

The only new material was Morton's recollection of his cellmate's *day-to-day MO*, which portrayed Ped more as mentor than Machiavelli. Morton, predictably for a double murderer, wasn't a big fan of the death penalty.

The *global manhunt* added little to the thousands of column inches, posts, hours of TV and radio time swallowed over the last few weeks by distant cousins, high school friends, jealous attorneys, and various other *acquaintances*, most of whom Ped couldn't recall.

The conclusion – expanded in a quote beside a photo of Morton showing a kid how to use a putter – was that *Ped Garland admitted in his book to worse things than he told me.*

Ped put down his cup, looked across at Carl Tyler, his right-hand-man.

'So how did they find Chase in the end?'

'Anonymous tip-off from a burner phone.'

'What persuaded him to open up after all these years?'

'Fifty K.'

'You drive a hard bargain.'

*****

Mike got plenty of sleep on the flight from India, so took an Uber from JFK directly to the Rockaways – a stretch of beach in Queens he'd never got round to visiting.

He spent most of the ride checking activity on the Aristotle channel. Reaction to their decision to go with drug trafficking had been mostly positive, with more dollars being pledged and some supporters of other suggestions switching to the chosen project. Mike also arranged to spend time with his daughter MJ while he was back at the center of the universe.

The Scott's beach house was four floors of cedar and glass on the edge of the swanky Neponsit neighborhood. Neil Scott had taken the afternoon off work and arranged for the three friends of Charlie's who had been in Bali with him to also front.

Introductions didn't get past first names.

'I've persuaded the parents of Ryan, James and Harvey to let the boys talk to you on the condition their names are left out of any story. They're all seventeen, so technically still under the guardianship of their parents, who are naturally concerned about the impact all this could have on their futures.'

Mike pegged Ryan as a born-to-rule smartass, James as the dumb jock, Harvey the serial rule-following introvert. He wasn't surprised Ryan did most of the talking.

Charlie was no kook surfer, 'but no way was the dude good enough for the Padang pipeline, especially in a monster south-west swell'.

The four friends had surfed Balangan, Toro Toro, Dreamland and Baby Pedang – an intermediate break on the other side of the channel from the infamous pipeline. Charlie, it seemed, was the most conservative of the group.

'He knew his limits. No way the dude would have gone near the pipeline if he wasn't... sky high.'

The boys were less forthcoming on the drugs. It was like they'd been schooled by a lawyer, so even behind shields of anonymity they weren't going to incriminate themselves. According to Ryan, Charlie had bought the blow, but he couldn't, or wouldn't say where or who from. Possibly at one of the nightclubs in Kuta. He mentioned the Strobe, Bounty, Kayseera. They'd been offered drugs by so many people, 'it was like all-you-can-eat'.

'Why were you staying in Ubud, so far from the surfing beaches?'

'We thought we'd booked the Nyalahutan place in Kuta, which is much closer to the action. Didn't realize there were three Nyalahutan resorts. But it turned out OK. Ubud's a cool place to chill, and only an hour from the beaches if you can avoid the traffic.'

Mike had difficulty extracting much information about the night before Charlie's death, but James eventually admitted they'd shot a few lines.

'We crashed before midnight. Had no idea Charlie had gone till the cops showed up next morning.'

Harvey avoided eye contact the entire interview.

When it became clear they weren't going to say any more about the drugs, Mike thanked them and reassured them he wouldn't use their names.

After they'd left, he shot some footage in Charlie's bedroom. The surf boards, surfer posters, large screen TV and gaming console could have been in any college dorm, though few students could afford the limited-edition Gibson J-45 guitar lying on the bed. There were also photos on the wall from family vacations somewhere in the Pacific, an unusual multi-legged wooden bowl, large red necklace.

'It's an 'ula fala, from American Samoa,' Mr. Scott said, noticing Mike's interest. 'We have a holiday home in Pago Pago. The necklaces are made from pandanus fruit, dried and painted red. The bowl is a tanoa fa'iva for preparing kava.'

'Can you surf there?'

'If you know where to look.'

Mike followed him onto the roof terrace, which gave three-sixty views over the Atlantic and across Jamaica Bay to Brooklyn.

Mr. Scott apologized for his wife's absence as Mike set up the iPhone and tripod on the coffee table, attached the microphone. 'She's too upset and wants to protect Charlie's little... our daughter.'

'Completely understandable.'

On the record, Mr. Scott said his son had the world at his feet. A talented sportsman and musician with scholarship offers from several Ivy League schools as well as Stanford and Duke, not that he needed the financial hand-up.

They went through his childhood and teen years, dominated by the beach, the surf and guitar. The progression from boogie-boarding to bodysurfing, learning to stand at Lido, Lincoln Boulevard, before taking on and mastering more challenging waves at Beach 92nd Street, point breaks at Sandy Hook.

'Had he surfed anything like the Padang Padang barrel before he went to Bali?'

Mr. Scott shook his head. 'Not as far as I know. We've been to Hawaii several times. Charlie would go watch the pros tackling the Banzai Pipeline, but I'm pretty sure he limited his time on the water to places like Kihei Cove, Guardrails, Kaanapali. You should have asked his friends.'

'They didn't seem that talkative, especially Harvey.'

'Charlie and Harv were real tight. Known each other since first grade. The kid's devastated.'

'Was there a girlfriend waiting back home?'

Mr. Scott smiled. 'There were a few who… before all this… would have told you they were Charlie's girlfriend. He hadn't settled on anyone.'

'Don't take this personally Mr. Scott, but is that something a father would know? My dad had no idea what I was getting up to at Charlie's age.'

'Fair point.'

'And I'm picking you're also going to tell me your son wasn't doing drugs.'

Mr. Scott bristled, then relaxed – almost slumped – his shoulders.

'I'm not saying Charlie was a saint, Mr…'

'Please, call me Mike. Mr. Bullard was *my* father.'

'OK. Mike. Charlie was a good kid, solid… everything ahead of him. My son made a mistake in Bali. A poor decision cost him… everything. But he didn't do this on his own.'

Mr. Scott leaned back on the sofa, linking his arms behind his head. He sighed, then looked across at Mike.

'I'm a businessman Mr... Mike. A very successful businessman in charge of an enterprise that spans the globe, has made me a wealthy man. If one of my software engineers screws up, the program he or she wrote is found to have caused death, the buck stops with me.'

His eyes narrowed, pupils contracting.

'Find me the lowlife responsible for the death of my son. Find me where the buck stops.'

As Mike was unscrewing the iPhone from the tripod, Mr. Scott asked him about Aristotle. Mike told him about Bec and how the name came from one of the philosopher's quotes: *No great mind has ever existed without a touch of madness.*

Mr. Scott looked puzzled. The guy was offering serious money so deserved an explanation. Mike told him about Bec's borderline personality.

'It's like bipolar, but with borderlines the bouts of anxiety, depression, the intense mood swings are usually much shorter. An hour or two, a day – rather than weeks with bipolar.'

Mr. Scott seemed genuinely interested, so Mike continued.

'Most people consider borderline personality a disorder. Bec refuses to. She's found a way to manage it, embrace it, even turn it to her advantage on occasions. It's what makes her a brilliant journalist.'

'Does she use medication?'

'Not anymore. Tried them when she was younger. Antidepressants, antipsychotics, you name it. Mood stabilizers. Some helped a little, though only for a short time, and she couldn't handle the side-effects. Nausea, seizures, blackouts. That was bad enough. Worst thing for Bec was that the drugs sucked all the color out of her world.'

'Sounds like you two are close.'

'Known each other since forever.'

'Has she tried therapy?'

'Been there too, got the t-shirt. After the shrinks finally got round to diagnosing Bec as borderline, she tried all sorts. DBT, MBT, SFT, TFP. The health field's awash with acronyms.'

'Tell me about it. Did any of them work?'

'Some helped at certain times. Bec still uses her own versions of calming techniques like TIPP and STOP. At the end of the day she realized the problem was inside her head, so it was up to her to find a solution. A way to manage.'

'What's Aristotle got to do with it?'

'It's like an alter-ego. Part of Bec's coping mechanism. She's got this scale, she calls Aristotle. Sees things going on around her in five colors depending on where her mind is at. Based on the terrorism threat levels that came out of 9/11. Green is low risk. Blue's guarded. Yellow elevated. Orange is high risk. Red is severe. When she's in the red zone she can be in a lot of pain emotionally, but there are also moments of intense clarity, creativity. Like – well – absolute genius.'

Mr. Scott seemed to be weighing up the information, and Mike wondered if he'd been too honest. Then the billionaire nodded, held out his hand to shake.

'Charlie's death was the result of a moment of madness. It may take a touch of genius to find his killer. I'm counting on you Mike, and your partners.'

5. The honest truth

It was the bottom of the seventh. The Braves were trailing by one but had set the table with runners on second and third and had a switch hitter on deck.

Ped and Patricia were in their regular spot at Sun Trust Park, in the Chairman's Seats behind home plate, surrounded by serial second-guessers.

The pitcher sent down a salad, easily read, and the home crowd rose in concert as the ball sailed into Chophouse Terrace.

It took longer than usual to reach the parking lot, as Ped was besieged by hand-shakers, back-slappers, selfie whores. All captured by the crew from Netflix, who were tailing the candidate for a day-in-the life doco.

They'd filmed him at the headquarters of his drug foundation in downtown Atlanta, on the giant slide at Piedmont Park with his grandson, enjoying a cup of joe with the mayor, signing books at Barnes and Noble.

The set-piece interview was in the living room at home, which had been *dressed* beyond recognition by a décor consultant hired by his press secretary. Sofas had been repositioned, the Fernando Botero paintings replaced with politically proper landscapes, the floor-to-ceiling shelves with books Ped would never read.

Pre-arranged questions covered his childhood in Atlanta and bilingual upbringing, thanks to his Colombian mother who immigrated in 1949 to escape La Violencia – the civil war ignited by the assassination of a Presidential candidate.

After law school at the University of Georgia in Athens,

Ped's fluent Spanish landed him a job at Weir and Stone, a boutique firm in New York that handled the international affairs of a large Colombian coffee producer.

By the time he married Patricia in 1986, he was making regular visits to Eje Cafetero – Colombia's coffee triangle – in the steep-sloped valleys between Medellin and Cali.

Warring cocaine cartels made Colombia one of the most violent nations on the planet at the time, but Ped never felt threatened because of his growing friendship with Jiménez, head of security for the coffee company.

'And when did you realize Mr. Jiménez was also head of security for the Rosario drug cartel?'

'Not till much later, near the end. Should I have picked up on it sooner? Probably, if I'd asked the right questions. But I was extranjero – a foreigner, just visiting Colombia a few days a month. I've never used that as an excuse for what I did. Just an explanation for why it took me so darn long to piece it all together.'

'And when you did?'

'That's when I started making bad decisions.'

'This was when, 1994?'

'Exactly right. I had my doubts before, but it wasn't until a trip to Tumaco – that's a port city in the south of Colombia – when Jiménez introduced me to the Lopez brothers. You had to be living in another galaxy not to know Felipe and Àngel Lopez were the kingpins of the Rosario cartel.'

'Yet you continued your work there.'

'Worse than that. I helped the cartel launder millions, knowing darn well where the money was coming from.'

'What made you give yourself up in the end?'

'A documentary. I was sitting in this room, on that sofa, watching TV with Patricia – who by the way had no clue what I was up to in Colombia. Our daughter was sleeping in the room next door. The documentary laid it all bare, the unimaginable harm cocaine was inflicting on American kids. Brutally graphic.'

'Like a lightbulb moment?'

'Your words, not mine. It took over a year of those blinding lights in my face before I mustered the courage to come clean with the DEA.'

'You got eight years?'

'Ten. They let me out after eight for good behavior.'

'And your friend Jiménez, who handed himself in at the same time, didn't spend a day in jail. That must have rubbed you the wrong way.'

'Not exactly. His testimony didn't just take down the Lopez brothers. It brought down a whole bunch of corrupt politicians, judges, police...'

'But no time inside?'

'Listen, I haven't laid eyes on Jiménez since the very day the two of us strolled into that DEA office in Miami. I did my time. He went deep into witness protection and has been off the radar ever since. But here's the kicker: I've heard that even after all these years, he's still sittin' high on the hit lists of at least three cartels. I wouldn't want to be caught dead in his shoes, that's for sure.'

'So, you served your time, wrote the book, set up the foundation, and here you are running for President...'

'You make it sound easy. Believe me, it's been a grueling journey. Sitting in that cell over at Hays State Prison, it hit me like a ton of bricks I was the luckiest guy on this planet. I had an incredible wife who stuck by me when Lawd knows most women woulda bolted. A beautiful daughter. Most importantly, a second chance, a shot at making amends. Which is why I've dedicated the rest of my life to fighting this drug nightmare.'

The interviewer looked at her notes.

'How do you respond to those who say you're a hypocrite

for calling for the death penalty for traffickers, given your… history?'

'They've got a valid point, no doubt about it. I'm tellin' folks that if someone today does what I did back in my wild days they deserve the harshest consequences. A vein for a vein. I get how some folks might see that as the pot callin' the skillet black. But here's the thing: if, on that day I was introduced to the Lopez brothers, I knew I could end up facing the needle just for breathin' the same air as them, I'da been outta there so fast you wouldn't have caught me for dust. And that's the unvarnished truth.'

'Straight up?'

'You betya.'

The interviewer smiled.

'Let's finish up with those words Mr. Garland. Several political analysts and marketing and brand experts are describing the term *Straight Up* – the way you used it as the title for the book that launched the foundation and made you a household name, and now as the slogan defining your campaign – as a masterstroke. You refuse to run negative ads on your opponent, don't use artificial intelligence, polling or focus groups, don't give press conferences, don't use a teleprompter, you speak unscripted… You've turned this nomination campaign into a referendum on… honesty.'

'Well, first off I reckon those so-called experts of yours need to step out of that D.C. bubble, get a breath of fresh air. They're spending too much time up each other's ass – behinds. Ain't nothin' masterful about the truth. I sure as heck don't need a swarm of overpaid folks in backrooms, or bean counters dictating what I think, what I say or wear, how to hold my tongue. I tell 'em straight up how it is. If folks agree, Lawd willin' an' the creek don't rise, they might just cast their vote my way. If they figure I'm all hat and no cattle they won't, and I can't say I blame 'em. It's a free country.'

*****

Bec's head was pounding as she spilled from the pressure cooker of the Lxxy Club onto the more manageable chaos of Jalan Legian, the strip dissecting Kuta's most popular nightspots. She and Jay had navigated through clubs with names like Bounty and Sky Garden that hinted at some botanic paradise rather than the mind-numbing musical anarchy and laser light mayhem chased by cheap booze and drugs.

As someone with such a tenuous grip on her demons, Bec struggled to understand why people with nothing to escape would deliberately dance on the cliff edge of emotional chaos.

Paddy's Pub, where they'd started their search for clues, had the least claim to innocence, thanks to a suicide bomber who walked into the nightclub in 2002 and detonated his backpack. Two hundred people died in that blast and another over the road seconds later, not that you'd know it from the slackness of the security. Jay got light friskings from bouncers outside two of the clubs. Bec and the contents of her handbag sailed through with high-fives.

They had a half hour before their rendezvous with a liaison officer from America's Drug Enforcement Administration, so grabbed a roadside table at the Mini Restaurant. The one-way procession of cars and motorbikes bordered on gentle after the blasting bass of the clubs, where meaningful conversation was impossible.

Bec ordered a blue margarita – the color Aristotle was chilling in the off-the-shoulder navy dress of a tourist, a stack of surfboards carried on the dreadlocked head of a Balinese beach rat, the lapis lazuli earrings of a petite maître d' hustling the sidewalk outside the restaurant.

28

Mentioning Charlie Scott or showing his photo had got them nowhere. Ditto Gusti Suardika. Jay reckoned a Canadian woman flashed recognition but clammed up.

'No-one wants to be associated with drug users, even dead ones.'

Bec nodded. 'His death got a lot of coverage here. No shortage of rumors on social media.'

The drinks arrived. The cocktail of blue curacao, tequila and lime juice almost took her head off.

'One thing I'm surprised about though is the lack of solicitation. You know, for drugs. I thought this place was crawling… Why are you smiling?'

'I've been offered hash, ecstasy, cocaine, a hand-job and something called shabu, which I think is ice.'

'When? Where?'

'Cab driver outside the Mini Mart, a security guy while he was padding me down, assuming you're only interested in the drugs. See that Indonesian guy leaning against the tree outside Surfer Girl, black bag over his shoulder? He's a seller.'

Bec wasn't sure if she should be annoyed or elated.

'Clearly, I don't look like a buyer. Unlike you!'

Jay held up his Bintang bottle. 'What can I say?'

Bec took another sip of the cocktail, catching a clump of salt to tone down the bitterness of the lime. The sidewalks were heaving with tank tops, body piercings, wide-eyed teens in beach gear trying to look older, ageing hippies with beer bellies and shaved heads trying to look younger, pale East Europeans just looking stern, with sunglasses perched redundantly on their heads.

An inebriated hen's party in Union Jack singlets pedaled by on a Bali-beer cycle contraption for the second time, past a Muslim woman peering out from the safety of her burka. Someone was butchering *Sweet Caroline* in a karaoke bar, drowning out the metallic gongs of a gamelan orchestra rehearsing a few doors down.

Evan Henley, the American drug liaison officer, was where he said he'd be at midnight – upstairs at the Bounty under one of the giant parachutes hanging from the ceiling like shimmering jellyfish. The corner table he'd chosen was marginally quieter than the dance floor, which was teeming with bikini tops, bare chests, hair tossing and air guitaring through a haze of cigarette smoke and blue neon.

There was only one spare seat at the table, so Jay excused himself to try his luck with the bar staff.

Bec realized recording the interview would be pointless, which was presumably why Henley chose this venue to meet. The American had to work alongside officers from the Bali division of Indonesia's National Narcotics Agency.

'The Government in Jakarta talks tough on drugs,' he said. 'They parade arrested tourists in orange jumpsuits and shackles for the TV cameras, even execute the occasional foreigner. But they give the narcotics agency jack-squat to police a coastline almost three times the size of the US.'

Cheers and whistles greeted the DJ's introduction of the next song – *Living Next Door to Alice*. Henley had to wait for the noise to subside.

'Money means everything on this island. If you've got it, you do what you want. The drug lords have obscene wealth and pay the police to look the other way. They control the gangs. The gangs run the distribution networks, the dealers, even the prisons…'

Cause for twenty-four years I've been living next door to Alice was the cue for dozens of voices chanting *Alice? Who the fuck is Alice?*'

Henley leaned further across the table. 'Corruption's uncontrollable. The cops know all the dealers, and vice versa. Scratch my back, I'll scratch yours. How else do you explain why Indonesia's the biggest drugs market in Asia when the authorities supposedly have orders to shoot dealers and traffickers on sight?'

Bec could see Jay talking to a blond guy in a Bintang singlet beside a large golden birdcage writhing with teenagers. She had to shout across the table to be heard.

'What can you tell me about the cocaine scene here? How easy is it to get, where does it come from?'

Henley took another sip of his soda, surveyed the nearby tables before answering.

'Gotta be honest with you here, Ms. Corelli. Cocaine's yesterday's news. The real story, the hot story in Bali and the rest of Southeast Asia for that matter, is synthetics. Methamphetamine, ketamine. The meth market alone has ballooned to more than sixty billion dollars a year...'

'That may be so Mr. Henley, but...'

'... while the markets for cocaine and heroin have contracted to the point where we've had to transition our limited resources to the fight against synthetics.'

'I hear you Mr. Henley, but our interest here is solely in cocaine, specifically the batch of cocaine that found its way into the bloodstream of...'

'Let me level with you Ms. Corelli. Sad as it is what happened to your boy Charlie Scott, he's one grain of sand on a beach. A mighty big beach. You want to waste your time on a single grain, I wish you luck. There's not much more I can do to help you.'

*****

Mike felt the chill wind off the Atlantic through his down anorak, so could only imagine how cold it must be in the water, even with a wetsuit and hood. He'd taken an early A train from

Manhattan to Beach 92nd Street, hoping to catch Charlie Scott's friend Harvey on his own.

He focused the binoculars on a group of hooded surfers one-hundred-fifty feet or so from the shore, finally recognizing the face that avoided eye contact with him the night before. The kid was pretty good but wiped out a second time and decided to give up. Mike watched him walk along the beach, board balancing on his head, towards the Rockaway Surf Club. He intercepted him as he was putting the board into one of the tall lockers behind the clubrooms.

'How ya holdin' up, Harvey?'

The kid did a double-take, and for a moment Mike thought he was going to bolt.

'Can't talk to you man,' he wheezed, scanning the beach. 'My mom. She's an attorney. I'll be, like, grounded forever.'

'She'll never know Harvey, I promise. Mr. Scott tells me you and Charlie were tight.'

The kid covered his eyes with his hands, took a couple of deep breaths. When his hands slid down to his mouth, Mike could see he was crying.

'I'm sorry about what happened in Bali, Harvey. Can't imagine what you're going through. But I gotta tell ya, kid, the story I'm working on is not about you. Or your friends Ryan and James. We're doing this for Charlie, and Charlie's dad.'

Harvey sniffed, wiped his nose on the sleeve of his wetsuit.

'Mr. Scott's solid, a stand-up guy.'

'And we're working on this for *him* Harvey. I'm not sure how much you've been told, but Mr. Scott has asked us to follow the trail of the drug Charlie took that night. All the way to its source, to the head of whatever scumbag organization is behind the trafficking. That's why we need to know where you guys got the coke. So we can head off on our trail. And leave you and Charlie's parents and sister alone.'

Harvey took another deep breath, then told his story.

Charlie bought the coke off a Balinese guy they met at Padang Padang, and who ended up staying at the resort in Ubud with them. He used the name Lompok. Harvey knew nothing about a Gusti. It was Lompok's motorbike that Charlie rode to the beach. The coke was pure high-end stuff only Charlie could afford. And it had a name. NuNu. Short for Nube Nueve, which was Spanish for cloud nine.

'And where can we find this Lompok?'

'He hangs out at the beaches, working the coast from Uluwatu to Tanah Lot.'

*****

Uluwatu, at the south-western tip of Bali's Bukit Peninsula, is a magnet for two reasons. The 11th century Hindu temple on the clifftop reels in the tourists, especially for the traditional Kecak dance performances at sunset. Two hundred and thirty feet below the temple lie some of the world's most legendary surf breaks, powered by monster Southern Ocean swells and south-east trade winds.

Jay and Bec, armed with the names Lompok and NuNu, had begun the day below the temple and made their way north along the coast, through Suluban, Padang Padang, Bingin and Dreamland. After lunch at a restaurant in Jimbaran, they skirted the airport to try their luck at the party beaches of Kuta and Legian.

They got a half-break when Jay spotted a deal going down beside the tourist information booth over the road from the Jayakarta Hotel. He parked the bike beside a fruit vendor and followed the beach boy with dreads through the split gateway onto the crowded beach. He sat in one of the hundreds of loungers lined in front of the cafes, lit a cigarette.

Jay took off his t-shirt, handed it to Bec.

'I'll meet you back at the bike.'

He pulled the brim of his cap lower, wandered over and parked himself in the lounger beside Dreads. A waiter appeared, and Jay ordered a Bintang. He kicked off his jandals, stretched out in the sun, closed his eyes, and waited.

Not for long.

Question three, after *where are you from* and *where are you staying*, was *are you looking*?

'Depends. Looking for what?'

'Anything and everything. Ecstasy, meth, dope, mushrooms, girls, boys.'

'I'm more a coke sort of guy.'

'Definitely doable man. One gram, two gram?'

Jay sat up, swinging his legs over the side of the chair to face Dreads. He glanced around, lowered his voice.

'A friend was telling me about some special blow he tried called NuNu. Scored it from a Balinese dude. Name of Lompok.'

There was a hint of recognition, before the eyes narrowed in suspicion, and the guy stood to leave.

'Can't help you man.'

Jay let him go. He slipped a 20,000-rupiah note under the bottle to pay for the beer and, keeping one eye on Dreads, went back to the bike.

They watched him hail a cab outside the Quicksilver Surf Academy, then followed him on the bike, north through Seminyak and Kerobokan, then back to the coast at Canggu. Dreads got out and walked into the Island Beach Bar.

Jay parked the bike and walked past the Batu Balong Temple onto the beach. Bali had loads of picture postcard places – this wasn't one of them. Mangy dogs roamed, sniffing at discarded polystyrene cups, plastic bags, coconut shells, candy wrappers, spilt offerings. The faded beach umbrellas looked tired. Even the sand here was a lethargic gray.

Not that it put off the surfers. Boards were stacked like coffins for rent. The sea speckled with hundreds of dots waiting for a wave. A tourist was standing on a surfboard on the sand, holding his arms out as an instructor gave him the lowdown.

Jay spotted Dreads head between two beach shacks. Fingering the zip tie in his pocket, he followed the young man into a shed used for waxing and repairing surfboards. The guy turned, realized his escape route was blocked, braced to fight. Jay stepped closer, lifting the zip tie to his mouth and biting it. The confusion, the momentary slackening of muscles, was all Jay needed.

He attacked one wrist with his left hand, stepping to the side and driving up with his right to drag him off balance, bend the wrist into a lock. Dreads yelped, but before he could react, Jay spun him around, yanked the other arm back and slipped the zip tie over his wrists.

He gradually increased the pressure on the arm until he had his answer: The Nyalahutan resort in Kuta.

Jay stuffed a wetsuit hood in Dreads' mouth, secured it with surfboard repair tape, then kicked out his legs, dragged him across the concrete floor, tied him to the post holding up the roof.

*****

Rodrigo Montoya surfaced and stroked slowly to the edge of the pool. Far below, beyond the beach and the rolling waves, the Indian Ocean spread to the horizon like a giant blue rug flecked with greens and blacks. He turned, leaned back, stretched his elbows over the side, letting the sun simmer into his shoulders.

He took in the view past the loungers and umbrellas, across the lawn to the arched entranceway over the path leading to the house. Putra appeared on the steps. The bracts on the yellow bougainvillea above the mayordomo's head were outshining the blues and reds, threatening the equilibrium. Montoya made a mental note to mention it to the gardener.

Putra paused at the entranceway.

'Call for you, bos.'

'Who is it?'

'Meneer Agung. Say it urgent.'

Putra insisted on using the old Dutch colonial honorific when referring to the leader of Kaluraha gang, and anyone else he disapproved of.

'Tell him I'll call back in five.'

Putra pressed his palms together in an exaggerated Sembah salute and retreated up the path.

Montoya hauled himself from the pool, pulled on a robe and lit a cigarette, taking several puffs before heading inside to make the call from the study on the second floor.

Agung reported that a New Zealand tourist and American journalist had been asking questions about Lompok and NuNu.

'And one of my guys in Canggu told them where Lompok lives.'

'Why would the dungu do that?'

'To stop the New Zealand bajingan breaking his arm.'

It was almost unheard of for anyone in their right mind to threaten a member of the Kaluraha gang, although a tourist might not realize who or what he was dealing with. Even more concerning to Montoya was the reference to New Zealand.

6. Butchers and bakers

'Youse wouldn't believe how many fighters dance around, bobbin' and weavin', waitin' for openings ain't never gonna come. You gotta create opportunities by pilin' pressure on your opponent. Be first or kiss the canvas.'

The former marine wedged into the seat beside Ped had trained eight Golden Gloves winners.

While Kate Hunter was in a hotel room on the Upper East Side analyzing re-runs of Florida and sweating the details of briefing notes with aides and psychology experts and focus groups, Ped was taking a breather to talk strategy.

'No fighter worth their salt gonna present you with no open target, Mr. Garland. The more you hold back, the more they relax, find their groove. Then, they'll kick your ass.'

They'd hired the theater in Brooklyn to prepare for the New York debate, and to test his new glasses. Behind the lenses lay transparent displays, camouflaged to blend with the frames, which were made from an advanced material that hid the embedded technology from security checks. A light touch on the side of the frame transformed the lenses into a live teleprompter, invisible to the audience.

The performance space was decked out to look like the debate venue, with hundreds of colored balloons showing the faces of butchers and bakers and candlestick-makers floating above the seats.

Other than the security detail, there were only four other real people in the theater. Jin Ly, Ped's message guru, Carl Tyler, his right-hand man, and two actors playing Hunter and the moderator. The woman was dressed in the same red Ralph Lauren pantsuit Hunter would be wearing on the night.

They knew this for the same reason they knew their opponent would be hardening her stance on drugs, gun violence and climate change, softening on healthcare and education, and throwing what she hoped would be a game-changer on illegal immigration. They had a mole in Hunter's campaign team.

The only unknown was how their opponent would react to two other pieces of intelligence – the first about to land anonymously on the political desk of the *New York Times*, the second scheduled to arrive in the inbox of the moderator an hour before the debate.

*****

Heading uninvited into the den of a drug dealer in a country with the death penalty would normally have Aristotle spiraling towards darker shades of yellow, even orange. But sitting on the back of the bike, arms around Jay's waist and the breeze kissing her face, Bec was hunting for distractions – the sapphire of a folded umbrella held by a woman on the bike in front, the blue of a Happy Hour sign, the liberty of the cloudless sky.

Jay had been vague about how he'd persuaded the guy at Canggu to reveal Lompok lived at the Kuta branch of the Nyalahutan chain, and Bec was learning not to push him on such matters.

They'd ridden down from Ubud on the Megapro, which apparently was a poor imitation of the Enfield Jay had used in India but handled OK. Bec was amazed how few people wore helmets, given the chaos, particularly after they left the relative order of the road bypassing Denpasar and headed toward Kuta. Four rows of cars squeezed into roads barely wide enough for two. Motorbikes whizzed up the inside, some carrying families of four, or pillion passengers balancing tables or porcelain toilet bowls on their heads.

Give Way was a rule either unknown, or at best a loose concept open to interpretation. Gridlock at uncontrolled intersections was overcome by a driver, usually in a large vehicle, forcing an opening for motorbikes to spill through until the flood was halted by an assertive driver from the opposing direction.

Jay appeared unfazed. After safely negotiating yet another potential pile-up, Bec was able to not only relax, but marvel at the temperament of the Balinese. She couldn't imagine New Yorkers being so patient if the traffic lights failed at the intersection of 8th and West 41st outside the *Times* building.

A block from the Nyalahutan, Jay swayed out towards the centerline to avoid a pile of rocks blocking part of the road. A red plastic bag tied to a bamboo stick on top of the pile flashed into Bec's vision an instant before a van roared out from a building site between a health spa and guesthouse.

She felt Jay's stomach muscles tighten as he accelerated, veered to avoid the idiot driver, then back hard left to miss an oncoming truck by inches. The bike wobbled as he fought for balance, leaning right again to dodge a mobile food stall.

'Hold on,' he yelled, revving the throttle. The front wheel lifted up and onto the sidewalk, the rear thumping into the curb as the bike shaved the base of a pengor pole, shearing off the wing mirror. Jay slammed on the brakes, tilted violently left, sending the bike into a skid and Bec tumbling into a stack of pots outside a homeware store.

Her first thought was anger at the idiot van driver. Her second was answered when Jay knelt beside her, checking she was OK. Her shoulder stung where she'd hit the sidewalk. The sleeve of her shirt was torn, blood was seeping from a graze extending to just above her elbow. Her knee throbbed, but felt no worse when she straightened it out, suggesting nothing was broken.

'The fricken hell did that idiot driver think he was doing?' she said, holding out her good arm for Jay to pull her up. 'He could have killed us.'

Concerned faces were floating on the periphery. Gangnam style music intruded from an upstairs window across the road. A man with both front teeth missing was picking up the motorbike, its front wheel buckled, headlight smashed.

Blood was seeping from a cut on Jay's forehead, but it was the look in his eyes that flung Aristotle into the orange star design on the sidewalk.

'The driver knew exactly what he was doing Bec. That was no accident.'

7. Go to the head

Kate Hunter chewed up half her opening address responding to the *New York Times* exclusive that she'd smoked weed in her freshman year at university. She was probably convincing enough to many of her supporters in the audience, though Ped could see the anger and stress in the lowered eyebrows, touching of the earrings, the hands balled into fists behind the lectern. He wondered how many hours of prep and angst went into those 45 seconds.

It went downhill for her from there.

Study your opponent. Boxer or brawler? Fast or slow hand-speed? The more you know, the easier it is to exploit weaknesses.

Hunter was pummeled in the opening segment on gun violence, internet crime and hate speech. But the exchange would be remembered less for her revised positions than for Ped's comeback lines on point after point.

Through a wireless connection hooked up to the Ciph's hybrid AI system, the teleprompter in Ped's glasses was streaming well-crafted rebuttals, relevant statistics, amusing anecdotes – all based on live analysis of social media comments while the debate was unfolding.

Punch punch punch. One to make them block, the next to make them duck, the next to make them retreat. Build the pressure so they lose composure.

By the end of the segment on drugs and healthcare, Ped's incisive interjections and hilarious one-liners had the audience in his corner and Hunter on the ropes. The best stage makeup in the world couldn't disguise the thinning lips, flaring nose, eyes blinking like a hummingbird.

Body shots not only take the breath away, reducing an opponent's mobility and endurance, they distract and demoralize.

The last segment before the break was on education and employment. They were arguably Hunter's best rounds because she was so punch-drunk, she reverted to autopilot. Ped still managed to land telling jabs before the bell.

The second half opened with immigration, and Ped raced through his spiel in half the allocated time. Then he turned to face Hunter.

Cut off the ring so your opponent has nowhere to run. They go right, you go right. They go left, you go left. Make them feel like they're forever in your headlights.

'Well Kate, that's where I stand. From the way you've been responding tonight, clearly based on desperation polling and think-tanks and AI rather than having real conversations with everyday folks, I'm pickin' you'll flip-flop on sanctuary cities, flip the script on border security funding, and call out local governments for not toeing the line with federal law.'

Ped hoped the cameras were zoomed in to catch the deer-in-the-spotlight eyes, the clenched jaw and bulging cheeks as Hunter fought to keep her cool. She failed, stumbling and mumbling her way to the last segment of the debate: ethics and integrity.

The moderator, probably sensing a need to re-level the playing field, turned to Ped.

'Mr. Garland, how can you be trusted to hold the highest office in the land, to be the ultimate role model to our nation's children, given your criminal background?'

Ped smiled, tilting his head subtly to one side, holding his hands palms-up.

'Well, I can tell you right now there are folks who won't vote for me because of that, and I respect their choice. I've made some lousy decisions in my time. But I faced 'em head-on, ate crow, and humble pie, learned from my mistakes. I *know* I'm a better person for it, and I'm darn sure I can use those lessons I've learnt to help make America better. My life's an open book. What you see is what you get.'

'Straight up?'

'That's got a nice ring to it. I reckon I might just use that.'

When the laughter subsided, the moderator turned to Hunter.

'Congresswoman, in your opening statement you admitted smoking marijuana at university, saying you did so only once as an experiment.'

'That's correct.'

'You sure about that?'

'Of course, I'm sure.'

It is a common myth that when right-handed people lie, they look to their right, because they're using their imagination to invent an answer. If they look left, they are said to be accessing their memory, telling the truth.

Ped was not surprised to see an experienced politician like Hunter glance to her left. Nor was he surprised to see her grip the lectern to stop her hands moving – a more scientifically-proven reaction to telling a lie.

The moderator moved in for the kill.

'So, if a roommate by the name of Belinda Archer was to come forward with an affidavit stating you smoked another joint two weeks later, behind her parent's garage, she'd be lying?'

Hunter was blindsided. And speechless.

Ped let the boos and shouts and background murmur hang for a few seconds, imagining the social media team already at work editing the moderator's question and Hunter's reaction, packaging it in multiple contexts ready to send to targeted recipients identified by the Ciph.

Feint to the body, go to the head.

He leaned toward his microphone.

'I, for one, am ready to cut Congresswoman Hunter some slack on this issue. She's admitted to smoking pot years back. I got skeletons in my closet too, believe me. Own up, learn, keep moving forward. Folks I talk to out on the streets, they wanna know what we're going do to fix this country today and tomorrow. They're not concerned with what happened behind some garage or in a hotel room decades ago when we were young and foolish.'

*****

Touché, thought Mike. Game, set and match to Garland.

He was watching the debate at a bar in Soho, with some former colleagues from the Wooster blog. He ordered another round. Zoe was sipping Bloody Marys, Rachel hot apple cider, their personalities summed up in their drink choices.

Zoe was adventurous, spunky, wild, and Mike still fantasized about the hotel in Arizona where she introduced him to the *Twist and Shout.* Rachel was a data analyst and sole mom who clearly still had a crush on him, despite knockback after knockback. Mike felt bad about the way he'd exploited the crush when he'd needed help with childcare while he was running hot on the virus story. With Zoe. He was counting on two women with such contrasting personalities never getting together to compare notes.

'What brings the great Mike Bullard back to New York? Last I saw on your social feeds you were on a beach somewhere in India.'

'Place called Varkala. You'd love it Rach. So would your daughter. What's her name again?'

'Abby. How's MJ – her old *playmate*?'

He deserved the dig. Their daughters were similar ages and Mike had traded on it. Shamelessly.

'MJ's cool. Took her to see the *Barbie* movie this afternoon. Turns out she'd already seen it twice. Didn't let on till I dropped her back at her mom's.'

'Can't imagine where she gets such a manipulative streak.'

Mike smiled.

Another round of drinks arrived, and Mike steered the conversation through staff changes at Wooster, stories Zoe was working on, to Rachel's take on new analytics tools being trialed at the blog. All the women really wanted to know was what Mike was up to, whether his bold leap into freelancing was paying off.

'Too early to tell. Pros and cons, I guess. Yes, I get to work on serious stories, but we're a small team, pretty much on our own. No data analysts, visuals wizards, leaderboards, and I can't just raid the gadgets cabinet whenever I need specialized kit like night vision scopes or a drone. That's one of the reasons I'm back for a few days, other than to catch up with MJ, do a couple of interviews. I'm sourcing kit.'

Mike wasn't going to tell them most of the gadgets he was buying would not be found in the cabinet at Wooster, whose journalists remained hog-tied by the laws of privacy and rules of transparency.

'How's the drug trafficking investigation going Mike? Your feed's gone strangely silent since you announced the project.'

'That's another advantage with freelancing. I haven't got a section editor screaming every ten minutes for an update to refresh the storyline. Good stories take time, not clicks.'

Zoe was shaking her head.

'Never thought I'd hear Mike Bullard badmouthing clicks.'

Rachel chimed in. 'What about the donors, Mike? All the

people backing your project are gonna want results. Have put their own money into it. Which I believe gives us more skin in the game than a section editor at Wooster.'

'You're one of the donors?'

'A small one, yes.'

'So am I Mike, and half the reporters at Wooster.'

'Seriously? I don't know what to…'

Zoe cut him off. 'We're aware of what you and Bec Corelli are capable of Mike. And I guess for some of us, the way the news media's headed, we need to know there's still a future in journalism. We want you… *need* you to succeed.'

'And I was only teasing about the clicks, Mike, and us donors demanding instant results. Take as long as you need.'

'I appreciate that.'

Rachel, ever the data analyst, asked him what he was doing to 'boost the Aristotle channel's visibility'. Mike realized that if he, Bec and Jay were going to make a serious impact with their investigation, they'd need a larger audience than subscribers to the YouTube channel. They needed digital allies who would share the results with their legions of followers. He told her about the relationships he'd been cultivating with a bunch of influencers who'd taken stands against drugs, or could be persuaded to.

Over another round, which the women insisted on *donating*, both declared they'd voted for the drug trafficking project over human trafficking and child labor. Turned out Rachel's estranged husband was hooked on fentanyl and one of Zoe's cousins overdosed on heroin at school.

'Maybe you should take a look at Ped Garland while you're here,' Zoe suggested.

'We're hunting bigger fish.'

'Bigger than the next President of the United States?'

'A different species.'

8. The baby grand

Tickets for the NatZ concert at Madison Square Garden had sold out in 84 seconds.

The singer opened with a medley from her most recent album, then the stage faded to black and the pulsating images on the giant screen were replaced with the still face of a young woman smiling. Twenty-thousand people buttoned up like someone hit mute.

NatZ, illuminated by a single pink beam that made her look delicate, vulnerable, gripped the microphone stand with both hands.

'Emma Larch was my ride-or-die back in Milwaukee. We'd ditch school, spill our secrets, learnt guitar together at Mrs. D's joint over in Bayside. We'd daydream about rockin' out together right here at the Garden. We'd chat on the blower every Saturday – no matter where I was globetrotting. Our last convo was just two weeks back. Em was in good spirits, y'know? Dealing with life's curveballs like the rest of us. But even from my crib in LA, I could sense that smile of hers. Just like in that pic up there.'

Her voice faltered.

'Told her I'd shoot her some tix to be here tonight. But a few hours later, Em got snatched away from us. Thought she was just poppin' a couple of chill bars – like I bet a few of you in the crowd have done. But those things were laced with a deadly hit of powdered Fentanyl. My homie got straight-up murdered by some scumbag drug dealer who didn't know her name, never heard her jam or shred the guitar, never saw that grin.

'Me and Em, we used to hit up this tiny spot by St. Johns in Milwaukee to busk. We'd set up shop at Cathedral Square…'

The crowd murmured in anticipation.

'I'll never forget the first time I dropped this track in front of people, right there in that park. Em was lurking backstage, tears flowin' because she understood what it meant. To both of us. It was a real moment, and I'm 'bout to bring out a special guest on stage in a sec. We're not just performing this jam in memory of my bestie, but also to throw a message out to all those lowlifes who mess with the lives of beautiful, vulnerable souls like Emma Larch.

'Yo, my peeps, let's give it up loud and proud for the dude who's gonna put an end to this madness. He's ditchin' the fancy suits and power tables with the big shots to be right here with us tonight. Give it up for the future President of the United States of America… Mr. Ped Garland.'

When a walk-on-water celebrity tells an arena full of fans to give someone a warm welcome, the response is a fait accompli. Ped had no idea how much of the cheering was genuine as the lights came up and he walked across the stage in a black t-shirt and Levi's. But the surge in volume when he parked himself behind the baby grand said it all. And the standing ovation at the end, when NatZ beckoned him over and wrapped her arms around him for a full thirty seconds, beneath the giant image of Emma Larch, was platinum.

As NatZ withdrew from the embrace and positioned Ped for a joint selfie with the delirious crowd in the background, he reflected on how this moment of marketing magic had come about. How the singer was identified as a key influencer of a prime demographic, how the Ciph found out about her interview in Wisconsin after her friend's death, how information about Ped was subtly planted with her influencers so the meeting outside the studio seemed coincidental.

The Ciph had already done the numbers. One hundred and fifty million followers, plus the anticipated shares, reshares and repeats on earned media, would give the post a larger audience than the hundreds of millions who watched Frazier beat Ali in the Fight of the Century at this very venue back in seventy-one.

While Ped's opponent argued policy and administration positions with a dozen Republican dinosaurs who still thought a hit was a positive soundbite on Fox.

*****

Jay felt Bec's grip tighten round his waist as they turned off the bypass and headed back towards the place where they were almost wiped out by the van three days ago.

Bec had recovered well physically. The graze on her arm was healing nicely, the swelling on her knee almost gone. The unexpected attack had shaken her emotionally, but also stiffened her resolve to *get back on the horse*.

The *horse* was a clapped-out Honda Scoopy with a sun-dead beginner surfboard strapped into hooks attached to the frame. Full-face helmets completed their disguises.

Jay scanned the roadsides for trouble as they passed a leather store and nail studio on Jalan Buni Sari. A blue Toyota taxi three spots back was a potential tail, so he shot up a lane beside a Mediterranean restaurant – against the flow of traffic – and doubled back. False alarm.

They sailed past the pile of rocks still blocking part of the road outside the building site. No van today, just barefoot laborers removing wooden reinforcing stakes between concrete floors. Bamboo – the workhorse of Asia.

The entrance to the Kuta branch of the Nyalahutan was tainted with the same giant gold letters, and the pretension didn't stop there. It was as if the designers had taken the layout and features of intimate Balinese family compounds and supersized them. With fries. Even the staff looked like they'd come off a production line tooled for chiseled features and robotic smiles. Children with remote-controlled plastic cars need not apply.

The two men behind the desk in the lobby had the strong clear bone structure of royalty and their flawless English left no room for misinterpretation.

'We have no-one by the name of Lompok or Gusti Suardika staying or living here. Sir.'

Jay and Bec were walking back to the scooter, contemplating their next move, when an Australian man with a brown towel over his shoulder caught up with them.

'Excuse me mate. Overheard you asking about a bloke called Lompok. There was a bit of a palaver outside my room in the early hours of the morning. Went out to tell them to shut the hell up and walked into a posse of cops in the hall. They had an Indonesian bloke in handcuffs, and I heard them mention Lompok. More than once.'

'You're sure that's what they called him?'

'Definitely. Funny thing though, they were all smiles and laughs. Especially your Lompok bloke. It was like he was being picked up for a night on the town, rather than inside a police cell.'

*****

Montoya was enjoying his second cup of tinto coffee on the private beach below the house when he heard the winch mechanism engage, the gondola car begin its descent.

He looked at his watch. Right on time. He liked that.

He'd asked for a report on the American journalist and her New Zealand friend. Montoya drained the coffee as Arief, his head of security, stepped from the car and walked across the sand carrying an iPad.

The meddlers had been identified as Jay Duggan and Rebecca Corelli. As well as persisting in their questions about Lompok and NuNu, they were also showing an annoying interest in the death of Charlie Scott.

'Who are they?'

'Haven't been able to find much on Duggan. He has no social media presence, so flies under most radars. The few hits we got online suggest he's some sort of green activist.'

'And his girlfriend, the American?'

'Corelli's far more interesting. Until recently she was a high-flying reporter for the *New York Times*. Bagged a few awards. But she's a retard. There's clips of her on YouTube throwing her toys at her father's memorial service in North Carolina. And this,' he said, handing over the iPad.

Montoya touched the play arrow. The video showed a woman screaming and lashing out at an airport security guard, kicking him in the balls, then being pulled away and carried off by a man in a Kingfisher singlet.

'Some nutjob, eh? We're pretty sure the guy with her is Duggan. The airport is Udaipur in India.'

Montoya replayed the clip, sucking in a breath of sympathy as Corelli's foot connected with the guard's groin.

He'd been wondering whether to let Carlos know about the mysterious pair. On this evidence the answer was *no*. They could do without the distraction.

9. The bagel man

'This is taking insane to a whole new level, Ped. You can't be serious.'

'Deadly.'

'This is … not just unorthodox. It's … well … plain rude. And the media will roast you for it.'

Garland smiled at his press secretary.

'Let them. It's a free country.'

It was the day before the New York primary, and Ped and Hunter had long-standing invitations to a black-tie lunch organized by Don Francis, a reclusive property developer and the Big Apple's most deep-pocketed Republican benefactor.

'Jesus F. Christ. What do I tell Fox and CNN? This is the first time the Don has let media anywhere near an event like this.'

'Tell them the truth.'

'Which is?'

'I had better things to do.'

'What could possibly be better than a check for half a million?'

'I'm gonna head down to East Village, have a good ol' chat with a store owner about the real deal when it comes to the economy.'

Exasperation summed up the look on Amanda's face, and Ped couldn't help feeling sorry for her. The right hand must find it frustrating not knowing what the left was up to. The Ciph and Jin were pigeon-holed away from the public face of the campaign.

'You realize how many cameras will cover your authentic little *chat* at such short notice? A big fat...' She completed the sentence with her thumb and index finger forming a circle.

We'll see.

The only *cameraman* present during the blink-and-you'll-miss-it with the owner and seven customers at a bagel joint near Tompkins Square Park had been hired by Jin to capture seven specific sentences.

From there, Ped and the cameraman were driven across town to a warehouse in Chelsea, where Jin and the rest of the crew had constructed prefabricated settings around a central lighting rig.

For the next few hours, they filmed versions of a post with Ped wearing a suit with red tie, yellow tie, blue tie, a blazer over an open-necked shirt, one with the black t-shirt and Levi's, from his front, left side, right side, lit or shot from angles to amplify authority, inferiority, toughness, concern. Even the background music changed to suit each target demographic.

The only common ingredients in each post were a clip of bagel man and his customer, and Ped ripping up a check.

The messages were variations on a theme: People who bankroll candidates' election campaigns always expect – and usually get – something in return: a federal contract, less regulation, lower taxes, a nudge here, a wink there. They have zero interest (Ped used Amanda's thumb and index finger symbol) in tackling drugs or improving healthcare or schools or making communities better places to live.

'And in return for having our TVs and phones bombarded with contrived poll-driven or AI political spin, bad-mouthing opponents, we have to pay more to visit the doctor, appliances catch on fire because safety checks have been outlawed, and gazillionaires like Don Francis flip the bird at the IRS.'

Ped was then shown ripping up the check for *five hundred*

thousand dollars only as he pledged not to accept another dime from a corporate or special interest and repeated his promise not to run negative ads.

Jin and a platoon of content strategists and creators then got to work producing thousands of personalized versions of posts which would land in targeted newsfeeds, email accounts and text conversations in the hours before the voting centers opened in New York City and the counties of Nassau, Suffolk, Westchester, Rockland, Orange, Putnam and Erie.

*****

Jay recognized *the look*. More specifically the pause. The point in the conversation where a bribe was required to move things along. It was the same the world over. He'd seen it at roadblocks in Tanzania and Myanmar, border posts between Afghanistan and Pakistan, East and West Timor, in the guardhouse of a prison in South Africa. The only thing that changed was the color and denomination of the currency.

This time he was at the Kuta police station, a multi-story affair behind a large billboard featuring the head of the Indonesian Police and the police minister. Both were decked out in military-style uniforms and towering over a menacing row of helmeted men with riot shields, body armor and batons.

Jay's requests to find out what happened to his *friend* Lompok had been stonewalled, until now.

Two million rupiah. $280 give or take.

Lompok was at Kerobokan Prison.

*****

The American Consulate in Denpasar was tucked behind a retail center near the Soldier Statue roundabout. Bec would have missed the entrance if it wasn't for the orange cones in front of a white wall crowned with razor wire.

She showed her passport at the little blue security box, which got her through the gate.

The consulate, according to its website, handled passport applications, witnessed legal documents, processed birth reports of American citizens and helped with absentee voting. It also gave permission for tourists to visit Americans in Kerobokan Prison.

Online searches had shown at least eight current American inmates. Bec zeroed in on Seth Crichton, a Californian doing four years for possessing cocaine.

From social media accounts managed by his family, comments and posts from friends and former inmates, and a web forum run by a prisoner support group, Bec gleaned enough personal information to convince a distracted consular officer she was Seth's cousin.

As she was leaving, she ran into Evan Henley, the Drug Enforcement liaison officer she'd met at the nightclub.

'Ms. Corelli, I hope everything's ok?'

'Yeah. Thanks for asking. Was just arranging to meet a distant... someone... in Kerobokan Prison. Thinking it might give an interesting perspective for my story.'

'Fair enough.'

'I'm also hoping to find out about an Indonesian guy who might be able to help with our story. Ever heard of someone called Lompok?'

Henley shook his head.

'Indonesians are mostly kept in the main part of the prison, as opposed to the foreigners' block. They'll only let you talk to your... distant... cousin?'

*****

Jay rode up to the traffic cones when he saw Bec come out of the consulate.

He handed her the helmet.

'All sorted?'

'Yeah. I guess.'

'What is it? You either got the permission or you didn't.'

'Sorry, yes, I'm allowed to visit. It was just something Henley, the DEA guy... He seemed to know Lompok was at Kerobokan. There was this spark of recognition – it was his eyebrows – when I mentioned the name.'

'It's his job to know that stuff, Bec.'

'I guess.'

They were hungry by the time they got back to Ubud, so instead of returning to their room Jay parked the scooter outside the Little Banana and they walked across the road for lunch.

The restaurant was perched on the hillside above the Camphuan Valley, named after two sacred rivers that met beneath the bridge into Ubud. They were led to one of the tables on the terrace decorated with clay pots filled with marigolds, and decided to share the Betutu Smoked Duck Feast.

Bec looked up from the menu. 'It says here the duck is baked under coconut coals and rice husks for eight hours. The cook must have got up early. I also like the sound of the lime tart with vanilla bean ice cream, if I've got any room left.'

As they ate, they watched a procession of people anting along the famous Camphuan ridge track, passing in and out of view between lush swathes of vegetation obscuring the bustle of the town.

The duck was good. Jay asked the waitress what spices they used.

'Cook use Balinese spices. Little bit secret.'

They paid the bill and were about to head out the door when

Jay noticed a police car parked outside the Little Banana, a cop looking at the scooter.

'Bec, I think you should go back and try that lime tart. I'll come and get you once I've checked everything's OK.'

He ducked through a side entrance, skirted the rear of neighboring properties, coming back to the road beside a guy setting up his mobile food stall. He watched him unpack baskets of noodles, eggs, vegetables, a wok, green gas bottle. A woman walked by on the other side of the road, carrying a basket of crackers on her head.

The cop was still standing beside the scooter, two hundred feet away. Jay stepped back into the shadow of a tree when he heard a siren approaching. It was a fire engine, with two guys in blue uniforms standing on top waving their arms to clear traffic ahead of them.

Jay chose his moment, then used the distraction to dart across the road into an empty lot beside the Mini Mart. A rough track led past the remnants of a temple being swallowed by the jungle, joining up with the path through the rice paddies at the back of the guesthouse.

Everything looked normal. The four-poster day bed with mosquito nets on the patio of their room. Clothes drying on a rack. Plastic hot water flask for all-day coffee and tea. Was he being paranoid?

He scaled the stairs two at a time and pushed open the ornate wooden doors, realizing an instant too late they were unlocked.

The spicy-vinegar smell of rice wine hit him the same time arms seized him from all sides and pinned him on the bed. His hands were pulled behind his back and roughly tied with a cord, before he was yanked to his feet, spun round.

Three of his attackers wore the brownish-gray outfits of the Indonesian Police, not that that meant much. Jay had heard the uniforms, badges, epaulettes and batons sold for a song at markets in Indonesian cities, although the car out front suggested they could be for real.

The fourth guy didn't bother – or need – cop regalia. His bright yellow t-shirt matched the traditional udeng wrapped around his head, and distinctive rings on the two fingers holding a cigarette to his mouth had black stones set in gold heads. He had a Saddam Hussein moustache, and the nails on both thumbs were long and sharp, like his cocksure expression. In his right hand he held up a plastic bag of white powder, but it was the tattoo on the inside of his wrist that got Jay's attention. A black circle bordered by yellow, with black dots spreading outwards like some contagion. He'd seen similar markings on the arm of Dreads, the drug peddler at Canggu beach.

Two-Rings blew a cloud of smoke into Jay's face, dangling the bag that no doubt contained drugs.

'Look what we found in your safe.'

Jay looked through the open doors of the closet, to the safe on a shelf below Bec's clothes. Even if he'd known the room had a safe, he wouldn't have used it. Never trusted them.

He smiled back at Two-Rings.

'You and I both know what's going on here. Let's cut the bullshit. How much do you want?'

Another foul blast of smoke swamped his face, forcing Jay to cough.

'Can't buy your way out of this, Duggan. Bawa dia ke lubang.'

Jay had come across the word *lubang* before. It meant hole, or pit. Which at least made things clearer. This wasn't about money. And they knew his name. They could have got it from the lobby at the Little Banana, but Jay thought that unlikely. The tattoo pointed to retribution for picking on the wrong guy at Canggu.

He considered Two-Rings and his uniformed sidekicks, assessed his immediate prospects of escape with his hands tied behind his back at somewhere between negligible and zero, so settled in for the ride.

10. The color white

'Congrats Daddy. Or should we say, Mr. President?'

'Still got a long road ahead Soph,' said Ped, as his daughter released him from the embrace.

He'd secured 58 of the 95 delegates on offer in New York, extending his lead over Hunter to 40.

Patricia and Sophie had been blitzing Manhattan in a surreal celebrity bubble since the NatZ concert. The family had escaped back to Ped's suite on the twenty-fourth floor of the Four Seasons, after the obligatory speeches, backslaps, high-fives, and endless *Straight Up* salutes of the victory party in the ballroom downstairs.

Sophie left to find her husband. Ped peeled off his jacket, loosened his tie, poured a bourbon, sank into the sofa. He kicked off his shoes, put an arm around his wife.

'You OK, Sugah?'

'Just tired Ped. Ready to get home. Back to the house.'

He buried his face in her hair.

'If Soph's right, your next house could be the color white.'

'Now who's getting ahead of themselves?'

Ped glanced at the TV on the wall. Barry Cosgrove was being interviewed. He reached for the remote.

'Let's see what the big-shot political commentator has to yap about.'

'... no-show at the Don Francis lunch another example. He not only rips up checks in their faces, he more or less accuses the golden gooses of tax evasion, leaving Hunter to explain what *she's* promised in return for the loaded money.

'Mr. Garland flips the bird – to use *his* phrase – at the mainstream media, and leaps head-first into highly contentious issues like the death penalty. This guy's breaking all the rules of political campaigning, yet he's just trounced the woman almost everyone – me included – considered a lock-in for the nomination a month ago.

'Kate Hunter's the candidate the Republican elite groomed to take over after the last failure. To bring the party back to *their* center of reality. But what these primaries are showing us is voters have a very different take on reality. And haven't shaken off the hankering for an anti-establishment candidate – particularly if he's smart like Mr. Garland.

'Time was when primaries were won by the candidate who raised the most money, kissed the most behinds – no exception. Voters see Congresswoman Hunter cocktailing it with billionaires and party insiders, as per the establishment playbook. Then they see Mr. Garland mixing with people on the street, hanging out in jeans at rock concerts. Even his social media posts are at a different level. Congresswoman Hunter's messaging is stilted, conventional. Have you seen Ped Garland's? They're amusing, real, about everyday stuff. His online following has gone ballistic since Florida, and he's being shared like there's no tomorrow.'

Ped made a mental note to thank Jin and the Ciph.

The interviewer gave a subtle shake of the head.

'Are you saying Ped Garland is the real thing? That there's a chance a convicted drug deal… lawyer could win the nomination, go even further?'

'Without the pardon he received from the White House, he wouldn't have qualified to stand for the Public Service Commission in Georgia, let alone the Presidency.

'As has been well documented, Mr. Garland secured his pardon because of his very public acceptance of responsibility and self-awareness of how serious his actions were, and the way he's conducted himself since his release.

'Conventional political wisdom would rule out someone with such a... colorful background. Mr. Garland seems to have turned it to his advantage. His book has been on the top of the *New York Times* bestseller list for weeks, is being seen by many as a kind of redemptive bible.

'You ask if he's the real thing? His remarkable political rise is on the back of what people are seeing publicly. I'm told privately he's getting multiple approaches from governors, congressmen, senators offering to endorse him in return for positions after November. As his lead widens, he doesn't need them so is blowing them off.'

The interviewer gave a hint of a smile.

'So, this *Straight Up* line is more than a throwaway election slogan?'

Cosgrove shrugged.

'Investigative journalists, Hunter's team, and now I'm told investigators for the Democratic frontrunners have been searching for cracks in the *Straight Up* line 24/7 since Mr. Garland announced his candidacy. They've turned up little more than he's admitted to in his book.'

'A 40-point lead, under two months to go. Is it too early to call it for Ped Garland?'

Cosgrove, a veteran of many campaigns, smiled.

'The man has 954 delegates after today. He needs 1237 to become the presumptive candidate. Seven weeks is an eternity in politics. Ask me in six.'

'Fence-sitter,' said Patricia, standing and heading to the bedroom.

'You comin', Ped, while your head can still fit through the door?'

'Got a couple of loose ends to wrap up, Sugah. I'll catch up with you real soon.'

He slipped through another door to the adjoining room, the private space set aside for him wherever they were on the road. The backroom. There was always a baby grand, his rocker recliner, three seats for guests.

One was occupied by Carl Tyler.

Ped poured a bourbon, sat at the piano.

'Whadya got?'

'Our plant in the Hunter camp's been outed. But the damage is done, and Hunter's not going to say anything because it makes her security look lax. She's also sacked the head of her coms team, hired Sebastian Woodhouse.'

'Who is?'

'A muck raker, mud slinger, take your pick. Helped Leadbetter topple Johnson in the mid-terms.'

'Should I be worried?'

'Don't think so.'

'Good. Any progress with Hunter's other matter?'

'Nothing solid yet, but we're closing in.'

*****

MJ had raved about *Hamilton* all the way to Queens, where Mike had dropped her off at school. Conservative friends had advised against taking an eight-year-old to a musical about politics laced with sex and bad language. Zoe, not surprisingly, had told him to go for it.

A scattering of *fucks* and *shits* was hardly alien to kids in New York, and phrases like *not being able to have intercourse over four sets of corsets* sailed over MJ's head.

Mike's attempt at explaining the American Revolution on the way to the theater almost certainly met the same fate. Didn't matter. The kid loved the dancing and the rap and was still churning out her favorite lines long after Mike had put her to bed in Uncle Robbie's apartment in Hell's Kitchen.

He would have preferred MJ focus on lyrics other than *the ten-dollar founding father getting farther by working harder*, but at this stage in the renewed relationship with his daughter, he'd take anything. He'd been an appalling part-time father during his time at Wooster, obsessed with his work and the chase, the clicks. Now Mia, his ex-partner, was giving him a second chance and he was determined not to blow it.

The current assignment might take him offshore for a while, but as soon as it was over, he'd get to spend an extended chunk of quality time with MJ. A year earlier that prospect would have scared the bejesus out of him. After the hug she'd given him as they said goodbye at the school gates, he looked forward to it.

Mike took the subway to Penn Station, then tried to phone Bec again. Still no answer. He tried calling the Little Banana. They hadn't seen Mr. Duggan or Ms. Corelli, but neither had checked out of their rooms, nor showed up for breakfast.

'Maybe they go to east or north for trip, Mr. Bullard? Many tourists do that.'

Mike told himself not to be paranoid. He replied to a message from one of the influencers he was cultivating – a travel vlogger who'd been posting about how drug violence had affected the places he'd visited.

Before boarding the Line 2 train to Harlem, he bought a print copy of the *Times,* craving some anchor to a safe and reliable – though tragically nostalgic – past.

Ped Garland was flavor of the month. There was a story about sales of his book heading, literally, straight up. There were quotes from an electrician in Brooklyn, a janitor from Little Falls, a sound engineer from the Bronx – all claiming to have screwed things up in their past, but seeing Garland's book as *shining a light*, a *reboot*, a *wake-up call.*

64

Mike got off at 103rd St and walked up to Lexington Ave, trying Bec again while he waited to cross. Not even voicemail.

Garland's drug foundation center was behind a church on East 103rd, but Mike struck the wall of true believers blocking the road before he'd got as far as Texas Chicken and Burgers. It was insane. Garland's political opponents accused him of renting these crowds. Mike was seeing something different. Diversity.

Teachers, addicts, soccer moms, tramps, transit workers, artists, hospital workers, uptown furs, downtown suits, grandparents, toddlers, everything in between. Talk about a cross-section. It was like someone sliced a chef's knife through Humans of New York.

The sea parted at the sight of Mike's old Wooster ID card, which also got him through the police barrier into the media section. His timing was spot on. A police motorcycle escort entered the street from the 3rd Avenue end, followed by a line of black SUVs. Mike was swept up in the soundbite scramble.

Political reporters at Wooster warned Mike to expect the unconventional, and the man who'd just aced the New York primary didn't disappoint. He stepped from the lead vehicle wearing an orange t-shirt and jeans, carved through the media pack and the barrier to shake hands with Everyman.

Mike thought the *Straight Up* words on the t-shirt a bit contrived, cheap, un-presidential, until he got inside the center and realized it was the uniform of the foundation's volunteers. Garland was mobbed by hundreds of them, and he worked the room like he knew every one personally.

Perhaps this guy was the real deal.

On his way out, Mike stopped at the merchandise desk and bought a copy of Garland's book, then tried Bec again. No answer. Where could she – and Jay – be?

His call to the Little Banana answered the question.

Mr. Duggan had been taken away by the police.

Oh shit.

*****

Seeing Jay bundled into the police car had pushed Bec into a lather of orange.

Too frightened to return to their room, she'd hailed a cab to the Ubud Police Station, ignoring the driver's attempts at conversation as she breathed and squeezed in a spiraling attempt to keep Aristotle from dragging her thoughts to the tangerine brickwork of the temples, rusted gas canisters lined against a wall like missile silos, the orange dregs of offerings wreathing the sidewalk outside the station.

Officers watching an Indonesian gameshow on television left her stewing at the front desk a full five minutes before an overweight goofball with a Hitler moustache, tin badges like you'd get in a kid's costume section at Walmart, and the nametag W. Winata finally showed any interest. He claimed to know nothing about a *bule* being taken into custody at the Little Banana guesthouse. *Bule* was the word many Indonesians used to describe a white foreigner. When W. Winata turned his back on her and returned to the television, Bec lost it.

She slammed her fist down on the fricken-joke-of-a-service-bell, and when the smug a-holes ignored her, she swept her arm across the desk, sending trays and papers flying onto the floor, the bell smashing into the wall. Arms grabbed her from behind and she was dragged by two female cops through a set of swinging doors, down a hall, flung into a cell.

The stench of sweat and spice and piss from the grimy squat toilet in the corner, the chipped tiles, moldy walls, peeling paint on the rusted bars, the crazed Aristotle faces and alien gibberish of her prostitute and track-marked cellmates, sent her screaming to another level.

Time and hope and reason blurred into an uproar of pushing, slapping, kicking, yelling, until Bec was being dragged again, along the hall of screaming echoes, through the door, down the steps, dumped on the sidewalk. Discarded. Worthless. Garbage.

Everyone had abandoned her. Jay. Mike. W fricken Winata. The drugged-out bitches and whores who couldn't stand to share a cell with her.

Aristotle hauled her eyes from the blood seeping through her ripped sleeve, across the road to the gangster red of the Never Quit R18 billboard. Advertising fricken cigarettes. Even logic had been abandoned.

Bec tried to hail a cab. None would stop. She started walking, not really knowing where she was or where she was going. Balinese cowered or crossed to the other side of the road. Tourists averted their eyes. She recoiled from the shouting red glow of an electronic currency exchange board and caromed into a parked motorbike, knocking down a line of them like dominoes.

Aristotle chortled red in the demonic face of a Walls ice cream logo, the chili fabric swaddling a deformed statue, a flashing of brake lights, the betel mouth of a witch, a diagonal red slash through a no-parking sign.

Prop roots of banyan trees flanking the road down to the bridge clutched at Bec's hair like the tentacles of a mutant Balrog, and souvenir sellers who had tried repeatedly to entice her with their cheap batik looked through her as if she didn't exist.

Aristotle was relentless, mutating the faded red of the hexagonal paving stones into uphill slog sand, sneering at the jilting by her so-called friends in the red of the Kings Tattoo sign, the clawing flames of heliconia flowers, scarlet graffiti splattered on a wall. The 24/7 beggars in the alcove next to the

Dharma café scattered as she approached.

Through some vestige of memory, Bec made it to the guesthouse, but found no respite. Aristotle had slunk ahead, underlining her abandonment in the fiery red bamboo trunks, the withered red flowers behind the ears of the demons guarding the gate, red cushions like dead weights on the day bed outside their room.

The doors hung open, the room empty, her desolation complete.

Aristotle hoisted her face to the painting above the bed, to the bloodied, shard-like leaves of a solitary palm.

She took Jay's Swiss Army knife from the table and stabbed through the canvas, dragging the red hilt all the way down.

11. Italian wool

'They're ready for you. At least try to be civil to them. Please.'

Ped grinned at his press secretary and followed her into the meeting room in the Crowne Plaza in Harrisburg, five days out from primaries in Pennsylvania, Maryland, Connecticut, Rhode Island, and Delaware.

He took his place behind the lectern, touched the frame of glasses, looked down over the assembled rabble. The hidden teleprompter gave him an instant breakdown of the audience. There were reporters from all the main American networks, newspapers, blogs, as well as several representing foreign news services like the BBC and China Global.

'Mornin', y'all. Now this here's the first – and Lawd willing, the last – press conference I'm fixin' to hold durin' this primary campaign. So, my advice to y'all is: don't let this chance slip away.'

He glanced across at Amanda, whose eyebrows were heading for the ceiling.

There was some paper shuffling, looking at phones. Someone coughed.

'Well now, folks, I reckon I'm a bit new to this game. But ain't these press conferences meant for y'all to ask your questions?'

Dozens of arms shot up. Ped pointed to a puffed-up muck slinger in the front row.

'Distinguished gentleman sportin' that fine red tie and Italian wool suit. Got a feelin' that ensemble didn't come from Walmart or the Buffalo Exchange.'

The elder statesman of the press corps managed to look embarrassed, insulted, confused, all at once. He stood, but before he opened his mouth, Ped asked him to state his name and employer, 'cos I'm seeing many of you folks for the first time'.

'Len Anderson, chief political correspondent for CBS. I'm sure one question on most, if not all, my colleague's lips is: why are you giving this press conference?'

Ped exaggerated the eye roll.

'Well, now, I reckoned I'd get me a tougher question from the chief political fall guy over at CBS, but if that's the best y'all got... I suppose I'm just here to get my press secretary off my case.'

Ped looked across at Amanda, who buried her face in her hands.

'She's been tellin' me a good number of y'all reckon I've been avoidin' press conferences and interviews 'cause I'm scared of them tough questions. I'm here today to set the record straight. But if that first question's any indication...'

He left Italian wool standing like an island and pointed to a woman in the third row.

She stood. 'Sonya Rowell, ABC. But why have you refused to give press conferences until today?'

Ped sighed, pretended to glance at his watch as he waited for the teleprompter feed to load.

'Because I've been hearin' folks say the mainstream media ain't representin' the American people no more. Truth be told, it's hard to argue when I look around this room. I can count the non-white faces here on one hand. Reckon if I took a little stroll down the ol' Google lane for an hour or two, I'd find that most of you have college degrees, a couple of you pull in over a million bucks a year, and seven of you are sittin' pretty in that top one percent of wage earners in the country. The homes you fine folks live in are worth three times the national average, and I couldn't help but notice one of you (he glanced at Italian wool) dropped a cool eight million on your penthouse over on Connecticut Avenue. Now, that don't look like a slice of the real American pie to me. I sure hope at least one of youse got a question that matters to the hard-workin', good-hearted folks of this great nation.'

It came from a woman with bulging eyes and a lace collar.

'And you are?'

'Sheena Francis, Wall Street Journal. Does your policy on the death penalty…'

'Now just hold your horses there, Sheena,' Ped interrupted, buying time for the teleprompter feed to load.

'Correct me if I'm wrong, but I seem to recall you've got yourself a master's degree in journalism from Georgetown, and you're a member of the Core Club with that initiation fee of fifty grand and seventeen thousand dollars in annual dues. I see you've been showin' some love on your social media for liberalizing marijuana use and supportin' the National Coalition to Abolish the Death Penalty. Now, what was it you wanted to ask again?'

'That's outrageous.' It was Italian wool, rallying from his humiliation. Mrs. Wall Street Journal was too stunned to speak.

'Why outrageous? It's all right out there in the open. Anybody with a bit of time and a hankerin' to type in a few keywords can find this information.'

'It's not relevant. Sheena, none of us here, is running for public office.'

'But y'all say you represent the public, that you're out here askin' questions on their behalf, that everything you broadcast or put in print is for the public's good.'

'But…'

'Seems to me the public ought to know who's givin' 'em the

news. If Mrs. Wall Street Journal over there's writin' about the death penalty, folks ought to know she's comin' at it from a place where smokin' pot's no big deal and where she's real heart emoji fond of the thought of them mass murderers livin' the high life on three squares a day in air-conditioned comfort.'

'That if Mr. Chief Political Reporter for CBS here starts talkin' about climate change, folks might wanna keep in mind he's been makin' a pretty penny, forty grand to be precise, speakin' at meetings for Consumers for Sound Fuel Policy – which we all know is a front for the petroleum industry. And that he sleeps with a public affairs executive at ExxonMobil. Assuming he sleeps with his wife.'

Ped held up his phone. 'Mind you, those are just the biases, the public biases, you can uncover with a half-dozen thumb swipes.'

He was enjoying himself, and the rising uproar.

'If y'all don't mind, can we have a simple show of hands? How many of y'all in this room hold at least a bachelor's degree?'

Three-quarters put their hands up. Some defiantly refused.

'Go on and raise your other hand if you reckon I'm bein' unfair.'

Before they realized what was happening, Ped, still holding his phone, pushed the photo button on the camera.

'Now I've got myself a photo of this gathering of America's finest journalists – and a few wanderers – all givin' the *Straight Up* salute. If I was willin' to be as carefree and liberal with the truth as some folks in this room, I'd go ahead and post this image...'

Italian wool stood and showboated toward the exit. The rest took their lead from him. As the last one left, leaving just Amanda standing at the back of the room, hands on hips, Ped leaned toward the microphone.

'How'd we do?'

'I thought I'd seen everything.'

'You didn't tell me it was gonna be so much fun.'

*****

The third beating was as good as self-inflicted.

Jay had discovered a way to cut the cord binding his wrists, but hesitated. Now his tormentors were returning for another round.

The uniformed guys who seized him from the Little Banana may have been real cops, but Two-Rings most certainly wasn't. Jay had been gagged, a rice sack put over his head in the cop car, so he wasn't sure where he was taken. Couldn't have been more than five miles before he was dumped, and the cops returned to their day jobs.

Other hands had seized his upper arms, lugged him over gravel, dropped him onto a rough concrete surface. There was a faint smell of poultry, and traffic sound told him there was a road nearby.

The first beating was from the Kidnapping for Dummies playbook. Superficial punches and kicks comfortably absorbed – even with his hands tied behind his back and limited vision – by bracing and breathing out to protect his gut inside a shell of muscle. His tormentors heckled away in Indonesian, though expletives have a similar ring in any language. Jay had managed to work the gag free, but held it in his teeth, so the conversation was one-sided. There was no sign of Two-Rings, so he learnt little.

He was tied to a post and left for a few hours. Before Two-Ring's journeymen returned he'd worked out what *lubang* meant in his context. The clues were revealed one by one in the scuffed court markings, glimpses of feathers, chicken shit, congealed blood, concrete steps and tiered seating, bright fluorescent lights suspended from an iron roof, bare timber rafters, flimsy supporting posts. The *pit* was a volleyball arena used for cockfighting.

For round two, Jay was slapped, kicked, and dragged round the arena. He couldn't figure out whether his adversaries were complete amateurs, intentionally avoiding serious damage, or softening him up. They soon lost interest, tugged him back and reattached the rope from his hands to the post.

This time they left enough slack to allow him to move in a radius of about a yard. Which is how he found the curved end of a razor blade used in cockfighting. He considered using it immediately, concerned how Bec would be coping in his absence, but needed more information. So he cut half-way through the cord binding his wrists, then maneuvered the blade into the hem of his shirt, beside the two zip ties.

The dawn chorus was tuning up as the goons entered the arena for round three. Jay was jerked to his feet. Two-Rings reappeared, with English subtitles. He claimed he was from the National Narcotics Agency, that the bag discovered in the guestroom safe had been analyzed and found to contain 50 grams of cocaine, well above the threshold for the death penalty. Unless he cooperated.

Jay was shaking his head, mumbling at the absurdity of *cooperating* with a gag in his mouth, when he was blindsided.

The blow doubled him over, and he realized immediately – from painful experience – he'd blown a rib. Or two. He winced, cursing himself for letting his guard down. Not splitting when he had the chance.

He was pushed back against the post, felt the coarse fiber texture of a rope noose slip around his neck. His head was yanked back, the other end of the rope tied somewhere above.

The balloon shape of Two-Ring's head loomed in front of

him. Smoke filtered through the sack into his eyes.

'I am a generous man, Mr. Duggan. You have one hour.'

Jay felt like yelling *One hour for what, you dumb shit?,* but kept biting on the gag.

They left him again.

He took deep breaths, forced himself to cough. It hurt like hell, but past experience – smashing into a rock white-water rafting on the Zambezi and the run-in with hired thugs at a soybean plant in Guatemala – had taught him it was the best thing for broken ribs. Something about helping the immune system of the lungs attack invaders.

Jay could hear a couple of Two-Ring's men playing kiu-kiu – an Indonesian version of dominoes – somewhere in the stands.

He manipulated the blade, cut through the rest of the cord binding his hands, then shuffled around on his backside until he was facing away from his chaperones. He sawed through the noose rope, leaving a couple of threads intact. Then spat out the gag and called out that he was ready to talk.

He threw in *bencong* – the Indonesian word for ladyboy, hoping the insult would lure both men within range.

He primed the zip ties, slipped them over his wrist, then squatted, coiled, ready to spring.

They approached, fuming in Indonesian and lulled by the noose round Jay's neck and sack covering his head. He identified the leader of the pair and took him out first, surprising him with a lightning jab to the throat, before rotating to lower his sidekick with a well-directed knee to the groin.

Jay's ribs burned as he trussed them up, noticing the circle tattoos ringed by yellow on both wrists.

*****

Montoya was the first to leave after desserts, making his excuses to the army general, two police inspectors and the senior administrator from the Denpasar Municipality.

The Lexus pulled up at the curb as he exited the restaurant. He took the call as the driver eased into the traffic.

The New Zealander had escaped, as planned.

Montoya hoped Duggan got the message. If not, they'd have to take things to the next level, which posed other risks. Foreigners going missing or dying in Bali tended to draw attention from embassies, which heaped pressure on the local politicians, who heaped pressure on the police, not all of whom were on the payroll.

He turned his thoughts to the American journalist, and the message she would receive on her visit to the prison tomorrow.

*****

Jay recognized the Suargan temple a few doors down from the headquarters of New Gangga Rafting on the road across the fields to the west of Little Banana. He cut across paddies to join up with the track near the swimming pool of Ananda Cottages. An old woman sweeping the soil beside a chicken coop looked up long enough to dismiss him as yet another disheveled *bule* returning from an all-nighter.

His ribs stung, but Jay was more worried about the state he'd find Bec in. She'd tried to kill him in India once, after he'd left her in a hotel room less than 30 minutes. That was when he found out about her borderline personality *issues*, how handling separation wasn't one of her strong points.

He slipped through the back gate of the guesthouse, paused behind a jackfruit tree to check the lay of the land. Everything looked, sounded at peace. Water trickling in the fountain, the drooping tip of a pengor quivering in the breeze, the Balinese dawn symphony in rooster and dove.

The padlock was missing, but Jay could see through the narrow gap between the doors that the wooden slide bolt had been pulled across from the inside. He knocked, gently at first, then more forcefully. No response. Hopefully Bec was in a deep sleep.

He grabbed two teaspoons from the tray beside the water flask, slid the handles through the gap above and below the bolt, then tilted them to get enough purchase to shimmy the wood to the left, a fraction of an inch at a time.

When he felt the bolt give, he braced his arms for whatever might come at him, then nudged the door open with his foot. The first thing to smack him in the face was the temperature. The aircon had been wound down to sub-Antarctic. Then he saw the painting, or what was left of it.

Bec was on the floor beside the bed, cocooned under a blanket, peering up at him through eyes that had cried to exhaustion. Jay slumped down beside her, eased under the duvet, cradling her until she fell asleep.

*****

Mike's first image of Bali, as the Emirates jet descended on its final approach, was a 400-foot hunk of copper and brass that made the Statue of Liberty look like a fourth grader dying to answer the teacher's question.

The colossal Garuda Wisnu statue on a hill south of Ngurah Rai Airport was dedicated to the search for the elixir of life in Hindu mythology. Right now, Mike would settle for proof of life.

As soon as he'd heard Jay had been taken away by the police, his only concern was for Bec. The New Zealander could look after himself. Bec could be a mess. Fear of abandonment, a trademark of people with borderline personalities, would have triggered a downward spiral into an emotional – and potentially fatal – abyss.

Mike had been fearing the worst since leaving New York, and his anxiety notched up even further when he couldn't get through to Bec during the brief layover in Dubai. Reading the opening chapters of Ped Garland's book *Straight Up*, particularly the one detailing how drugs had driven a close friend of the candidate to commit suicide, didn't help.

Mike expected Customs to show interest in some of the toys in his suitcase, but he sailed through the *nothing to declare* lane and into the arrival hall, where the heat whacked him. He felt every one of the 30 degrees difference from Manhattan.

He slowly scanned the line of signs being held by men wearing sarongs and pieces of cloth folded around their heads. There was no Mr. Bullard or Little Banana, but on his return sweep he noticed a printed sign on A4 paper *edited* with red scrawls. The *B* in Bullard had been changed to a *P*, an *h* inserted after the second *l*, and *er* added at the end. Pull Harder.

Jay's face appeared over the top. He was smiling, but it looked like he'd been in a brawl. His right eye was almost closed, there were cuts on his forehead and arms, a bandage round one knee and he flinched as they shook hands.

'What the hell happened? And how's... where's Bec?'

'She's fine. She's gone to prison.'

*****

This was not what Bec was expecting.

After passing through tedious security checks, metal detectors, bag scanner, getting patted down in a windowless room and surrendering her phone and passport in return for a visitor's pass stamped on her hand, she walked through an open steel door into a park-like space the size of half a football field.

Kids were running, skipping, laughing on the lawn, in and out and around family groups and couples sitting, hugging, kissing, chatting, sharing food in the shade of trees.

Family day inside Kerobokan was more festival than funeral, although Aristotle was glimmering gold in the dome of the mosque and yellow in the frangipani, reminding Bec not to be fooled by the once-in-a-month aberration from the brutal normality of life in Bali's notorious prison.

Behind the smiles, she noticed a visitor absentmindedly playing with a wedding ring, laughter from an inmate that didn't reach his eyes – tell-tale signs of strain, façades of happiness.

Bec recognized Seth Crichton's face from a news photo of him being paraded in an orange jumpsuit after his arrest. He'd lost weight since then, but was still a bull of a man, dwarfing the prison guard he stood beside.

She introduced herself and Seth pointed to a table with a handwritten sign, *Pendiam pergilah!*

Bec asked for a translation as they sat on red plastic stools.

'Reserved, so fuck off!'

'Your sign?'

Seth nodded, his eyes straying over her breasts, reminding Bec he'd been inside two years.

'The fuck you here for lady? You think this is some theme park peep show for fucking tourists?'

From comments posted on a crowdfunding site set up to provide materials and equipment for a jewelry workshop at Kerokoban, Bec knew how Seth spent most of his free time in the prison. She took the silversmithing magazine out of her bag, which brought a smile to his face, loosened his tongue.

Bec gradually moved the conversation to drug trafficking, their investigation into Charlie Scott's death. Seth was more interested in complaining about inconsistencies in the police case against him, which Bec hinted she could investigate.

A group of Indonesian inmates started hovering nearby, showing too much interest, so Bec leaned across the table to keep the conversation private.

Her mention of *Lompok* was like flicking a switch. There was a sparkle of recognition in Seth's eyes, an instant before two of the inmates lunged across the table.

There was a flash of yellow headscarves as Bec was squashed against the wall and passed out.

12. The Ciph

More than two centuries of political wisdom since the first Presidential election, and billions of dollars on campaign strategists and media consultants, had been reduced to this.

Numbers on a laptop.

When Jin Ly and Nadia Zapora had knocked on his door the morning after Super Tuesday, Ped had called security.

'You need us,' Jin had said. Calmly, with no hint of danger.

After throwing everything and more into campaigning in the week leading to the all-important first Tuesday in March – with fifteen states on the line including the monsters of California and Texas, Ped had ended up trailing Hunter by an embarrassing 122 delegates.

Some influential media were already calling the contest, and *the talk* had shifted to potential running mates for Hunter and *when*, not *if*, Garland would withdraw.

And there he was, standing in a white Beverly Hills Hotel bathrobe, confronted by a power-dressed Asian-American and a kid with half her head shaved, the other flowing in aquamarine, rods of steel through her nose and cheek, hugging a laptop. Like salt in a wound.

Three words made Ped send Mack, the security guard, back along the hall.

'SpreadEagle on steroids.'

The state-of-the art voter engagement app that combined conventional campaigning techniques with the power of artificial intelligence was set to rewrite the electioneering landscape, and rumors were that Hunter's campaign was experimenting with a prototype.

'We've taken it to a whole new level.'

That got them into Ped's backroom, where Jin did all the talking. She was the daughter of a fifth-generation Chinese immigrant, had a master's degree in communications, PhD in social media marketing, and five years crafting social messaging for one of the biggest ad agencies in California.

Jin's sidekick looked like she should have been at school, one with relaxed dress codes. But she possessed an extraordinary gift: an uncanny ability to sift through the vast sea of digital information and uncover hidden patterns. As well as an insatiable appetite for hacking.

Over the past few months she'd been refining a micro-targeting program that incorporated the most advanced features of SpreadEagle and its two main rivals.

Jin described the kid's hybrid program as a digital masterpiece.

'She can seamlessly weave together the intricate threads of social media posts, smartphone use, consumer behavior data, cross-referencing all the information with the latest polling analysis, creating a profiling engine that peers into the very souls of… whoever you want it to.'

'From public or private sources?'

Jin inclined her head and smiled.

'What's the real question here, Mr. Garland?'

'Is what she's doing traceable?'

'No. And what we are offering you is far more advanced than what your opponent is paying two hundred fifteen grand a week for.'

Ped was about to ask how she knew this, but figured if the kid could hack into the big platforms and private polling companies, Hunter's firewall would be a piece of pie.

There was more.

'The kid's a prodigy. She's cracked the code on using keyword combinations that go way beyond simple identification of individual targets. She's dug deeper, unravelling what truly ignites people's passions, discovering the precise times their guards are down, even deciphering the days of the week they're most open to persuasion. And that's not all. She's found a way to double-tag them, subtly influencing their decisions by tapping into the people who hold sway over them.'

Jin paused, letting it sink in.

'And here's the kicker, Mr. Garland. She's translated all this into an app that's light years ahead of anything anyone else – including your opponents – are doing with peer-to-peer texting.'

'Which does what, exactly?'

'It allows us – you – to send anonymous text messages to target's phones, without their permission.'

'That's gotta be illegal.'

'Not yet Mr. Garland. We've found a loophole in the federal regulations.'

'And the kid does this all by numbers and combinations and codes?'

'Correct.'

'Like one of those, what are they called, ciphers?'

'Call it what you want.'

Which was where the nickname Ciph was born. For obvious reasons, the kid didn't want her real identity known.

The odd couple had joined the backroom team under Carl Tyler and, in the fortnight between Super Tuesday and the bundle of primaries centered on Florida, refined and tested the software, resulting in the *vein for a vein* line. Ped had put his faith in the numbers and never looked back.

Until now.

They were four days out from a clutch of primaries in the north-east. The Ciph's data pointed to a speed hump in

Pennsylvania, the biggest prize of the day with 71 delegates.

Ped refused to believe what he was seeing on the Ciph's laptop in the hotel backroom in Pittsburgh. Everything he was hearing, the vibe on the street, in the cafés, at rallies and factories throughout the Keystone state yelled slam-dunk. He doubted Hunter would score a single delegate.

His phone beeped. It was his campaign manager.

'You've got to make the call now, Ped. The advance crews can't wait any longer.'

'Cancel Philly. We're out of here. I'm shifting resources to Connecticut, Delaware, and Rhode Island.'

'We still staying clear of Maryland?'

'Publicly, yes.'

*****

Mike looked at his phone in disbelief. Garland's social media following had ballooned to forty million since the image of the roomful of journalists with their hands in the air at the Harrisburg press conference went viral. Mike had become follower number 32,574,002 after seeing the candidate in Harlem just four days ago.

He yawned as their driver turned sharp right before a statue of some Hindu god wrestling a dragon. Mike's body clock was still ticking on eastern standard time.

The rest of the article on Garland's relationship with the mainstream media concluded he was doing just fine without it. By the time one of his updates was reposted or forwarded and pinballed through cyberspace, he was reaching seventy million. Audience numbers for the top-rating primetime TV news shows wavered round the three-million mark, and the weekday print-run for the *New York Times* had dipped below half a million. Influence over your audience was limited when the other guy's bullhorn was 35 to 140-times louder.

It reminded Mike to get back to the social justice influencer who was warming to his messages about the devastating impact of drug trafficking on vulnerable communities in countries like Indonesia.

They were dropped off outside the BIMC Hospital, and Mike, still looking at his phone, followed Jay through the main entrance to the elevators.

Jay pushed the button for Bec's floor.

'Knew this guy who flushed his phone down the toilet when it told him he was spending more than an hour a day on the screen. Can you believe that? *Sixty* minutes. *Every* day.'

Mike tapped a few keys and held up the phone to the Neanderthal. Jay took in the numbers, shaking his head. It showed Mike's screen time for the previous seven days averaged 5 hours 24 minutes. The biggest chunks, highlighted in orange, were on social media.

Bec was sitting up in bed, looking at *her* phone, and Mike could see Jay's head shaking again. She looked up and smiled.

'About time you showed up, Bullard. How you doin?'

'How are you, more to the point? Jay tells me you were…'

'I'm fine. Wrong place, wrong time, end of story. Now that you're back, I'm thinking…'

'But Jay…'

'Wasn't there. So is just guessing I was the target. Will you guys stop worrying about me and get with the program.'

Mike glanced across at Jay, who raised his palms in mock surrender.

'Ok, so what did you learn at the prison, Bec?'

'Don't remember much. I was knocked out.'

'I rest my case,' said Jay. 'According to the doctor, who was told by the ambulance driver, who heard it from a guard – so we're talking a serious case of Chinese whispers here – Bec was knocked out when her head hit the wall. The guard couldn't, more likely *wouldn't* say whether the attacker was going for Bec or Seth, but it seems Seth shielded her from more serious injuries. Could have saved your life, Bec.'

Mike turned back to her.

'Did Seth tell you anything about this Lompok dude before your head accidentally bumped into the wall?'

Bec gave him a filthy look. 'He knew something. The way he reacted, his eyes when I mentioned Lompok's name, just before…'

Mike knew nobody who could read a person like Bec Corelli. Her ability to decode the unspoken language of emotions – from the subtlest furrowing of a brow, tremble of a lip, twitch of a cheek – was freakish. And a double-edged trait of her borderline personality. Heightened empathy towards the feelings of others could also drag Bec down with the weight of their unspoken pain.

'So where does this leave us? What's our next move? How long will you be in here?'

'The doc wants to keep me in for a few days. He thinks it was just a mild concussion but wants a scan to be sure.'

She sat up straighter, adjusting her pillows.

'Seth is still our best option. Now you're back Mike, you could go visit him, as a fellow American.'

'Not a good career move.' It was Jay, looking out the window with his back to them.

'You got a better idea?'

'Actually, I have.'

*****

Kerokoban Prison. A ten-acre hellhole made famous by the incarceration of a blue-eyed Australian girl-next-door caught with nine pounds of cannabis in her bodyboard bag.

Built to hold 300, the prison was currently home to more than five times that number of drug users, mules, sellers, traffickers, gangsters, murderers, rapists, pedos, pickpockets. And Lompok. Possibly.

A stack of books had been written about life in the joint, including the dog-eared paperback Jay held in his hands as he sat in the third-floor room of a guesthouse he'd rented near the prison.

From the window he looked through binoculars across a large open field, past scrawny cows grazing on waist-high weeds, garbage, bits of plastic and mounds of abandoned building material to the high whitewashed walls capped with corroded spirals of razor wire.

His vantage point was level with one of the prison's four watchtowers, beside ten-foot gray doors with a tiny grilled window.

After scouting the main entrance building and exterior walls, Jay decided the side gate held the most promise.

13. Sheets to the wind

Ped had spent the morning of voting day in the shopping centers and strip malls of Wilmington, Delaware, then split the afternoon between Rhode Island and Connecticut before flying to Philly for the five-state victory party being set up in the Terrace Ballroom of the Pennsylvania Convention Center.

Several muck slingers, including the great Barry Cosgrove, had ridiculed him for not spending a minute of the previous three days in either Pennsylvania or Maryland, which between them had almost twice as many delegates as Connecticut, Rhode Island and Delaware combined.

Under the heading *Opportunity lost to bury Hunter in home state*, Cosgrove described Garland's decision to bypass Maryland as his 'biggest blunder'.

Ped's public line, that Congresswoman Hunter was doing a fine job for the people of Maryland, and it didn't feel right to campaign against her in her home patch, had been widely reported.

Privately, Jin and the Ciph had been carpet-bombing swinging voters and their reinforcers with under-the-radar third-party posts and texts in Hunter's home patch for weeks. Carl had also been active in the dark recesses of Baltimore. Ped didn't want to know the details.

Exit polls throughout the morning pointed to wins for Garland in Connecticut, Delaware and Rhode Island, a respectable loss in Maryland, a pounding in Pennsylvania. Little had changed by the time Ped boarded the plane in Hartford for the flight to Philly, and the results were confirmed minutes before he stepped onto the stage at the convention center. His lead had been trimmed to 32.

The bulk of his speech to the faithful concentrated on the plus side – that he'd done better than expected in a region Hunter was predicted to dominate, he needed just 201 more delegates to secure the nomination, positive speculation about his chances against the two clear candidates emerging on the Democrat side. Ped had instructed Carl to shift resources from the team shadowing Hunter's campaign to focus on the two Dems.

But as he faced the balloons, banners and saluting hard-core, he sensed a flatness, lack of vigor compared to previous victory rallies. A large contingent of delirious Delaware supporters – many of them three sheets to the wind – had made the trip up the interstate from Wilmington, along with smatterings from Bridgeport and New Haven. Most of the faces, though, were roll-your-sleeves-up Pennsylvania vols who knocked on the doors, made the calls, talked the talk. He'd taken them for granted. Let them down.

He tried to apologize but was shouted down and eventually left the stage to saluting chants of *Ped, Ped, Ped* that reminded him of black and white newsreels from Berlin.

What had he unleashed? Was he starting to believe his own bullshit? And could he actually pull it off? He'd misread the mood. A kid with steel rods through her nose was more in touch with folk than he was. And he couldn't see the Ciph getting security clearance to enter, let alone work, at the White House.

*****

It took Jay three days. Every vehicle passing through the gray doors – trucks delivering food, utility and tradesmen's vans, prisoner transports with fresh meat, a pizza delivery truck, even a busload of suits from the Indonesian Ministry of Law and Human Rights – was searched thoroughly inside and out, including a sweep underneath with bomb-detection mirror.

Every vehicle except this one. A matte black Hummer.

From his vantage point in the guesthouse, Jay watched it arrive each morning between 5.50 and 5.55. The gates swung open, and the driver reversed the vehicle into a covered bay. Then each evening between 6.35pm and 6.40pm, the gates opened and out it came. Like clockwork.

Jay spent the morning with Mike at a cafe near the Taman Sari market, trawling through images and video and posts on social media from Facebook to YouTube, and sites Jay had never heard of. It was alarming what you could glean from public sources if you knew what you were looking for. Jay wasn't fooled by the occasional PR whitewash when prison authorities let selected journalists inside to interview ass-lickers and film choreographed routines.

He convinced Mike to loan him his smartphone, show him how to connect it wirelessly to a tiny camera the journalist had brought back from the States.

After Mike left to check up on Bec in hospital, Jay visited hardware stores to get the equipment he'd need. Screwdrivers, hex keys, pliers, small hinges, a slender piece of metal, can of spray paint, hand drill, nuts, bolts, small mirror. He was sitting on his motorbike down the road from the gray doors by 6.30pm.

He slipped into the traffic behind the Hummer and followed it along the busy Teuku Umar Barat towards Denpasar. It crossed a canal with blue utility pipes along the side, then turned into a small lane beside a footwear store. Jay watched from the corner as the Hummer went up the narrow lane and stopped outside a two-story house. A man in the blue uniform of the prison service got out of the passenger side and entered the house. Jay guessed he was the prison's governor.

The Hummer reversed out of the lane, and Jay followed it to an executive parking yard behind the Ibis Styles Hotel.

*****

'He's done it before, apparently.'

'Fricken hell Mike. This is insane. I can't believe you went along with it. Encouraged him.'

'He didn't need any encouraging.'

Bec signed her discharge papers at the front desk and followed Mike to a cab waiting outside law offices next to the hospital. The sun hadn't been up long, but the heat was already sapping after the air-conditioned ward.

She'd been buoyant at the thought of seeing the blue of the sky after three days in a windowless room waiting for a scan. But news Jay was planning to break *in* to Kerobokan Prison had Aristotle smothering in the amber cloths bundled round roadside shrines.

'What do you mean, he's done it before?'

'Told me he sprung a friend out of a prison in a country called Timor-Leste, which I'd never heard of. It's a former Portuguese colony north of Australia. Jay and his friend, who lives somewhere here in Bali by the way, were trying to stop a Portuguese company chopping down a forest of sandalwood when the friend got busted. Jay was a bit vague on the details, but it seems he got into the jail dressed as a Catholic priest. The guy's like a cross between Jack Reacher and Greta Thunberg.'

'That doesn't make this right, Mike.'

Before leaving the hospital room, Bec had gone through her morning routine of breathing and squeezing – her version of the TIPP distress tolerance technique recommended for people with borderline personality. TIPP was short for lowering *Temperature*, *Intense* exercise, *Paced* breathing, *Paired* muscle relaxation. Bec shortened it even further to *breathe* and *squeeze*, adding in *splash* and *dash* when Aristotle played up, like he was now by drawing her attention to the yellow in the Hypermart sign in the median strip.

'What else did Jay say? You know, about his past?'

'Not much, I thought you knew.'

'He keeps a lot to himself. From what I've been able to piece together, he's worked all over the world as a kind of elite environmental activist. I'm pretty sure most of what he's done is outside the law, which is why he doesn't broadcast it. I know he's sabotaged a gold mine in Egypt and a copper mine in Myanmar, as well as blowing something up in India. Something happened in Zimbabwe he refuses to talk about. And he was involved in protests against toxic waste being dumped in Alabama. Stopping sandalwood deforestation would be right in his wheelhouse.'

Mike was smiling. 'Breaking into a prison sounds a breeze.'

Bec looked out the cab window at the passing commuter chaos. Thought about what she'd learnt online about Kerokoban Prison during her research into Seth Crichton – the unchecked violence, murder, rape. Prisoners catching rats, breaking their necks, eating them raw. Death row inmates setting themselves on fire.

'It's the most irresponsible, hair-brained idea I've ever heard, and I need to talk him out of it. When's he planning to attempt this suicide mission?'

Mike palmed his phone. 'About now.'

*****

Fuel economy was the last thing on the minds of executives at the Indiana heavy vehicle manufacturer AM General when they decided back in the 1990s to convert military Humvees into civilian SUVs called Hummers.

During his online research with Mike, Jay had laughed out loud at a review describing the Hummer as *the perfect example of an SUV done right when your scoring is just based on badassery.*

The spec of most interest to Jay was the dimensions of a lock box he'd spotted in the cargo area of the Hummer when the hardtop was opened by guards as the vehicle entered the prison each day. They'd poked around the box, never opened it.

Breaking into the parking lot behind the Ibis, and into the Hummer, had been straightforward. Loud gamelan music from a nearby temple had drowned out the sounds as Jay got to work on the lockbox.

After tracing the edges of the panel with his fingers, probing for vulnerability, he'd carefully inserted the tip of a small screwdriver into a seam. The panel resisted initially, so he'd adjusted the angle of the screwdriver, applying pressure until the first screw yielded.

Once he'd detached the panel, Jay removed the expensive-looking kites stored inside and turned his attention to the latch. Using the piece of metal, which he'd painted matte black, he'd crafted a latch that could be opened from inside the box.

Satisfied the surface of the panel would appear untouched to a casual observer, he'd attached the tiny camera under the chassis and tested the connection with the phone.

Jay got an undercarriage view of the black and white curbing popular in Bali on the drive to the governor's house and back to Kerokoban. There was a moment of anxiety when the Hummer passed through the prison gates and was surrounded by several pairs of boots and raised voices in Indonesian, before Jay felt the passenger door open and watched the governor's shiny black shoes walk away.

14. Pawn your TVs

If trusting the Ciph over the death penalty was a leap of faith, this was jumping out of an airplane at thirteen thousand feet without a parachute. Naked.

It was Indiana and Kansas week, and after the misread in Pennsylvania and an eye to November, Ped had asked Jin and the Ciph to identify an issue and pitch that would resonate with their target audience *and* appeal to soft Democrats he needed to woo later in the year.

So here he was, rolling up to a General Motors plant in Noblesville, Indiana, to tell three hundred auto workers and grease monkeys their eight hours-a-day plus benefits were... unsustainable.

When he'd tried to explain to the Ciph the state was the home of the Indy 500, and tens of thousands were employed in its auto industry that pumped billions a year into the local economy, she looked at him like he was talking a foreign language.

'You asked for the cohort, Grandpop. This is it. Straight up.'

They'd driven up from Indianapolis on the campaign bus, giving a ride to half a dozen local muck slingers – ruffling the feathers of the national media reps forced to follow in their own vehicles. Ped didn't mind; he wanted to get a handle from the locals on how his pitch would be received.

Like a lead balloon, political suicide, death wish summed it up.

The security team had a busload of reinforcements waiting nearby just in case.

They were greeted in the parking lot by dozens of supporters holding *Ped for President* and *Straight Up* posters, a handful of serial anti-death penalty protesters, and a dopehead with a handwritten *Peddling for Ped* sign. Which was kinda funny, so Ped made a beeline for him, shook his hand. The media lapped it up.

The mood inside the cafeteria was tense. Ped guessed the local reporters had tipped them off about his *death wish*. So he tapped the frame of his glasses and ploughed right in.

'Republican politicians have been telling folks in your industry for years everything's just peachy keen', climate change is a hoax, they're gonna ease up on environmental regulations like fuel economy targets. Dangling the promise that your jobs are rock solid, go buy a bigger flat screen.

'The Democrats, on the other hand, figure all these climate scientists and Swedish teenagers with Asperger's could be onto something. Not only do they want tough vehicle pollution standards, they also want to ban the sale of cars with internal combustion engines – completely in twenty years, and by fifty-percent inside ten. Which would be a death wish for plants like this. And your jobs.

'Now y'all might have noticed I'm campaigning under the motto *Straight Up*. Tell it how it is. Well, both parties are feeding you a line. Partisanship and kowtowing to special interests are plaguing this country, right alongside drugs and dishonest politicians who profit from pushing their own agendas. The truth is almost always somewhere in the middle.

'*Almost* always. But not on climate change and the damage your industry is doing to the environment.'

He paused, to let the seething intensify, and double-check he was reading the teleprompter's suggestion correctly.

'I'm not here today to sugar-coat it. I'm here to tell you your jobs are fucked. Combustion engines are history. Pawn your TVs.'

Ped braced himself for hell to break loose. All he got was

open mouths. Three hundred of them. He wasn't sure if it was the language or the message. Or both.

It didn't last long.

*****

Jay eased himself out of the lockbox, careful to avoid any rocking that might give away his presence. Using the torch on the phone, he located the lever for the tailgate mechanism.

His most immediate danger was being detected by the guard in the watchtower beside the gate. Each morning he'd watched from the guesthouse, the guard had moved to the south side of the tower to concentrate on inmates assembling for the headcount on a tennis court adjacent to cellblocks Seminyak and Kuta. Only a masochist would name prison buildings after beaches.

Jay sucked in a few deep breaths to calm himself, then gently released the tailgate, supporting it to prevent it slamming open. Once out, he angled the small mirror to check the surroundings were clear, then sidled round the wall of the courtyard and through an arched gateway to the back of a Hindu temple to wait for the siren signaling the end of the headcount.

He knew from social media postings certain categories of prisoners were now free to roam the open zones until the early evening count. The ones who paid for the privilege or were tampers – senior inmates who helped settle disputes. Standard practice was for eight guards to be on duty at any one time – four posted in the watchtowers, four patrolling the grounds.

Close to one hundred of the 1700 inmates were non-Indonesian, from more than twenty nationalities. Jay was counting on those numbers putting enough doubt into anyone he come across as to whether he belonged.

Half of the foreigners, including Seth Crichton, lived in

relative luxury in the foreigners' block in the north-western corner of Kerobokan. Those who couldn't afford the monthly fee took their chances in blocks of cells built to hold three prisoners but stuffed with a dozen. Jay had considered trying to find Seth in the foreigners' block, but decided the chances of being outed were too high. New arrivals did not get into the privileged space immediately and there would be a waiting list.

Video footage smuggled out and posted on TikTok suggested the faded batik shirt, tattered denim shorts, Bali United football cap and flip-flops Jay was wearing wouldn't look out of place, nor the bamboo broom he scored from the back of the temple.

He studied the map he'd sketched from his research, then walked down the path beside the intake and release building used to process new and departing prisoners.

Groups of inmates returning from the headcount paid him no attention. He turned right into a path between a utility building and laundry, then ambled along the sideline of a volleyball court where inmates were preparing for a game near the cellblock known as Jimbaran. He gagged at the stench from blocked toilets, waved the broom through a swarm of mosquitos.

Jay knew to expect constant announcements over the PA speakers, but the first surprised him so much he ducked and turned his head. Too quickly. A Balinese prisoner, one arm obliterated by tattoos and reeking of clove cigarettes, blocked his path.

'What have we here? A fresh meat bule boy.'

Other inmates started showing interest.

'Yeah, Got in yesterday man. Looking for the kitchen near dining room Sanur. Can you point me in the right direction?'

Words – peppered with laughter – were exchanged in Indonesian.

'Why sure bule boy. It's back there, through the archway and right. Just ask for Taman. He'll show you what to do with your broom stick.'

Jay knew he was being directed to cellblock Lovina, notorious for sex offenders.

He played the innocent and walked through the archway, but turned left across the edge of a large open area he guessed was the park Bec had been in for the family day. Prisoners were weeding the gardens. It was closer to the main administration building than he wanted, but he made it to the library without further incident.

He ducked into the entranceway, had another look at the map. The silversmith workshop was in a building beside the chapel. The most direct route would take him past cellblock Amed, controlled by the Kaluraha gang. From Jay's research, he knew the gang was dominated by outsiders from the neighboring Indonesian island of Java and had expanded from humble roots in the villages of Surabaya into one of the largest and most ruthless in Bali.

Jay slung the broom over his shoulder, headed down a path between the infirmary and a building containing isolation cells for prisoners on suicide watch or mental health cases. An emaciated Irish prisoner with a pockmarked face tried to engage him in conversation outside a room he knew from a book was used for hookers on sex nights, organized by guards who took outrageous commissions. Used condoms blocked the drain.

Jay rattled off a few sentences in Māori, pretending he didn't speak English. Paddy quickly lost interest, though Jay could feel eyes on his back as he walked past a classroom and turned right before the mosque. Sandals and flip-flops had been abandoned on the concrete step. Through the door Jay saw a dozen or so prisoners kneeling in prayer.

He moved on, past a large dining hall, the din of tables and chairs scraping on concrete, pots being stacked, the starchy smell of rice cooking. Ahead was the building housing the various workshops. The silversmith room was at the far end.

A guard was chatting to two prisoners outside the chapel, so Jay waited until he moved off, then walked over to sit on a low stone wall outside the workshop, considering the padlock on the door. Seth had told Bec it was opened by a guard after lunch each day. Chosen prisoners who had earnt the right – or paid for it – were allowed to work there. Jay fingered the picking tool in his pocket, waiting for the path to clear.

It took less than twenty seconds to get inside.

He was surprised how well resourced the workshop was. A homemade propane furnace, gas stoves, heat bricks, stainless steel mesh, hairdryers, a jeweler's saw, buffing machine, drills, copper tongs, metal stamps, a silver solder, oxy-acetylene torch, rolls of ceramic fiber for lining the furnace. Porno pictures from magazines pinned to the wall.

There were two side rooms. The first, easy to unlock, was a storeroom with tubes of silver clay and epoxy putty, gas bottles, molds, stamps, small boxes for presenting jewelry for sale. The second room had a lock Jay couldn't open. He returned to the workshop, waited.

Through a crack in the window, he spied vignettes of the daily grind. Drug deals. A fight. Group yoga session. Consensual and non-consensual sex. Prisoners stumbling past, drunk.

The siren sounded for lunch. Jay's stomach rumbled in sympathy. The signal for the end of lunch was his cue to get into position behind the door, prepping the zip tie by looping the strap, inserting it loosely into the head.

Jay expected the opened padlock on the door to put the guard on alert, but it made little difference. The little guy's breath smelled of arak and he was easily immobilized. Jay taped the guard's mouth, squirted putty into his ears, pulled a bag over his head – all from behind so his face wouldn't be seen.

He found a key to the second side room in the guard's pocket. As suspected, it was where the finished jewelry was kept. Jay dragged the guard into the room, secured him to a wall bracket, then walked back through the workshop into the storeroom.

The inmates turned up soon after. Three accents. German, Balinese, American. Seth came into the storeroom. It took some effort, with a broken rib, for Jay to subdue and stop him calling for help. Bec hadn't mentioned his size.

Jay felt the tension go out of the big American's shoulders as soon as he mentioned he was a friend of the woman journalist who'd visited him.

Lompok was well known to the inmates of Kerobokan, though Seth had never met him. He was always *entertained* in the VIP section. Meaning private room, the latest smart TV, Wi-Fi, beer fridge, women on tap, come and go as you please.

'But if you fuckers are looking for the source of NuNu, you're wasting your time with Lompok. He's perantara. A middleman. You need to check out a limo company called Eksek, near the airport.'

Jay persuaded Seth to get the other two inmates to leave the workshop for ten minutes, then told him about the guard tied up in the other room.

The American's demeanor changed instantly, from macho to panic.

'Calm down mate. He has no idea who jumped him, and you can be the white knight. I'll make it look like someone broke in to steal some bling.'

'But he would have heard...'

'Nothing. He's heard zilch Seth. Relax. I took care of it. But I *will* need your help with something. How long before they'll notice the guard missing?'

'He usually hangs around twenty minutes or so after opening up. Checking the lockup. Taking his cut.'

'Ok. Give me ten, then *discover* the door to the lockup is open, find the guard, rescue him.

'What are you going to... How the fuck did you even get in here?'

'Probably better you didn't know. I'm not planning on a long stay. Tell me, which gang controls cellblock Nusa Dua?'

'The Iblis. Why?'

'How do they get on with the Kaluraha?'

'With knives.'

'What color do the Iblis use?'

'Red. What the...'

And if the Iblis wanted to insult the Kaluraha, what would they do, or say?'

Seth thought for a moment.

'They'd call them putra pelacur. Sons of whores.'

Jay looked around the room. There was a red tablecloth on a workbench. He tore off a strip the size of a headscarf, grabbed an industrial Sharpie pen used on metal jewelry, handed them to Seth.

'Write it on this. In Indonesian.'

'You're out of your fucking mind.'

'Quite possibly.'

Jay stuffed the cloth in his pocket, picked up a bucket and mop, retraced his steps, this time diverting past the rear of cellblock Amed. He picked up a loose paving stone, wrapped it in the red cloth, tossed it through a window.

15. The stock certificate

The response from the auto industry was turbo-charged, high-octane and predictable. As well as reckless.

Ped and Carl were watching the attack ad on a TV in the backroom at the Westin Hotel in Kansas City. It had been hot-lapping screens throughout the day in Indiana and Kansas, after debuting nationally during *Fox & Friends*.

There were clips from the Noblesville visit about combustion engines being *history*, and *pawn your TVs*. But the crux of the ad attacked Ped's line about *dishonest politicians profiting from pushing partisan barrows*.

A voice sounding suspiciously like a four-time Indy 500 champion then revealed Ped *Straight Up* Garland had invested in a company making electric vehicles, which had just got a federal grant for five million dollars to research robotic manufacturing. A stock certificate from the EV company in Georgia filled the screen, zooming in on the name *Ped Garland*, then the bottom line: *is the owner of 100,000 fully paid shares.*

Mainstream media reaction to the Noblesville encounter had been mixed.

The big hitters in Indianapolis and Fort Wayne were unanimous the naïve greenhorn was going *Straight Down*, as were most Republican cheerleaders in the national media. Columnists and analysts from the left used terms like *method in his madness*, but still expected Garland to get smoked in Indiana.

'How much you figure they dropped on those ads Carl?'

'Them polished productions don't come easy on the wallet.'

'Even though they got that tip off about the stock certificate for free?'

Carl chuckled. 'You think I oughta send 'em an invoice?'

'I reckon they'll be beggin' for a refund once Jin and the Ciph get through with 'em.'

High-resolution images of the stock certificate had been emailed anonymously to the chief executive of the Auto Alliance and to Hunter's new attack dog soon after Ped, shielded by a dozen beefcakes from out of town, had been extricated from the angry mob at Noblesville.

Social media postings and press releases featuring Pedzi Garland, an indignant African American environmentalist from Savannah, proud owner of a BMW electric car – and no relation to the candidate – were in the can ready to start going out from midnight.

*****

The sirens catapulted Bec from the uncomfortable but manageable realm of yellow into deep orange, cascading down the crumbling tiles of the main prison building, bulls-eyeing from the orange of the Alfamart sign to the fluoro carrot of a kite tangled in a power line like a fly trapped in a spider's web.

She'd spent the last hour with Mike in a cafe over the road from the main entrance to Kerobokan, reading with increasing anxiety stories about a recent gang clash sparking a riot inside the prison, two inmates being killed, and the mayhem spilling onto the streets of Denpasar.

Bec flinched as the sirens were tailgated by whistles and breaking glass, the shouts of angry men, agitated Indonesian words over PA speakers. Then the *thud-thud-thud* of dozens, hundreds of saucepans being beaten against bars drifted across the road, loaded with anger, foreboding. And accusation.

This was her fault. Jay wouldn't be on a suicide mission if she got the information from Seth Crichton when she had the chance. Every shout amplified the guilt gnawing at her chest.

'Don't be so hard on yourself,' said Mike, reading her thoughts.

'Aristotle's winding you up, Bec. Spinning you lines that almost certainly aren't true. He knows nothing about Jay and what he's capable of. Slow down. Breathe in, hold, breathe out.'

Before she got to exhale, the sounds of sirens from the east grew louder, morphing into flashing red lights of police cars, ambulances. Black armored vehicles – Aristotle at every wheel – swept into the parking lot in front of the main building, riveting Bec's eyes to the stark red walls, the blood red of the Indonesian flags herding the freaks in their unearthly body armor, helmets, shields, batons, teargas grenade launchers.

As the riot police streamed through the entrance, Aristotle stretched Bec's eyes back to the east, through the red of the Circle K logo, a Bintang beer flag, a suckling pig sign, before homing in on the flashing warning beacons of motorbikes piloting a beast of a vehicle with menacing red wheel rims and front bumpers. It roared towards the gray side door of the prison, smothering Jay's escape route.

*****

Riot police the world over dress to intimidate. The black contour-molded suits, black thermo-composite helmets, black neoprene forearm, elbow and knee protectors, shatter-resistant poly-carbonate shields, stiff jaws, the way they march in lockstep, are all designed to scare the bejesus out of rioters, unruly mobs, peaceful protesters sitting down in the middle of a road holding flowers.

But from the waist down, a squad of riot police appeared a

lot less frightening – almost comical. From Jay's vantage point in the lockbox, peering into the smartphone connected to the camera under the Hummer, the groin protectors on the cops spilling from the Komodo armored personnel carrier looked like incontinence diapers.

A riot police callout wasn't quite the distraction Jay intended when he lobbed the brick into Kaluraha basecamp, but a guy had to work with the cards he was dealt.

It took the best part of an hour for the sirens to stop, the riot police to clear out and the prison to return to its addled state of normal. Soon after, footsteps on the concrete signaled the driver returning to the Hummer. As he switched on the engine to crank up the air-conditioning, Jay glanced at his watch and smiled. 6.38. The governor, after discovering all his prisoners and guards were accounted for, wasn't going to let a little riot interfere with his clockwork.

As the Hummer left the prison and turned onto the road towards Denpasar, Jay rotated the dial on the smartphone app to swivel the camera to face backwards. He recognized the license plate on Komang's car on the inside lane as the Hummer pulled up to traffic signals.

He released the tailgate, slid silently to the ground, and rolled to the curb just before the traffic moved off. He waited for Komang to draw level, then climbed into the back seat.

Bec was staring straight ahead, red-eyed, breathing deeply, straight-jacket arms. The silent treatment. Jay let it ride until Komang turned to follow the canal north towards the bypass.

'I'm fine, thanks for asking.'

Bec laid into him.

'You're out of your fricken mind… *You* mightn't give a damn about your own sorry ass, but you could have put our whole project at risk, not to mention the likelihood of implicating Mike and me. And Komang…'

Jay caught Komang's eyes in the rear-view. He looked more uncomfortable at Bec's language and being drawn into the conversation than a run-in with the riot police. Balinese hate confrontations.

'… all the people who've backed the project, put their money where their mouth is, are bankrolling this investigation…'

'Well I…'

'What imbecile pulls such a hair-brained low-percentage stunt? What the fricken hell did you hope you could possibly achieve? Are we any closer to Lompok?'

'Not exactly…'

'Did you see Seth?'

'You keep out of this Bullard, you complicit fricken a-hole.'

Jay could see Mike was smiling. Bec wiped her eyes, her jaw tightening for another verbal onslaught. Jay got in first.

'Yes Mike, I did see Seth.'

'And?'

'He said Lompok's living it up in the VIP quarters in the staff section, comes and goes as he pleases.'

'So we wait till he comes out?'

'No. According to Seth, Lompok's just a wholesaler. If we're serious about getting closer to the source of NuNu, we need to look into a limo company in Kuta.'

Bec turned to face Jay, eyes spitting.

'That's it?' she hissed. 'That's all you've got to show for risking everything? Surely Seth knew more.'

'Probably. He was getting a bit agitated about the guard locked up in the next room. I had to come up with a distraction to calm him down.'

'Don't tell me the riot police was your doing?'

'Possibly. Might have overplayed my hand a touch.'

'Lighten up Bec', said Mike, leaning his head back and grinning at her. 'We agreed we'd use unorthodox methods.

Even said so on the Aristotle website.'

Bec's eyebrows hiked north.

'I'm surrounded by morons.'

*****

Locating Eksek Limousine Services wasn't easy. Mike eventually tracked it down to a dead-end lane in the Segara district on the northern fringe of the airport.

The video camera glasses seemed a good idea back at the guesthouse, but Mike was having second, third, fourth thoughts the further he got into the lane.

Everydayness – women bent over sewing machines, old men sitting on the ground shooting the breeze as they whittled away at hunks of wood, the fresh smell of a backyard laundry – had succumbed to imposing walls of concrete-block, graffiti, and the oily recesses of an auto repair business. No statues or offerings, no birds, trees, flowers, or anything to embrace the Balinese image of being at peace with itself and nature. A call to prayer sounded from a nearby mosque but was drowned by the rumble of a departing jet.

Mike touched the button on the arm of the glasses to begin recording. An HD video camera was built into the frame of the glasses, with the lens in the bridge. He was crossing more than one line here. Recording people without their consent breached the code of ethics of every media organization he'd worked for. Right now, Mike was more worried about the physical consequences of being caught.

Teardrop-shaped banners with black and yellow motifs arched like fake pengor poles on each side of high steel gates. Through the bars Mike saw a two-story compound, colorless like an abandoned hotel, clothes drooping over the upper railing. Faded t-shirts with the same black and yellow motif.

Dozens of motorbikes lined up facing a wall, beside piles of garbage overflowing from black plastic bags.

Beyond the gate, and behind the concrete wall topped with broken glass, Mike sensed a large body of men. The pungent smell of weed mingled with beer and sweat.

According to his research, the limousine base was the last building on the left. There was no signage, at least not in English. Just a rusted roller door padlocked to a bolt in the sidewalk beside a solid metal door with a round opaque window like you see between compartments on ships.

Mike knocked. No answer. He tried the door. It wasn't locked, so he went in. It was an office of sorts. In the thick of oil filters, brake cables, wiper blades, cans of touch-up paint and chauffeur caps was a desk with a reasonably modern computer and cheap particle board shelving sagging under the weight of colored binders. Through an open side door Mike could see the rear ends of two white limos. He was looking around for a buzzer when a woman burst through the door, waving her arms in the air, yelling at him in Indonesian.

So much for customer service.

A Balinese guy appeared at the door, wearing overalls, wiping his hand on a greasy cloth. Mike noticed the tattoo inside his arm – the ringed circle with expanding dots Jay had mentioned.

'You lost?'

'I'm looking for Eksek Limos.'

'Why?'

Mike wasn't prepared for that question.

'Ah, to book a limousine?'

'We no booking. Limo only for airport, Nyalahutan guests. You stay at resort?'

'No.'

The guy shepherded Mike towards the door.

'Limo only hire you stay resort.'

*****

Bec put her face into the hole and tried to relax, focusing on the Egyptian blue of the bowl on the floor beneath her rather than the bumblebee caution in the marigold petals.

The petite Balinese woman knew her stuff, but Bec knew the science. Which always made it difficult to get pleasure from a massage. She'd met borderlines who swore by it, relied on it to get through the day. For Bec, understanding pressure from the woman's fingers was supposed to trigger nerve cells in the skin to tell the brain to release endorphins, that the fragrance of the aromatherapy oils could boost serotonin or produce enkephalins, tended to defeat the purpose.

Instead of surrendering to the masseuse's touch, she fought with Aristotle over who was in charge and whether her mind could or should be manipulated. Bumblebees and Egyptians. Couldn't help herself.

She was stretched out on a lounge chair beside a pool at the Nyalahutan Ubud, wearing a one-piece swimsuit with sleeves to conceal her scars, and large, red-rimmed sunglasses and a floppy hat in case she was recognized from the previous visit.

They'd decided to stake out the chain's three resorts, after Mike's report on his visit to the limo base. Research into the yellow and black motif revealed Eksek Limousine Services was housed beside the headquarters of one of Bali's most notorious gangs – Kaluraha.

Jay had wanted to Rambo his way into the place, but Bec persuaded him to at least try the stake-out option first.

The masseuse platform, the pool, and the restaurant where she'd spent most of the day, provided views of the entranceway and driveway. So far three limos had pulled up to take guests from Australia, Russia, and the States to the airport.

Two arrived with couples from the UK and Japan.

16. The rizz

News of the first exit poll from WIBC in Indianapolis reached Ped in the kitchen of a brick ranch home 285 miles away in suburban West Virginia.

It showed he had his nose in front in Indiana, as the Parkersburg housewife was showing him the contents of her refrigerator.

The Ciph had unearthed another target cohort ahead of next week's contests in West Virginia and Nebraska: mothers. The Ciph's numbers showed him level-pegging with the female Democratic frontrunner in support from moms, and streets ahead of the male Dem. There was also political capital to be made against Hunter, a woman whose support from her own gender was softening.

Different kinds of moms were likely to respond to Ped on different issues, so the day's filming schedule had the candidate crisscrossing the city to meet with a professional mom, a welfare mom, a foster mom, a grandmom, and an eight-month pregnant mom-to-be. Each one identified by the Ciph as highly influential Garland supporters from their likes and language on social media, emails, texts.

The stay-at-home mom complaining to Ped about misleading labels on yoghurt was likely to vote for him because he told it like it was. She'd sent an intern from Hunter's campaign packing because *the guy was so windy he could blow up an onion sack.*

By the time he'd talked death penalty with a financial advisor over her marble counter in Meadowcrest Drive, the exit polls back in Indiana had him opening a lead, and Kansas was looking like a lock.

Harper Miller was planning a homebirth *the way my body instructs*. She was terrified about the state of the planet her baby would inherit, so liked Ped's stance on climate change. As he left her to envisage the child's *entrance Earthwise*, he was looking comfortable in Indiana.

Clarice deMoyne had to battle, barter, beat down or beg for every dime she needed to keep her family together. She was impressed that Ped, who met her in her mobile home in Boaz, had the backbone to stand up to *them Hoosier auto workers*.

Mrs. Maybelline Grant never had children of her own but had provided a loving home to thirty-seven – the first when Ronald Reagan was starring alongside Lee Marvin and Angie Dickinson in *The Killers*. Ped would get her vote because he wasn't *acting like a big bug, getting above your raisin'*.

Yes ma'am, thank you ma'am, 'preciate it ma'am.

When Ped's driver reversed out of the driveway of her weatherboard cottage with the Stars and Stripes out front, he had Indiana and Kansas – as well as tiny Guam – sewn up.

Jin handed him the talking points for the last appointment of the day.

'Is this for real? Did the Ciph tell you why she thinks I might appeal to grandmothers?'

Jin smiled. 'The word she used was *rizz*.'

'Meaning?'

Jin hesitated.

'It's a young person's phrase. I believe it comes from charisma. I guess the numbers suggest grandmothers find you… charming.'

Several retakes were required during filming at the brick and stone Mediterranean-style manor, because the old girl had difficulty concentrating on the script.

They watched the final result in her media room. Despite all the doomsday predictions that Ped had committed political suicide in Indiana, he took 38 delegates to Hunter's 19. With 28 delegates from Kansas and seven from Guam, he now had 1109, needing only 128 more to secure the nomination.

*****

Mike was thinking back to the bar in New York and the question about whether he was enjoying freelancing.

The answer right now was *hell yes*. He was sitting on a submerged stool in the swim-up bar at the Nyalahutan Kuta, sipping a pina colada, chilled out by a duet of bamboo flute and acoustic guitar, one eye on the driveway, the other on the parade of bikinis and unconstrained vacation mode.

Mike had even avoided the five-million-rupiah room rate, after Jay told him about *the towel*. Each resort had its own branded pool towel which, draped over the shoulder, was as good as an entry ticket to the pool area. Jay had scored two of the Nyalahutan's from the beach while their owners were in the surf, flouting Bali's conservative expectations on public displays of affection.

As well as monitoring the arrival of limos, Mike had consolidated his online relationships with several more influencers. The biggest catch was a popular *culinary explorer*, with whom he'd shared stories about the connection between the drug trade and food production, how trafficking was hurting farmers.

From the pool bar, Mike could see through the lobby with its hanging metal spheres, bronze ceiling fans and yellow parasols to the driveway. A whistle-happy security guard in a white shirt, gold epaulets and aiguillette helpfully announced the arrival of every vehicle.

Mike made a note of each limo, discretely photographing the occupants, finding out as much information as he could about them, where they flew from, where they were heading next.

17. Neither the time

Mother's Day in Lincoln, Nebraska should have been about breakfast in bed, home-made cards, brunch at The Egg & I or Greenfields, or just kickin' back with the kids.

For Avery Snyder, it was about visiting the Lincoln Memorial Cemetery.

Her daughter Brynlee had died of an overdose twelve years earlier, and every one of the four thousand three hundred ninety-eight days since had been as black and barren and lonely as the one before.

'Got to be honest with you, Mr. Garland. The five stages of grief are just not holding up for me. I've gone through denial and isolation, the anger, the bargaining – maybe not in that exact order. Depression's been with me from day one. But I can't bring myself to move on to the last stage. And I won't.'

'Acceptance?'

'How am I supposed to do that, Mr. Garland, and still face myself in the mirror when I'm in Bryn's room?'

Mrs. Snyder, clutching a framed photo of her daughter, had been ID'd by the Ciph from her posts to a Facebook group called Moms Against Drugs.

Ped could see over her shoulder his press secretary having trouble keeping the muck slingers behind the ropes set up a respectable distance from the headstone.

He put his arm on Mrs. Snyder's shoulder. 'Shall we?'

'Of course. A vein for a vein.'

She never got to say the words. The douchebag pounced before Ped finished his introduction.

'Can you clarify, Mr. Garland, why we haven't been able to locate anyone in West Virginia who has made a contribution through your campaign website?'

'I beg your pardon. What are you talking about?'

'We've spent...'

'Who's *we*? And who are you? The hell you think you're doin'? This is a cemetery, for heaven's...'

'I'm with the *Charleston Gazette-Mail*. We've spent...'

'Well, I'll be speaking with your editor sir, this is neither the time nor...'

'I serve as the editor, Mr. Garland. Our story is scheduled for publication tomorrow regardless of whether you choose to comment. According to your website, over two thousand West Virginians have contributed to your campaign. We've conducted interviews with five thousand individuals across the state, including Charleston, Huntington, Parkersburg, Morgantown, and Wheeling, and we haven't been able to find a single person who claims to have donated.'

Ped glanced around. Where was his press secretary when he needed her?

'Where's the money really coming from Mr. Garland?'

*****

During a mission several years earlier to Egypt, where Jay had been sent to investigate an imminent environmental disaster at a gold mine near the Red Sea town of Marsa Alam, he'd been forced to spend several days on a stake-out at a beach bar.

Jay had traced the whistleblower, whose tip warned of a dangerous pile-up of cyanide tailings behind a dam, through the informant's use of a poste restante service. The bait had been set, and Jay had laid claim to a corner table in the beach bar that gave a good view of the town's post office.

The bar wouldn't have been such a bad place to while away a few days if it wasn't for the irritating presence of a whining expat Englishman.

Jay thought about him now as he sat in the Jukung beach bar at Jimbaran. He had drawn the Nyalahutan Jimbaran, and after forty-eight hours was past bored. He was ready to answer any question about the architecture of the restaurant, bar, lobby, or pool. The fancy weave in the bamboo panels, the carving on the teak beams and posts, the lotus motifs on the cornices and lintels, the thickness of the grouting between tiles at the deep end. Hell, he could write the quiz – and throw in sections on the gilded frames around the puri pura artwork and the workmanship in the Hindu statues. It was light years from the trinket junk sold in tourist stores, as you'd expect for the room rate.

The final straw for Jay was discovering the roles of two of the Nyalahutan's staff. One did nothing but swoop on frangipani flowers that dared land on the marble paths; the other spent his entire shift making sure nobody walked on the lawn.

Jay would have broken his promise to Bec to give the stake-out three days if he hadn't stumbled across the Jukung. The bar, named after the traditional wooden outrigger canoes anchored offshore, was Jay's sort of place. Cheap Heinekens, all-day breakfast of scrambled eggs, smashed avo, bacon, mushroom, tomatoes, and reggae. And by positioning a bean bag on the sand beyond the last lounger, line-of-sight to the driveway of the Nyalahutan.

The rafters of the open-air joint were covered in nautical paraphernalia – life preserver rings, anchors, spear guns, starfish, ceramic turtles – and a Bintang beer sign was nailed to a stunted ketapang tree, next to a shrine for the daily offerings. Modern Bali summed up on a tree trunk.

The only downside of the Jukung was Shane, an overripe Australian hippie who'd adopted the sign over the bar, *Beer is the reason I get up in the morning,* as his mission statement. The loser spent his days bordering on comatose, doing violence to local place names like Seminyak and Canggu.

After ten hours of Shane, and no sign of any pattern with the limos collecting and depositing guests at the Nyalahutan, Jay was ready to take the direct route.

18. Just like Dylan

Even usually conservative commentators were calling Nebraska for Garland hours before the voting centers closed, so supporters had been showing up early for the victory rally in Omaha.

Volunteers were stitching the nets above the stage for the balloon drop, and merchandise sellers were unpacking the limited edition *Straight Up* coffee mugs and buttons and pins and *Ped for President* bumper stickers.

By the time the result was made official on the giant screens, the warm-up acts had whipped the crowd into a state approaching delirium.

Ped, across the road in his suite at the Marriott, had begun the day on a high, and on the cover of *Rolling Stone* magazine. The think-piece inside was the first by a major publication to take his candidacy seriously and speculate about the sort of President he would make.

Ped had also been buoyed by the Nebraska exit polls. But news out of West Virginia, the other state holding a primary, kept the cork on the champagne, and was the reason he was holding off addressing the crowd over the road.

Polls pointed to a close contest in the Mountain state, with the lead toing and froing. Analysts out east were pointing to the *Gazette-Mail* story about his public donation site for his failure to dominate a South Atlantic state that two weeks earlier seemed his for the plucking. Fortunately, the story ridiculing his claim to be a straight-up man of the people, hadn't been picked up outside West Virginia. Yet.

Ped waited as long as he could, but the final count was still on a knife-edge as he headed across the road.

He entered the Grand Ballroom to the revitalizing cries of *Ped Ped Ped Ped* and quickly hit his stride.

'Back when I was a kid grinding through piano lessons with Mrs. Lintott in Atlanta, trying to crack the code of that *Cannon in D* chord progression, I had this wild dream that one day I was gonna make it to the cover of the *Rolling Stone*. Just like Dylan, Kristofferson, Linda Ronstadt.

'*The thrill that'll getcha… when you get your picture… on the cover of the Rollin' Stone.* Well, here we are. This,' he said, holding up the current edition, 'isn't exactly how I imagined it happening.'

He had to wait for the cheering, whistling, foot-stamping to taper off.

'I've gotta hand it to 'em, folks. This magazine, this journalist right here, they're the first ones who've really gotten us. Only took 'em eight months!

'Let me read y'all a coupla lines here… *Ped Garland is resonating with everyday Americans feeling out of place and on edge in their own country… These people — and there are many of them — are searching for someone to blame, and high on the list are establishment politicians, the government and political correctness… In Ped Garland they've found a candidate who refuses to play by the established rules, who says what he thinks, to hell with the consequences. The ultimate consequence could see him trading up from a bunk in a prison cell to a seat in the oval office.*'

The crowd broke into a chorus of *Trade Up, Trade Up, Trade Up* as his press secretary slipped him a note.

Ped raised his hands for quiet.

'Sorry to be the bearer of bad news folks. I've just received the final word from West Virginia. It didn't quite go our way.'

Boos echoed around the ballroom until they were drowned out by a chant of *Stolen, Stolen.*

'We didn't exactly come out on the losing end. It was a tie. Seventeen delegates to Congresswoman Hunter, and a matching seventeen for yours truly.'

The crowd wasn't sure how to take that news. Some booed, others resumed the *Stolen* chant.

Ped silenced them again.

'Let's be straight up here folks. A tie in West Virginia wasn't exactly the outcome we were gunning for. Sure, it means we've now locked in 1162 delegates and we're only 75 away from the goal. But it also means a bunch of folks bought into the fake news about nobody chipping in for this campaign. *Your* campaign.'

As he let that sink in, Ped thought back to the night at Madison Square Garden, had an idea.

'I see we've got some members of the fourth estate with us here this evening.'

That set the crowd booing again. A redneck in the front row was waving a faded sign saying *Rope. Tree. Journalist. Some Assembly Required.*

'How 'bout this, folks? Raise your right hand if you've pitched in and donated to the campaign.'

Every right hand in the room – other than those in the roped-off media section – shot towards the ceiling.

'And if you see yourself as a good ol' everyday American, go ahead and raise your other hand.'

Ped leaned into the microphone and managed to blurt out *I rest my case,* before he was overwhelmed by an avalanche of *Straight Up, Straight Up, Straight Up.*

*****

Bec tried to shut out the Irish family playing charades too loudly at the next table, with porcelain faces like they'd just stepped off the plane from a Dublin winter. 'Book. Two words. First word sounds like…'

Team Aristotle was sitting on cushions around a low table upstairs at a funky eatery on Hanoman Street in Ubud, trying to make sense of the limo movements they'd recorded.

Breathe it all in, love it all out whispered a sign on the chalkboard above the dessert specials – organic mulberry pie, carrot, and beet cake. If only it were that easy. Bec had entered data from their days of observations into a spreadsheet and was applying different formulae in search of patterns or anomalies.

Every table in the café was occupied by people dressed for permanent summer, many staring at phones or wearing headphones, blind to the tops of pengor poles swaying in the breeze outside the window and the platter of accents – French, American, Japanese, Dutch. Full-volume Irish.

Mike and Jay had spent so much time arguing over a prediction on a box of steel straws – that by 2050 there would be more pieces of plastic than fish in the ocean – they were only half-way through their meals.

Jay was tackling a large Indian plate of dhal, eggplant bharata, aloo gobi, raita and sautéed spinach over red rice. Mike had embraced the spirit of local cuisine by ordering a Californian burrito.

Bec had forgiven Jay for the prison episode, as had Aristotle, who was flittering over the table in the indigo flash of a butterfly's wings, the aquamarine earrings of the waitress clearing away her plate, the denim coaster beneath her Tamarind Sensation.

Her mind needed a reboot. She closed her eyes, narrowing her focus to block out everything but the smells around her. The warm, spicy notes of ginger. The rich, creamy scent of coconut. The sharpness of basil, whispered crispness of mint, citrus undertones of frangipani.

Bec had used this heightened sensitivity technique before – while poring over boxes of invoices during an investigation into fraud at a non-profit in New Haven. It helped her identify patterns she'd overlooked.

When she opened her eyes, her attention was drawn to a different section of numbers on the screen. She entered a new formula, applied it.

Three of Eksek's four limos were used for all but two of the 73 rides they'd observed, delivering and picking up guests of all ages from Australia, Russia, the States, Britain, China, Japan, Germany, France, Spain, Israel.

The fourth limo – with a registration plate ending in GI – was used only twice, both times to deliver elderly New Zealand couples from the airport.

19. Between the eyeballs

Desperation can be a powerful motivator. Kate Hunter's team – just 75 delegates away from blowing a shoo-in for the nomination, wasted no time heaping salt into the crack opened up by the *Gazette-Mail* story on donations to Ped's campaign.

Thirty-six hours after West Virginia, the attack messages appeared on TV, radio, social media, on posters, phones, and doorsteps across Kentucky and Oregon, scenes of the next primaries.

Ped was in the backroom at the Seelbach Hilton in downtown Louisville, analyzing the ads with Jin and Carl Tyler.

Screenshots from Ped's campaign website showed how many people had supposedly donated how many dollars in each state, with a woman's voice saying: *We asked everyday Americans on the streets of Kentucky straight up if they donated – or even knew someone who donated.* The face of a man appeared saying *no*. His face morphed into a second face, *no*, then a third, *no*.

The morphing faces gradually sped up into a *no-no-no-no-no-n-n-n-n-n-n-n-n…* ending with the face of a local celebrity enunciating a very deliberate and rounded *NO*.

Hunter's spin doctors had underlined the messaging so successfully the media were framing the upcoming primary as the Second Battle for Kentucky, in reference to a critical clash during the civil war.

Several muck slingers were paraphrasing the famous Abraham Lincoln quote that '*to lose Kentucky is to lose the whole game*'. Hunter was being likened to the Union's Major-General

Buell, Garland to the Confederate's General Bragg – deliberately misspelt by some as *Brag*. Hunter was visiting the Perryville Battlefield Museum for a photo op that afternoon.

'The ads aren't bad,' said Jin. 'You can see the fingerprints of Hunter's attack dog Seb Woodhouse all over this. But he's made two – possibly three – mistakes.'

'Enlighten us.'

'He's used your *Straight Up* slogan. People who think that's clever were never voting for you anyway. The rest will see it either as a cheap shot in a negative ad, or it reinforces your platform to them.'

'And the second mistake?'

'Look at where these ads have been placed. There's no focus. It's like he's lobbed a hand grenade into a crowded square and is counting on the shrapnel to do the damage. This war's not going to be won with hand grenades and Bren guns. It's going to take a sniper hitting individual targets between the eyeballs at five hundred yards.'

'Like the Ciph?'

'You got it.'

'You mentioned a possible third mistake?'

'I'm not sure, but something about one of the faces used in the ad seems familiar to me.'

'So?'

'If I'm right, he's not from Kentucky.'

'Let's find out.'

'It won't come cheap. We'll have to buy facial recognition software, and depending on what the Ciph comes up with, we might need to hire a private investigator.'

'So?'

'These are unbudgeted items Mr. Garland. The war chest's virtually empty.'

'Do it. I'll find the extra money.'

*****

The Lepas Landas restaurant was ideal. Close to the airport, with a clear view along the main road from the international terminal, and room for Jay to park his scooter on the sidewalk.

He had a list of arrival times of flights originating in New Zealand, so settled in to wait for limousine GI.

*****

'What's that funny sound, Dad?'

'That's a band called Oasis. *You're My Wonderwall.* Very famous song,' said Mike, assuming his daughter was referring to the voice of Liam Gallagher being squeezed from a small speaker on a table in front of one of the cafes edging the sand.

'No silly. Like, the chiming sound.'

Mike had to think for a moment.

'Oh *that*. It's a gamelan orchestra practicing in the temple up above the beach. They have these bronze instruments like xylophones they hit with metal hammers. You hear it all over Bali.'

Mike was Facetiming MJ back in New York from Padang Padang beach, where he'd spent the morning shooting backdrop, discretely interviewing surfers, waiters, souvenir sellers, death-wish photographers who ventured inside the barrel with their dome port and fisheye lens in search of the perfect image.

It wasn't difficult to spot the experienced and inexperienced surfers. Amateurs emerged from the stairway through the cliff with a swagger and who-gives-a-flying look similar to those Mike saw at the Rockaways. Once beyond the reef, they paddled east towards the long, gentle break known as Baby Pedang.

The pros shared the swagger, but their eyes were all focus

and ice, betraying the respect of a warrior knowingly putting their life on the line. These guys – and girls – paddled west to where every takeoff, drop, stall, and blast out of the shoulder was roulette.

The small beach was gridlocked. Tourists, wannabe and never-gonnabe surfers occupied every square foot of shade under umbrellas, rocks, overhanging cliffs, while hundreds stood cooling off in the shallows.

Mike chatted away to MJ, asking her about school, her mom, whether the spring had finally arrived, until he noticed a Balinese guy in a red *Make America Stoned Again* cap in front of a stack of blue surfboards for rent.

'Gotta go sorry, MJ. There's this guy I need to interview for our story.'

He ended the call, put on the video camera glasses, wandered over.

*****

Bec was beginning to pick the difference between New Zealanders and Australians. One clue was the way they used the vowels *i* and *e*. Jay and other Kiwis pronounced words with an *i* as a short *u*, so fish came out like *fush* and sex as *sux*. Aussies pronounced them as if they had multiple *e*'s. *Feeesh* and *seex*.

She was flitting between the Nyalahutan resorts at Kuta and Jimbaran, looking for New Zealanders, then striking up conversations to see if they'd arrived in Eksek limos.

From a lounger beside the pool at Jimbaran, she watched a couple she guessed were in their sixties enter the bar and get directed to a table by the Ganesha statue. The man was wearing a black cap with a silver fern embossed on the bill. Another Kiwi identifier. Bec finished her mango matcha smoothie, headed for the bar for a refill, smiling at the couple as she sat at the table next to them.

Jason and Megan Hopper were from a place called Tairua on New Zealand's North Island. He was a retired police prosecutor; she a teacher-aide at a primary school: 'What you'd call elementary school in America.'

They'd flown in from Auckland five days ago. Jason had spent weeks researching accommodation online before choosing the Nyalahutan.

'We wanted to come to Jimbaran because it seemed a bit quieter than Kuta and the other beaches. In the end it came down to a choice between this place and the Four Seasons.'

'I've heard the Four Seasons is excellent as well,' Bec lied. 'What tipped the balance for you Jason, if you don't mind me asking?'

They looked shyly at each other before he replied.

'Free limo transfers. We'd never ridden in one before. Decided to treat ourselves.'

Bec had heard similar stories from two New Zealand couples at the Kuta resort. A retired school principal and teacher from Tokoroa; and retired therapist and insurance executive from Auckland's North Shore.

All had chosen Nyalahutan resorts because of the free limo pick-up from their homes in New Zealand and the limo transfer from the airport in Denpasar.

'It's a one-and-three-quarter-hour drive from our home on the Coromandel Peninsula to Auckland Airport, dear,' said Megan. 'We felt like royalty.'

Bec pretended surprise. 'That's an amazing deal. Did you book it through a travel agency near this Tie-raw?'

'*Tairua* dear. It's a Māori word. No. Jason booked it online through the Aventura agency in Devonport.'

People who investigate things for a living – police detectives, insurance fraud inspectors, financial auditors, freelance journalists tracing the source of drugs – use different terms to describe the revelation moment: lightbulb, eureka, epiphany, the penny-dropping instant when two plus two adds up to five.

The name Aventura triggered such a revelation for Bec, sending Aristotle skipping from the yellow of the flower in Ganesha's ear to the euphoric aqua of the pool and blue kamen bands of the waitresses.

'Isn't that your bag over there?'

The urgent tone in the voice of the retired police prosecutor snatched Bec from her moment of self-congratulation. She turned, relieved to see the bag still sitting on the umbrella base beside the lounger.

'Yes, why?'

'That bloke heading towards the entrance, in the yellow shirt, he was looking in the bag. Is he a friend of yours?'

Bec watched with increasing fear as a young Balinese man, brown Nyalahutan towel draped around his neck, walked out through the metal detector, and climbed onto the back of a motorbike.

Aristotle started pulsing in the orange trumpet flowers hanging upside down from a Datura tree.

'No. I've never seen him before. Are you sure?'

'Absolutely. Might pay to check nothing's missing.'

Bec felt suddenly alone, in need of security in numbers. She studied the New Zealander, weighing up whether to trust him.

'Can I ask you a favor... Jason? Would you mind checking the bag with me. It's just... I've heard of people having drugs planted in their rooms... I'm probably just being paranoid...'

'I'd be happy to.'

They walked over to the lounger. Bec could see the sunglasses she'd left on top of the bag lying on the ground.

'There's this scam,' she said as she picked up the bag, 'where they plant drugs then the police turn up and demand a bribe to make it go away.'

'Doesn't surprise me in this country. I've heard far…'

'Oh shit,' said Bec, as her fingers settled on a small plastic packet.

She pivoted, searching the faces of people around the pool, the garden, the restaurant. Everyone was staring at her, talking about her, accusing, judging.

Her hand was still firmly clasped around the packet inside the bag. She looked down, turning it over to reveal the brand stamp. NuNu.

A memory flashed. A therapist at The Balance mental wellbeing center back in Greenville, North Carolina. Letters on a whiteboard. DB. Dialectic Behavior. And the therapist's words:

Acknowledge your intense emotional reactions. Allow yourself to feel fear, anger. No judgment. Accept it as a natural response. Understand it is a temporary wave passing through.

Jason's voice interrupted her thoughts.

'Don't worry, Rebecca is it? I saw the bloke put it there. You've got a witness. We should go to the police.'

Bec steeled herself. She'd coped with worse than this before. Much worse.

'That's very kind of you Jason, but I'm sure you've heard what can happen to people caught with this sort of stuff in their possession. Yes, you can tell them you saw the guy looking in my bag, but for all you know the stuff could have been there already. I've gotta get rid of it, then worry what to do next.'

He looked confused.

Bec glanced around, her eyes settling on the restrooms.

'I'm gonna flush it down the toilet. You go back to your wife, Jason. I'll join you once I've got rid of it.'

The restroom was a tiled expanse of frosted glass walls with plants in an open-air garden at one end, heated toilet seat, bidet, sweet-scented frangipani petals arranged in bowls on a teak vanity.

Bec put the NuNu packet on the vanity and took a photo of it. She emailed the image to Mike, then deleted it off her phone. She lifted the toilet seat and was about to tip the cocaine into the bowl when she had an idea.

She walked over to the garden, tucked the packet behind a rock, then returned to the bar, putting her bag in the middle of the table.

Megan eyed it like it was a bomb. Bec couldn't blame her. Jason was scrolling through his phone, all business and procedure.

'My advice is your first call should be to your embassy. As I said I'd be happy to…'

He was interrupted by a flurry of activity by the front counter. Two police officers in brown uniforms marched toward their table.

'I don't believe this,' said Jason, starting to stand.

Bec put her hand on his arm. 'We have to assume these cops are in on the scam. Best not mention what you saw.'

The officers reached the table.

'Are you Rebecca Corelli?'

Their first mistake, thought Bec.

'How did you know my name?'

The cop, if he really was a cop, ignored her: 'Is this your bag?'

She handed it to him, emboldened by the presence of the former police prosecutor. 'It is. Be my guest.'

The cop emptied the contents onto the table. Megan looked away in embarrassment at the condoms.

Bec's phone sounded. She could see it was a call from Mike, but ignored it.

The cop pulled out a small knife, cut the lining of the bag, tipping it up. His eyes moved to Bec's chest. She thought for a moment he was going to strip-search her. Then he looked at Jason towering over him, thought better of it, and left.

Bec thanked the couple for their help and walked past the pool, doubling back to the restroom to retrieve the packet of NuNu. She tucked it inside her bra, then headed out to hail a cab and call Mike.

She explained what had happened, asked if he'd heard from Jay.

'That's what I was calling about. Limo GI has finally changed its pattern. Instead of returning to the base next to the gang HQ, it's headed towards Uluwatu.

*****

The small folding drone was much quieter than the clunky one Jay had flown in Brazil to film convoys of barges, known as comboios, transporting genetically modified soybeans to the port of Santarem. Mike had brought this machine back from the States and given Jay a demonstration while Bec was in the hospital.

He'd followed the limo to the heavily guarded entrance of a private property on a road running parallel to the south coast of the Bukit Peninsula. Backtracking a quarter mile, he'd turned down a gravel road which ended at the parking lot between two fancy resorts. Steps cut into the rock led down to a platform with a dramatic view over the Indian Ocean. A group of Balinese youths were flying kites from a ridge over his right shoulder.

It took Jay a few minutes to get used to the controls, check the camera was recording. He moved the joystick to propel the drone out beyond the cliff face. Waves crashed against the shore hundreds of feet below. On the beach to the west, a dozen transparent spheres dotted the sand like beads from a gigantic bubble gun. Jay had read about the Zorb-like hotel *rooms* that allowed guests to sleep under the stars without getting eaten by mosquitos.

He maneuvered the drone high above the breaking waves to the east, descending briefly for a closer look at a large, thatched structure on the beach, beside a gondola lift. He followed the cable line up the cliff. It ended at the edge of a marble deck beside a swimming pool in front of a three-story mansion.

Jay pushed the throttle and the drone rose, then did a three-sixty of the building from about 300 feet. The back of the limo was visible through the open door of a four-bay garage off the rear. Jay sent the machine higher, then did a grid sweep to assess potential entry points. A high concrete fence ringed the property on three sides, topped by cabling suggesting some form of electrical barrier. No fewer than six watchtowers. The governor of Kerobokan Prison would have given his right testicle for this level of security.

Jay pushed the left stick along the x-axis. The drone headed back out to sea, then he lowered it to about ten feet beneath the top of the cliff and swept it back and forth for a closer look. The face was steep, but not impossible, and the scrubby bush provided some cover. Glinting glass gave away the positions of two fixed cameras three-quarters of the way down the cliff, facing upwards on both sides of the gondola cable.

Jay had seen enough. He hit the button to bring the drone back automatically to its start position. He folded it up, tucked it into his backpack, headed up towards the kiters.

Vibrating strings hummed in the air like large vehicles in low gear as the teenagers gazed skywards at kites of different shapes and sizes – all in the symbolic Hindu colors of red, white, black, yellow. Discarded lengths of bamboo and fabric were anchored by rocks behind the group, and Jay was able to score the broken remains of a small fish kite without being noticed.

Fifteen minutes and multiple scratches later, he dropped from the last bunch of bush cover onto the sand. Keeping as near as possible to the base of the cliff, he edged closer to the beach house and gondola, stopping at a point he estimated was beneath the western camera. He scampered up, reaching the camera and positioning the broken kite over the lens. He continued up until he reached massive bamboo poles supporting the decking. Sweat was dripping off him and his rib was protesting, so he climbed into the shaded cavity under the pool to catch his breath.

When his heart rate settled, he crept round a pool pump, ducked down the side of the house, keeping beneath a line of bougainvillea he calculated should conceal his movement from the watchtower in the south-western corner of the property. Noise from an Indonesian gameshow came from an open window. He stretched up to have a peek. Two Balinese dressed in security guard uniforms were glued to a television on a wall. A bank of monitors pulsed above the desk behind their backs. Through an internal door Jay could see a Lexus and the front fender of the limo. The security post must back on to the garage.

The last section of the wall would be in full view of the watchtower, so Jay had no choice. He sucked in a couple of nervous ones, walked calmly up the side of the house, round the corner and into the garage. No bullets, sirens, or movement from the security room. He exhaled.

Jay couldn't get a decent look at the limo without risking one of the security guards losing interest in the gameshow and spotting him. He positioned himself beside the door, took a couple of zip ties out of his pocket, then kicked over a carton of oil filters.

The response was immediate, but half-hearted. One of the

guards stepped through the opening, yawning, his eyes shut and arms chicken-winging, showing the Kaluraha tattoo. It made lowering, gagging, and binding him a walk in the park. It took more than five minutes for the second guard to step through the door to look for his mate. Same result.

Jay knew he didn't have a lot of time. He walked around the limo, looked under the chassis. Nothing unusual. He opened the driver's door. He'd never been inside a limo, but everything looked like what you'd expect. He found the levers for the trunk and hood, but nothing out of the ordinary in either compartment. He took another walk around the vehicle, then stepped back a few paces, scratching his head.

Then he noticed it. There was a gap of about two feet between the back of the rear seat and the trunk. He opened the back door and had a closer look at the seat. The black leather looked just as expensive as it had the first time.

Jay flipped the trunk again. He activated the torch on the phone Mike had loaned him, reached in, tapped the felt panel behind the seat. Seemed solid enough. Perhaps the designers deliberately wasted space. But that wouldn't make sense. They could have allowed more room for luggage. He looked closer at the panel, running his hand under a ridge along the top. His finger caught on a flap. He pulled it, revealing a cavity big enough to conceal a small person – like your average Balinese male.

Jay shot some video of the trunk and cavity, then a wider shot of the garage, before his eyes fixed on a steel door at the far end. It was locked. Still no alarms or sirens, and Tweedledee and Tweedledum weren't going anywhere. Jay unclipped a set of keys from the belt of one of the guards.

A sweet, flowery odor like incense, mixed with the tang of cheap plastic, intrigued him until he found the light switch.

He could have been in the air-conditioned backroom of a

pharmacy. Measuring scales, plastic powder trays, weigh boats and weighing papers, powder brushes, blades, funnels. Cartons and cartons full of small clear resealable plastic bags bearing the NuNu motif, others with latex gloves, face masks.

Dozens of copies of a popular and particularly thick guidebook to Bali were stacked on metal shelves along one wall. Jay took one down, noticing immediately the absence of weight. He opened it. Most of the inside pages had been hollowed out.

He positioned the open cover in front of the shelves of books and took a photo, then switched to video mode and panned round the room, noticing the flashing light of a security camera – at the same time a siren sounded.

*****

Montoya was sitting at the desk in his office, entering figures into a ledger book, when the alarm went off. A fucking monkey, no doubt. The ultrasound repeller kept them away from the cliff-face at the front of the property, and the electric fence on top of the perimeter walls worked most of the time, but there was always one stupid or hungry enough to tempt fate.

The siren stopped, so Montoya continued with his calculations while he waited for Arief to confirm the primate intrusion. Protocol was for a report within three minutes. The numbers added up. He made a note in the margin and still hadn't heard from Arief, so lit a cigarette, headed downstairs.

The control room was at the end of the hall past the billiard room in the west wing. He punched the code into the keypad, pushed the door open, ready to give his head of security and his sidekick a blast.

The two chairs were empty, the screens on all the monitors above the control desk blank. Montoya picked up one of the handsets to call the towers. All he got was static. And a spike in his heart rate.

He walked quickly to the door to the garage. Everything appeared normal. Where in hell were they?

He stepped down, walked between the Lexus and the limo, out onto the driveway. Blue sky, kites, birds singing. Nothing unexpected. He spun around and saw the boots.

Two pairs, wriggling under a tarpaulin.

Arief and his partner were face-down on the concrete floor, their feet bound with zip ties and hands tied to a metal conduit. Both had rags stuffed in their mouths held in place with tape.

Montoya grabbed pliers from the workbench, snipped the ties, then noticed the door to the lab was ajar, keys still in the lock. He left the guards to remove their gags, rushed over to the lab, yanking the door open.

Nothing seemed disturbed. But the light beside the camera was off. He moved closer, saw the cord had been cut.

'They jumped us boss.'

Arief had appeared at the door, reluctant to enter.

When it became clear neither man got a look at the intruders, Montoya marched them back to the control room, got Arief to power up the standby system. The monitors came back to life, revealing nothing out of the ordinary. Calls to the tower guards had the same result. All six assumed a monkey had triggered the alarm, especially when the siren stopped so quickly.

Montoya ordered Arief and his partner to search the house and front of the property, after showing him how to access the recorded footage from the cameras.

He punched keys to pull up the view from the camera in the lab, clicked on the red circle at the bottom right of the screen, dragged it back, stopping when a face filled the frame.

Duggan.

He pulled the red dot further along the progress bar until movement stopped, then let it play in real time. It showed the

New Zealander entering the room, switching on the light, snooping around, choosing a guidebook off the shelf, opening it, then pulling out his phone, taking a couple of stills, switching to video mode to shoot the equipment, ending up facing the camera.

Duggan lowered the phone and smiled, casually forming his fingers into the shape of a gun. He pulled his imaginary trigger, then reached up beside the camera, ending the recording.

Montoya looked at the timer, then at his watch. Ten minutes had elapsed since the alarm sounded. He slammed his fist into the desk. A light pulsed on the control panel. He pushed the *answer* button.

It was Arief.

'No sign of them boss.'

Them.

Montoya suspected Duggan acted alone. Journalists couldn't have pulled off such a surgical hit and run.

He returned to the screen, dragging the dot to the frame showing the smartass New Zealander taunting him. This time he'd have to let Carlos know.

First things first. He took out his phone and hit the speed dial for Agung. It was time to call in that debt from the leader of the Kaluraha gang.

*****

Bec had to admit it. The energy smoothie bowl – packed with cashews, sunflower seeds, dates, chia, coconut, banana, and raw cacao, topped with crunchy granola and chocolate and fruit – was a pick-me-up.

Mike had convinced her to return with him to Ubud to work on the video package, to regroup, recharge and reboot *the old Greek dude* after the near-miss with the drugs and police at the resort in Jimbaran. They were at the quaint Yellow Flower café, a short walk through the rice paddies from their guesthouse. Surrounded by Bohemians, bulimics, and beguiling bamboo flute.

Bec was having trouble concentrating on Mike's laptop. He'd shot some great footage at Padang Padang, and in covert interviews with drug addicts in Kuta that pushed the ethics envelope. They'd agreed on several edits, but Bec's thoughts kept heading south, jittery about what Jay might be up to.

Aristotle was meddling, diverting her eyes to yellow flashes in the cushions, a painting on the wall, tassels on a parasol half hidden in bush, the headscarf of a woman struggling past with a large rock on her head.

The walk back along the path to the Little Banana turned into a maddening tussle of cat and mouse.

Bec fought to see only blues or greens in the windmill fronds of palms silhouetted against the sky. When that failed, she tried the neutrals, one after another. Doves rising from legions of rice in various stages of growth. The trickling of the irrigation channels and serendipitous waterfalls. Roosters cockadoodling from the confines of bamboo cages. Plastic bag scarecrows tied to string. Wind through trees competing with the barking of dogs, laughter of children playing.

All the while, Aristotle was strobing. In the hovering chili red menace of a dragonfly, the glinting bronze of a lizard sashaying across the path, bunches of over-ripe papaya, an explosion of bougainvillea over a stone wall.

They came to the large shrine in the middle of the path, clambered round it, then jumped across the gap in the channel. Plastic bottles were banking up in a foaming eddy.

Mike was explaining how a telephoto lens he'd brought from the States could be attached to an iPhone or used by itself, like a mini telescope.

'Let me see.'

Bec peered through the lens, adjusting the dial to focus on a mechanical plough, its wheel sunk into the mud of a paddy. She panned across the fields to the coconut palm above the gate at the back of the Little Banana. The enhanced detail was impressive. Bec detected movement, so edged the lens to the right, past the frangipani tree beside their room. Two Balinese men were sitting on the day bed, smoking. She tilted down, saw another man sitting on the stairs. His yellow headscarf and ringed circle motif zoomed into focus.

Bec felt a shudder. From memory. The innocence of a smile a moment before impact, dark glasses in an airport queue, fragments of human bone in an incinerator.

'Fricken h…'

She froze at the sound of running feet on the path.

'What is it?'

The answer came from behind them.

'Time to go boys and girls.'

Bec swung round, suspended between fear, elation, and heart-thumping disbelief.

Jay stood there, shirt ripped, dried blood congealing over a new cut above his eye, but grinning.

'What the…'

'I'll explain later. We've gotta split.'

'They're outside our room Jay, Waiting…'

'I know. There's another lot in a car out front of the guesthouse. More on their way, I'm guessing. Have you got all the important stuff?'

Mike held up his backpack. 'All here.'

'Sweet. This way.'

Bec's million questions went unasked in a flurry of orange as Jay led them down a narrow track flanked by the high stone walls of villas to rent, rejoining the path beside the Intuitive

Flow yoga retreat. A tan dog limping on three legs, the rusting wheelbarrow of a workman carrying shingle, the clay soil of the worksite, tiger wheel rims of a motorcycle, the carrot paint of a wooden duck in the window of a gallery.

At the junction above the Camphuan steps, they turned right, past a long line of motorcycles, a fruit stall. Signs blurred like a meaningless message thread: Ubud Heaven Villas, Santra Fine Art Gallery, Session in Progress. Across a bridge, up a flight of stone steps, into a waiting cab.

Jay told them what he'd found on the south coast, and Bec filled him in on what she'd learnt from the New Zealand tourists and the link to the Aventura travel agency in Auckland.

Mike wanted to go to the police.

Jay didn't trust them.

Bec, once her pulse rate slowed enough to think, agreed, for different reasons.

'Even if we managed to find an honest cop who wasn't on the take, it would trash whatever chance we have of finding out who is really behind all this.'

20. A dog barking

Any lingering doubts Ped had about micro-targeting and the power of social over mainstream media were obliterated by the results in Kentucky and Oregon.

Hunter had peppered television, radio, newspapers with her face-morphing ads implying Garland's public donation site was a con. She also got plenty of free airplay from her Battle of Kentucky re-enactment from a media desperate to engineer a closer contest. Slam-dunk elections were ratings killers.

Sniping from beyond the 500-yard line, Jin and the Ciph had zeroed in on voters and reinforcers with morphing faces of real people – often from the targets' neighborhoods – saying they'd donated. The battery of morphing faces saying *Yes* ended with a dog barking – a clever play on the concept of *every man and his dog*, and a humorous counter to Hunter's tired use of celebrity.

Jin had also been right about one of the faces in Hunter's ad. The Ciph tracked him down not to the streets of Kentucky but to Hunter's campaign office in Washington, where he worked as a search engine optimizer. His name was Walter Binchy, and Jin's take on the *Where's Wally* puzzle books went viral until he was outed.

Ped took Kentucky 24 to 22, Oregon 15 to 13 – narrow victories but hugely significant given Hunter's Second Battle of Kentucky gamble. He now needed just 36 delegates to get over the line – Hunter an unattainable 148. Ped's spin doctors went into overdrive to convince the media their man was on track to the White House.

*****

The cab ride to the port of Padangbai on Bali's south-eastern coast had been a diversion, though Bec only found out when they arrived.

Jay had chatted away to the driver about how they were heading to Lombok, more specifically to the Gili islands popular with backpackers, peppering him with questions about travel options. A fast boat direct to Gili Trawangan was recommended, along with a hotel near the night market.

As soon as the cabbie was out of sight, they walked out the back of the ferry terminal to where a Balinese man was waiting in a black Toyota Hilux. Jay introduced him as Wayan, *an old mate*. Bec knew from experience the gaps between the lines would only be filled when Jay was ready.

They doubled back across the island via a bewildering series of minor roads to avoid Ubud and join up with the highway to the north near Mengwi. Bec hovered in the yellows, even though she knew Jay's account of what went down after the alarm went off in the drug lab down south was sanitized for her benefit. Orange was banished to the sidelines as Jay and Wayan jabbered and joked like they were heading down the road to a picnic at Reedy Creek.

The road started climbing after Luwus, and they got their first view of mountains to the west, dominated by the 7000-foot Batu Karu. They passed motorcycles laden with brooms, chickens in baskets, plastic toys, household goods, and schools of waving girls hanging over stone fences with blue and green ribbons in their hair.

By the time they reached the town of Batu Ritu, Bec needed a restroom. Wayan obliged, pulling into a parking lot beside a raised podium. Bec would later look back at the fiberglass cat-like animals mating on the railing, and the woman in the orange fluoro vest who greeted them before her feet touched the gravel, as a double warning unheeded. But when a girl's gotta go....

On the path down to the restroom, Bec declined several offers of *the tour*, agreeing to a *quick coffee* to get the woman off her back. What she didn't realize, as she squatted uncomfortably over the porcelain pan sunk into the ground, was that the cute cat-like creatures in cages outside were luwaks – Asian palm civets with a penchant for coffee berries.

After nearly wiping her hands on a towel that would have defeated the purpose of washing them, Bec allowed the woman, as promised, to lead her further down the path for a coffee. They arrived at a platform overlooking a valley terraced in dark green bushes, with a wooden seat beside a table covered in jars and small glass cups.

Bec would later claim she was just being polite, had difficulty understanding the woman's accent, that she told her repeatedly all she wanted was a quick cup of coffee for using the restroom.

Fifteen minutes later she'd sampled Bali Coffee which, according to the laminated A3 information sheet, *spurs the brain positive thinking*; Robusta Coffee which *slows down aging*; and Ginger Coffee, *make your brain send the active message on the body*. Bec only got two sips into the Luwak Coffee before she grasped the woman's explanation of how it was produced. The battery-caged animals were force-fed coffee cherries, then pooped them out ready for collection and roasting.

Bec tried to pay for what she'd tasted so she could escape, but the woman refused, leading her up another path to, surprise, surprise, *the store*. She was trying to choose between Mangosteen tea or turmeric and ginger when Jay rescued her.

The ribbing from her two friends – underscored by Wayan's exaggerated head-shaking – lasted all the way to Bedugal, a town on the edge of Lake Bratan with lime green and blue-domed mosques. Soon after they'd left the main road to head along a ridge high above Lake Buyan, Wayan got a phone call. The conversation was in Balinese, but Bec read concern on his face through the rear vision mirror.

'Translation?'

'At Munduk, police road block. They only check foreigners.'

'Might be nothing to do with us,' said Jay, 'but I'd rather not chance it Wayan.'

'I know quick way.'

Emotions Bec had been keeping in check roared into focus. Embarrassment at being duped at the coffee place, her pathetic inability to extract herself, the helplessness and loss of control over the change of plans and unfamiliar route, the fear of being hunted.

Wayan left the ridge, charging down steep, narrow, potholed, un-signposted roads, with Aristotle howling orange from the roof tiles, flags on bamboo poles, segments of umbrellas shading food stalls, in water tanks, cloth around shrines, in stacks of fluoro plastic crates full of trapped chickens on a flatbed trailer.

Bec, breathing and squeezing, and clinging to Mike like a life preserver, caught a glimpse of the north coast and Bali Sea. She held on to the image as Aristotle oscillated in the reds of graffiti on roller doors, the comb of a rooster scurrying across the road in front of them, until finally they reached the open flats on the outskirts of Lovina.

'Now finish the dangerous road,' announced Wayan.

*****

'You must do something make Kaluraha gang very angry.'

Wayan was scrolling through social media posts on his phone, as he and Jay relaxed on beanbags in the tower room of

Desa Global, the ecotourism venture Wayan ran with his wife Nyoman. The tower, above the yoga barn, gave three-sixty views over the fields to the town and sea in the distance.

'What are you seeing online mate?'

'It all over the Facebook and Instagrams. Kaluraha mengerahkan… how you say?... creep... spread... block road in Klungkung, Badung, Gianyar, Tabanan, Jembrana… I think you finish work, Jay. You plant jungle. No more new missions.'

'She's a long story mate. And what we're doing here is a bit different. I'm sure the Kaluraha lowlifes will soon forget about us, get back to their money-making rackets and stand-over tactics. There's bugger all in it for them hunting me and my friends.'

Jay drained the bottle, changed the subject.

'What about you mate, and your wife? Tell me about your little operation here. Haven't heard a squeak out of you since… where was it? Irian Jaya?'

Wayan handed Jay another beer and updated him. Life was good. Nyoman ran the not-for-profit café and yoga retreat. Wayan took tourists on personalized adventure tours, trekking, mountain-biking, snorkeling, and diving – off reefs near Pemuteran and in the national park on the north-west corner of the island. Profits from the social enterprise went to the poor and disabled in villages along the north coast.

'Good for you mate. You still, you know, active in the movement?'

'Not any more. Not from Irian Jaya time. We want make business big, have family. Nyoman hamil… how you say…?'

Jay shook his head. 'You got me there, mate.'

Wayan made a ball shape with his hands in front of his stomach.

'Pregnant? You mean Nyoman's having a baby?'

Wayan beamed.

'That's fantastic news mate. Congrats.'

He held up his bottle, clinking a toast.

Jay watched two kites, shaped like birds with tails at least a hundred feet long, dueling above paddies to the west.

'What about flying? Or is Nyoman and your impending fatherhood keeping you grounded?'

Wayan smiled.

'I still have airplane. Tourists like see whales. It better than chasing dolphins with boat.'

'You were also into hang gliding, if I remember rightly.'

'I sell hang glider. Now, I try paraglider.'

Nyoman's voice came up from below, calling them to dinner. Jay drained his beer.

'Look mate, before we go down, I've got a favor to ask.'

'Whatever you want, Jay. I owe you.'

Jay had told him about their project to uncover the source of the drug that killed Charlie Scott, and most of the highlights reel from their time in Bali. But not everything.

'I don't want to put you and your family at any more risk than…'

'Now who talk nonsense, man? What you want me do?'

'OK. I told you about the packet of NuNu they tried to plant on Bec in Jimbaran. I thought she'd flushed it. Turns out she's still got it. Wants to courier it to a lab in the States for analysis. Is that possible from here?'

Wayan nodded. 'I will arrange.'

'Cheers. We'll be out of your hair soon. Bec's booked flights to Auckland for Saturday.'

*****

Bali is not a large island. Ninety-five miles west to east, seventy north to south. Smaller than the state of Delaware. With the resources and street smarts at the disposal of the head of one of the island's largest gangs, Montoya expected a quick outcome.

The stakes had been raised even higher by the arrival of the American journalist Mike Bullard, who had teamed up with Duggan and Corelli. Mugshots of the three targets were in the hands and on the cellphone screens of thousands of Kaluraha members, prospects, associates, business partners, and hundreds of cops and local government officials on the payroll in Denpasar and all eight of Bali's regencies.

Montoya's offer of a three-million-rupiah bounty – roughly two hundred dollars – had whipped the island's underbelly into a frenzy. The bounty and the mugshots were being widely shared on social media, grabbing the attention of even law-abiding but cash-strapped Balinese outside the tentacles of Kaluraha.

Like the cab driver who had just reported taking three people fitting the targets' descriptions to the eastern port of Padangbai. The tip-off earnt him the equivalent of a year's wages, and the hunt was extended to Lombok and the neighboring Gili islands.

21. Truckload of enemies

The *Washington Post* story broke online an hour before the town hall meeting in Atlantic City.

It claimed the private security outfit looking after Ped was an offshoot of the Ángeles – one of America's Big Five motorcycle clubs designated by the FBI as outlaw gangs because of links to criminal enterprises. The gang's sergeant-at-arms was part of Garland's close protection detail, members of the club's Indiana chapter had escorted the candidate from a speech to auto workers in Noblesville, and heavies from the Idaho, Illinois and Pennsylvania chapters were behind disturbances at Hunter rallies in Boise, Springfield, and Harrisburg.

Hunter swooped in from the get-go, demanding to know if Mack *The Knife* Mendez, the Ángeles sergeant-at-arms – otherwise known as the gang's enforcer – was lurking in the audience.

Ped, reading from the teleprompter, countered by laughing the claim off as the desperate death rattle of a candidate who would stoop at anything to score yet another cheap shot. He dabbed his nose with a tissue, then tried to dodge and parry to change Hunter's point of attack.

'Is Wally in the audience tonight, Kate?'

'You're not answering the question Mr. Garland. Is Mack The Knife, the sergeant-at-arms for a criminal gang outlawed by the FBI, part of your close protection detail here tonight? Let's have it, straight up.'

Ped smiled, contracted his forehead.

'No Congresswoman. Is Wally…'

'Do you have someone by the name of Mack Mendez on your security team?'

Ped couldn't lie.

'Yes, but…'

A section of the audience reacted the way you'd expect a bunch of Hunter goons to react.

Hunter pressed.

'But *what*, Mr. Garland? I'm sure the audience would love to hear your explanation?'

'Mr. Mendez has been part of my security team. I would be flabbergasted to learn he was associated with a criminal organization. As soon as I was made aware of the *Washington Post* report, Mr. Mendez was stood down pending an investigation.'

The meeting shifted to questions from the audience on healthcare, the economy, family values, with no telling blows landed by either candidate before the break. Ped had noticed Hunter's subtle lack of eye contact with the questioner during the discussion on access to abortion, but doubted the audience picked it up.

During the interval, Ped learnt that the Ciph's AI-driven audience analysis showed strong negative sentiment over the way he handled the Mack Mendez questions. As soon as they resumed, he moved to cauterize the wound, set up Hunter for a counterpunch.

'My campaign manager tells me Mr. Mendez has confirmed he is an office holder with the Ángeles Motorcycle Club. His employment with us has been terminated immediately.'

The orchestrated cries of outrage from Hunter's goons were quickly shut down by the moderator.

The next question from the audience came from a soccer mom in the front row, whose postings on the ballooning federal budget deficit had come to the attention of the Ciph.

'Mr. Garland, why does someone who claims to be a man of the people need security protection in the first place, and how much is all this costing us?'

Ped walked toward her as he answered.

'Well, that's a fair question. Truth is, when I 'fessed up to the bad decisions I made when I was younger, information I passed on to the DEA led to a whole heap of people working for the drug cartel being taken out of circulation. Some astute people in the media have estimated my information prevented the deaths of hundreds of vulnerable young people, kept thousands of potential drug addicts out of hospitals, rehabilitation programs, the criminal justice system, and saved American taxpayers billions of dollars.'

Hunter tried to interject. Ped ignored her, maintained eye contact with the questioner.

'But sharing that information with the DEA also made me a truckload of enemies. I still get death threats after all these years later, and they've only gotten louder since I called for *a vein for a vein.*'

Hunter had another attempt.

'That doesn't explain why you're using a private security company, with...'

'I'll tell you why I'm using private security Congresswoman. Two reasons. Firstly, *I* get to call the shots... which means I have more quality face-to-face time with folks than I'd ever get if, like you, I was under the protection of the Secret Service. When was the last time your minders let a real person get within ten feet of you?'

She tried to answer. Ped cut her off, as the teleprompter gave a pulse to indicate incoming new material.

'Secondly, to answer the young woman's question, my security costs taxpayers like her a mere fraction of the staggering two hundred sixty-six thousand dollars a week it costs to keep Congresswoman Hunter's adoring fans at arms...'

'You're just making those figures up,' Hunter chimed in, 'like you made up the number of people donating to your...'

'They're not *my* figures Congresswoman. They come from the chief political correspondent of the *Wall Street Journal*, which you praised just last week as, quote, *informative, responsible, and credible*. Unquote.'

*****

'Mind if I join you?'

'Sure. Drink?'

'Just coffee thanks.'

Mike took a seat opposite Jay's friend in the café of Desa Global. The place was like a throwback to the 1970s. Mismatched tables and chairs, walls covered in masks, friendship bracelets, hand-made mosaic jewelry boxes, Buddha heads and busts, incense sticks. One hundred percent natural, no palm oil, no animal testing.

The seductive chimes of gamelan shimmered from speakers sharing the rafters with revolutionaries, freedom fighters, activists – posters of Yasser Arafat, Martin Luther King, Che Guevara, Gandhi, Abdul Sattar Edhi, Malala Yousafzai.

Mike was grateful for the cooling draft of the ceiling fan. He was feeling decidedly rough after testing Wayan's selection of local arak cocktails into the small hours. The drinking session hadn't slowed down Jay, who was coming into view on his umpteenth circuit of the property, after an exercise workout exhausting just to watch.

Wayan returned with the coffee.

'So how do you know Jay?'

'We worked same place two time. One time in Papua. One

time in Timor.'

'What sort of work are we talking about?'

Wayan's eyes narrowed. 'How much Jay talk to you?'

'A little. He mentioned Timor. Was that where he sprung a friend from prison, dressed as a priest, something to do with sandalwood?'

Wayan nodded, smiling.

'The friend, that was you, wasn't it?'

Another nod, followed by silence. Mike continued.

'Well, we know the guy's been some kind of eco-warrior, that he's... done stuff in India and Egypt, Zimbabwe, back in the States in Alabama. Toxic waste. And Myanmar. Haven't heard about Papua. Where is that exactly?'

'West side New Guinea.'

Wayan drew the veil back part-way in his broken English, but Mike managed to piece it together.

Several years ago, Jay had been working for a British company in West Papua – also known as Irian Jaya – escorting ecotourists up the Ajkwa River to stay with the Komoro tribe. He became incensed with pollution in the river from a copper and gold mine on the Jayawijaya Range, a sacred mountain of the Amungme people. He planned an operation against the mine, and Wayan – who he'd worked with in Timor-Leste – flew in to help.

Wayan's role was to organize hundreds of tribespeople to blockade a road to the mine. It was a diversion, which allowed Jay to penetrate the mine's security, sabotage the pipelines, make the river run clean for the first time in decades.

On his way out, Jay ran into a team of elite British activists from the Forest Liberation Front, who'd spent over a year planning something similar. They were so impressed with what Jay achieved on his own, in little over a week, he was invited back to London, where he became a cell leader for the Front.

Mike was intrigued. 'What did he get up to after that?'

'He do plenty things. Jay need tell you.'

There was an awkward pause.

'But if I get in trouble I want Jay… how you say in English… be my support.'

*****

Bec watched as Wayan's wife floated silently around the compound, placing tiny palm leaf baskets of offerings beneath a statue of Ganesha, beside a fountain, on a ledge at the entrance to the family temple, in the middle of the path leading to their rooms.

She'd seen women performing the ritual everywhere they'd been in Bali, but never given it much attention. After placing each basket and sticks of burning incense, Nyoman dipped a frangipani flower in a bowl and sprinkled the water over the offering, ending with a graceful twist of her hand. She placed the last basket on the step to the veranda, where Bec had been trying unsuccessfully to draft words to go with Jay's drone footage.

Bec had been lost in a fog of amber since learning scores of cops had – unofficially – joined the hunt, thanks to a bounty on their heads that seemed to rise by the hour. Nyoman's movements were a welcome distraction, suppressing the streaks of yellow in the dying leaves of banana palms, the logo on the Amnesty International poster, highlighted words on a sign: *All cultures, all beliefs, all sexes*.

'That's a beautiful ritual, so peaceful. What does it mean?'

Nyoman stepped onto the veranda, put the silver tray on the table, sat in the next chair.

'Are you a spiritual woman, Bec?'

'I'm not religious, if that's what you mean.'

153

'Religion is a *system* of faith and worship of a superhuman power. Spirituality is about how we *connect* with a higher power, which can mean different things to different people. For some it is simply nature. It, he, she has many names.'

Bec was thinking Aristotle, but didn't want to go there.

'You speak very good English.'

'I spent four years at an international yoga instructors' school in Rishikesh in northern India. English was the language of instruction.'

'Well if you mastered yoga as well as English, your students are very fortunate. Tell me about the offerings. I'm intrigued.'

'Canang sari is about balance between positive and negative forces. The offerings are to the Hindu gods for peace. It symbolizes the balance between good and evil, God and demon, heaven and hell. We use white lime for Shiva, red betel for Vishnu, and green gambier for Brahma.'

'The colors are important?'

'Critical. Also, the positioning of the flowers is important. White to the east, red to the south, yellow to the west, green to the north.'

Sounded familiar. Perhaps Bec was more spiritual than she thought.

'What about the cloth wrapped around the statue, those black and white checks?'

Nyoman clasped her hands together.

'The pattern represents the duality of life. The harmony found in the balance between light and shadow, doubt and hope.'

The edges of the cotton were torn, reminding Bec of frayed threads on the old corduroy jacket of her father's she'd retrieved from the attic of their home in Greenville. That jacket had been a sanctuary from the emotional storms that raged through her teenage years. She'd drape it over her shoulders like a shield, breath in the musk, the memories, run her fingers over the ridges and grooves of the corduroy. A tactile reminder of her father's tenderness, unconditional love, the promise of safety.

As Nyoman turned to leave, Bec's phone sounded. Jay had warned her not to answer unless she was certain of the caller. This one had been trying repeatedly for the last two hours. There was something familiar about the number. She wracked her brain, finally recognizing it: Ethan Henley, the DEA liaison from the consulate.

She tapped *Answer.*

*****

Montoya was losing patience and sleep, thanks largely to his demand for hourly updates.

There'd been reports of the trio heading west to get the ferry to Java, south to the island of Penida, some suggesting they'd already left the country. One Kaluraha lieutenant returning from a business meeting in Singapore was sure he'd seen them queueing for a flight to New York.

The Star-Spangled Banner ringtone sounded. Montoya hit *Accept* and put Henley on speaker.

'Selamat pagi Ethan. I'm hoping this isn't a social call.'

'They're up north, in Lovina.'

'How...?'

'I just spoke to the woman, Corelli. They're hunkered down with a friend of Duggan's, at a place called Desa Global. You're gonna have to move quickly, Rod. They're booked on a flight from Denpasar to New Zealand Saturday.'

Montoya thanked him, swiveled the chair to face the desktop. He opened Google Maps, typed in *Desa Global Lovina.* The red arrow symbol hovered just below the main road, the image in the box to the left was of tables in a café below a poster of Che Guevara. He tapped the symbol to expand the map.

It was time to take control. He called his driver.

Before they turned onto the Mandara Toll Road, truckloads of gang members were being pulled from towns in the east and west to set up blocks along the dozens of local roads dissecting the island north to south through the central mountains. The main highways were already under 24-hour surveillance. Specially selected squads were converging on Lovina with instructions to rendezvous with Agung and keep Desa Global under surveillance until Montoya arrived to supervise the assault.

Montoya realized the trio had to be prevented from getting inside the perimeter of Ngurah Rai Airport – virtually the only chunk of land, other than embassies – beyond his influence. Manpower was being tripled on roads leading to the airport, compliant cops were delivering mugshots and *instructions* to staff in all the ticket booths vehicles had to pass through.

As the Lexus sped across the plain on the north side of the mountains and closed in on Lovina, Montoya raised the bounty to five million rupiah.

*****

Jay closed his right eye, adjusted the central wheel to focus on one of the outrigger fishing canoes on the beach more than half a mile away from the tower above Desa Global, where he and Wayan were weighing options.

The faded black Indonesian script was razor-sharp against the duck blue of the wooden hull. Jay closed his other eye, tweaked the diopter to bring his right into focus, then scanned across the line of boats, some flying red and white Indonesian flags, past couples walking on the gray sand, hawkers lounging in the shade, stopping at the dolphin statue topped by a golden crown.

The detail was impressive. He swept back to the east, past kids playing volleyball in the parking lot, thatched meru towers of the Puri Dalem temple and the roofs of stores flogging cheap batik, Bintang t-shirts, stubby holders, fake designer clothes.

'They're good Wayan. Where'd you get them?'

'Jerman. Germany.'

'Imagine they come in handy on your bird-watching tours?'

'They already cover their cost. Last week, we see black-winged starling, first time this year.'

Wayan's phone sounded. While he took the call, Jay had another look through the binoculars. He fingered the central focusing dial as he brought the view back across the rooftops of houses, hotels, restaurants, palm trees, communication towers, to the main road running parallel to the beach. Motorbikes monopolized the traffic, alternating with SUVs, small trucks, the odd bicycle.

Jay zoomed in on movement near the intersection with the road leading to Desa Global. About twenty men were congregating in front of a flat-deck truck beside a black Lexus. The image was sharp enough to pick up the Kaluraha logo on the t-shirts and yellow headscarves, the iPhone in the hand of the man in Mykita sunglasses leaning on the hood of the Lexus. The other hand was pointing up the road towards Desa.

'Terima kasih,' said Wayan, pocketing his phone.

'Bad news Jay. They put roadblocks on main road, both east and west of town. Also, on Jalan Damal, Gambuh-Celuk Buluh and Setra.'

'They're the roads to the south right?'

'Yes.'

Wayan's phone sounded again.

Jay looked back at the intersection. The men were piling onto the back of the truck, which had been joined by a second. Sunglasses was walking round to the driver's door of the Lexus.

'More bad news, Jay. My boat driver call me. He say preman with guns surround the boat.' The Indonesian word for gangster had come up several times in their conversations over the past twenty-four hours.

Jay hadn't taken his eyes off the Lexus. It pulled out from the curb, turned into the side road, shadowed by the trucks.

'Looks like Plan C mate.'

Plan A had been to use backroads south to Denpasar and the airport.

Plan B was to take Wayan's boat to the village of Pemuteran, which opened up more options, including approaching Denpasar from the west or even heading across the strait from the port town of Gilimanuk to Ketapang in East Java.

Bec and Mike had been briefed on both options and were ready with their backpacks as Jay and Wayan descended the ladder. Jay figured they had two minutes, tops.

They ran across the family courtyard and through a gate in the concrete block fence at the rear. Four mountain bikes were leaning against the wall of a bamboo hut. Wayan led them along a track between rice paddies to a stand of coconut palms rising from a gully, from where they were concealed from the compound.

He tossed Jay the key to one of two dirt bikes beside a water pump, along with a pair of orange clip-on pillion pegs.

'So, are we talking Plan A or B?', Bec asked as she climbed onto the seat behind Jay.

'C.'

'Which is?'

'A work in progress. I'll explain later.'

*****

Hold on tight and lean with me were the only words of advice from Jay before the bike rumbled into life and they bolted out of the gully, across broken fields towards the hills rising to the south of Lovina.

Nothing could have prepared Bec for the ferocity of the ride. It was like Jay's jinking maneuvers to avoid the van in Kuta multiplied by a factor of ten. Peering over his shoulder, seeing Mike bouncing and jerking on the back of Wayan's bike made it worse. Closing her eyes, tucking her forehead into Jay's back, wrapping her arms around his waist, concentrating on keeping her feet planted on the pillion pegs was the only way to achieve anything remotely like balance.

Aristotle receded into a shadowy blur as the jolting motion, the foliage brushing her arms and legs, the constant growl of the bikes left little space in Bec's head to think or worry about the reason for the sudden departure, change of plans.

They were climbing. Mostly. Once, when the growling ceased, she opened her eyes to find them coasting down a smooth gravel road past masses of brown-gray spices laid out on mats to dry. Before she could ask Jay what they were, the flashing red of Wayan's brake lights signaled a return to jungle paths and the angry roar of the machines.

Searching for visual anchors to latch onto became pointless, so Bec tried the opposite: embracing the blur. Letting her focus drift, imagining she was observing their flight from above, a movie camera hanging from a drone. It helped for a bit, dulling the sound of the bikes, pausing time, numbing the panic.

A sweet scent began dominating the air, transporting Bec back to her first childhood visit to a dentist. She opened her eyes, breaking the spell. They were weaving through a plantation of trees with shiny dark green leaves giving off the unmistakable scent of cloves.

The land leveled out and they turned onto another gravel

road, this one leading to an iron-roofed building perched on a grassy ledge. Wayan had already dismounted and was fiddling with a padlock on a large roller door. By the time Bec had climbed off the bike, rubbed life back into her numb legs, taken in the impressive view over the treetops down the hill all the way to the sea, Jay and Wayan had emerged from the building with two large purple backpacks and contraptions that looked like oversized children's car seats.

Aristotle stirred when Bec realized they were unpacking and assembling paragliders, and flashed red as it became obvious from Jay's questions, he had never flown one of these things.

'What the fricken hell is going on Jay?'

He looked up and smiled.

'We've been forced into a little diversion, detour, bypass… whatever you want to call it.'

'Forced by what?'

'Mike's friends in the Kaluraha gang. They nearly got us at Wayan's place, and they'll probably turn up here soon, so we need to shake a leg.'

'What do you…?'

'I'll explain later. The gang have sealed off Lovina with roadblocks. Two truckloads of the thugs were on their way to Wayan's place, which is why we had to leave in a hurry. The road is out. Ditto Wayan's boat. So, we're left with, well, Plan C.'

He smiled again. His calmness, complacency in the face of such obvious danger was… infuriating.

'What about…?

'It'll have to wait Bec,' he said, attaching lines from the canopy to karabiners on the harness, which she now saw had two seats.

'Tell me you've flown one of these things before. Preferably on multiple occasions.'

'A paraglider, no. Flew a hang glider once though.'

'By yourself?'

'Not exactly. But I'm a quick learner. All we've got to do is copy Wayan and Mike.'

'We?'

A whipping sound spun Bec round. It was the wind filling the canopy above Wayan. He and Mike were pulled a few feet into the air. Wayan tugged on levers and floated back to the ground, looking across at Jay.

'Remember, when sail get full, lean into harness.'

'Got it. See you on the other side mate.'

'Semoga. Good luck, my friend.'

Wayan told Mike to lift his legs, took a few awkward paces forward, and they disappeared over the ledge. A few seconds later they came into view, rising out above the trees.

'See. Piece of cake.'

Bec turned to see Jay standing with the canopy stretched out on the ground behind him, holding the harness out for her.

Aristotle was whooshing like a maniac in the watermelon red of the canopy, every flap an exclamation mark of what would go wrong. The sail ripping, lines tangling, harness breaking, stalling, spinning, losing control, falling, plummeting…

'There must be another way.'

'No Bec. We need to go *now*.'

She surrendered to the urgency in his voice. The smile had gone. Bec had only just climbed into the harness when a gust partially filled the canopy – and carried the sound of vehicles approaching from below.

*****

Jay was thinking about the way a pilot back in New Zealand once described paragliding to him as *the simplest form of human flight*. The guy was an instructor with a gazillion hours hang time, but surely it couldn't be that difficult.

As soon as he felt another gust, he grabbed a bunch of riser lines in each hand, shuffled a few paces forward as the wind filled and lifted the canopy above their heads. He pulled lightly on the brakes to steady it, as Wayan had told him, then turned and crabbed forward to keep the sail loaded, the lines taut.

Two noises surprised him. The crackling of the sail – so different to the utter silence during his one and only parachute jump more than a decade ago. And the gunshot.

He looked up to see Wayan circling above the ridge, wriggling his legs in an exaggerated running motion. Time to go. Two more gunshots forced Wayan to take evasive action, throwing the paraglider into a corkscrew spin Jay hoped was controlled.

'OK Bec. Lift those legs. It's show time.'

He leaned to take her weight, then started running towards the ledge.

The launch was easier than expected but followed immediately by a third unexpected sound. A rapid *beep-beep-beep-beep* that sounded ominous. Wayan had mentioned something about audio varios and altimeters, but Jay had been distracted by Bec at the time.

He tugged on the left control to wheel away from the direction of the shots, and as he gained altitude he rotated and looked down to see the Lexus and one of the trucks pull up outside Wayan's shed.

The fourth unexpected sound was the ringtone on Bec's phone. She squirmed around to get it out of her backpack, take the call.

'It's Mike. For you,' she said, putting the phone on speaker, thrusting it forward so Jay could hear.

'I give you seven-point-five for launch.'

It was Wayan.

After a few pointers on technique and an explanation for the beeps – it was the variometer indicating the speed of climb and fall relative to the ground – Jay was able to start enjoying the flight. And view.

Orderly rows of clove trees gradually gave way to terraced rice paddies dotted by the splayed tops of banana and coconut palms. Moonlight reflected off the iron roofs of small sheds and ponds. As they descended, Jay could make out a roadblock about a mile east of Seririt, where the main road south left the coast.

Wayan came back on the phone to talk Jay through the landing. Their target was Celuk Pengastulan, although Wayan indicated celuk – meaning harbor – was an overstatement.

'It's like big rock wall at road end.'

With Wayan giving instructions from behind, Jay shifted his weight, released pressure on the left control to hang a sharp right round the dome of a mosque. He descended over a narrow street lined with stores, pastel-colored houses with run-down fences. At one point he was low enough to see shock in the eyes of a woman in a burka.

Up ahead he focused on what looked like a school building to his right and, beyond that, the remains of a concrete jetty – the landing site. It looked ambitious, to say the least, with piles of discarded plastic and large chunks of concrete piping to one side...

'Power line!'

Wayan's warning came just in time, but the evasive action to avoid the cable strung across the road between two poles took Jay too high, overshooting the landing point.

22. The exchange program

Ped could tell before Jin opened her mouth there was a problem.

He'd walked through to the backroom adjoining his hotel suite in Albuquerque, for a progress report. They were four days out from a clutch of primaries – winner-take-all New Jersey and Montana, as well as South Dakota, the Virgin Islands, and here in New Mexico.

'Where's the Ciph?'

It was Carl who answered.

'You better sit down, Ped.'

The Ciph had been busted. Not by the cops, not by Hunter's team. Not by the muck slingers or social media platforms or polling companies. By her parents.

'Turns out Mom and Dad were under the impression the Ciph was living in Sydney, attending boarding school on an exchange program organized by her school in Brooklyn. They decided to fly to Australia this week to surprise her on her seventeenth birthday…'

'I thought she…'

Carl held up his hand.

'You might as well hear the full story, Ped.'

'She fooled all of us, Mr. Garland,' Jin began. 'She hasn't spent a day at the Brooklyn school since hacking into its IT system at the beginning of the year. The school's database was amended to show the family had moved upstate, with all the necessary permissions and notifications signed off. As far as her parents were concerned, the Ciph'd won a fully paid scholarship for the exchange in Sydney. She Zoomed them every night using a fake background from her room, even changing the view out the window to match the seasons. The parents were emailed weekly progress updates from the boarding school, received gifts from Australia on birthdays and special occasions. Mom got a personalized Down Under care package of Aussie treats for Mother's Day.'

'Unbelievable,' said Ped, though he realized it wasn't.

'I had no idea, Mr. Garland. She told me she was nineteen, and her CV stacked up online. I realize now she'd doctored the websites, given me false links.'

'What about references? What did they say?'

'I got a message from the PA to the top one on the list saying he was too busy to talk but would reply to email questions. I was so blinded by what the Ciph demonstrated to me on her laptop in five minutes – how her talents could be used – I didn't dig any further.'

Ped rubbed his eyes.

'I wouldn't beat yourself up too much, Jin. We've all become a bit intoxicated by the Ciph and her numbers. Where is she now, and where does this leave us?'

'They got home from Sydney last night. The Ciph's gone back to Brooklyn to sort things out. I'm afraid the chances of her returning to the campaign are slim. Mom and Dad are staunch Democrats.'

Ped turned to Carl.

'What's our exposure here?'

'Low. I've spoken to the father. They're honest, straight-forward, extremely protective of their daughter. They're not going to Hunter, or the media or Dems. They wanna shut this down.'

Ped rubbed his eyes again. Perhaps it was a blessing in disguise. He always knew he'd have to start trusting his own gut at some point.

Carl had given him the signal he wanted a word in private.

'OK. We can't change the past. We need just 29 delegates on Tuesday, out of a possible 140. Where did the Ciph get to before she left?'

Jin looked at her tablet. 'She's given me all the targets and reinforcers for New Mexico and South Dakota. Those messages are being churned today, go out tomorrow. We're flying a bit blind in New Jersey and Montana, but Fox has you ahead in both.'

'Excellent.'

'And the false flag we'd discussed Mr. Garland – using bots shadowing Hunter's account to make it look like she's getting backing from that Mexican cartel…'

'I'd rather not know the details, Jin.'

'Sure. It doesn't matter now because she hadn't completed the set-up.'

'Never mind. I probably wouldn't have used it, anyway, given how things are unfolding.'

Once Jin left, Ped poured two bourbons, handed one to Carl.

'I take it you have news?'

'You could say that. We've finally tracked it to a private clinic in Bel Air.'

'California?'

'Maryland. Small place north-east of Baltimore.'

'You'll be able to get what we need?'

'I believe so.'

'Why the smile, Carl?'

'We think there's more. I'll have to fly to Canada to check it out.'

'How long will you be gone?'

'Just tonight. There's a flight back into Helena in the morning.'

'It's worth it?'

'Oh yes.'

'Do it.'

'You still want the resources we were using to monitor Hunter's day-to-days to be split between the two Dems?'

'Absolutely. Hunter's campaign's dead in the water,' said Ped, moving to the piano.

'Anything else?'

He sat and played the intro to Cathedral Square.

'We might have a little issue in Bali?'

'Anything that should distract me from these primaries Tuesday. Or choosing a running mate?'

'Na. It's under control Ped.'

*****

Mike hadn't felt too bad while the boat was moving. Now they were anchored, bobbing like a cork, he was struggling to keep the contents of his stomach in his stomach.

He looked across at Bec, who, illuminated by the moonlight, was unplugging her phone from a portable power bank. She seemed to have recovered from the crash-landing into the sea at the Muslim fishing village, though Mike wondered what shade Aristotle was etching. Jay had tried to claim he'd aimed for the water to avoid a hard landing on concrete. Bec hadn't bought it. The only thing that prevented a stand-up argument had been their need to cut and run.

Wayan had been outstanding – landing on a dime, calmly freeing Jay and Bec from the tangles of their harnesses and cords, finding a boat to *borrow* for the night.

The narrow wooden dugout canoe with outriggers each side and a triangular cloth sail had taken them in a wide arc out to sea then back to this point, known as Gede's Reef. According to

Wayan, they were about a mile and a quarter offshore, and the lights Mike could see to the south were the town of Pemuteran.

Wayan was telling Jay about a reef conservation project he had worked on in this area – something about an underwater temple garden – when his phone sounded.

The only word Mike recognized from the conversation was *Nyoman* – Wayan's wife – but he didn't need to be fluent in Indonesian to understand the concern on the Balinese man's face.

The good news was that Nyoman had been roughed up only a little, and the preman had left as soon as they heard their quarry fleeing on the dirt bikes. She was now safely ensconced with her brother in Singaraja.

'And the bad news?'

'Preman in Pemuteran. Three trucks full.'

Mike felt the bile rising again. He looked across at Jay: 'So the game's up?'

'Ye of little faith.'

*****

Jay slipped over the side and settled into steady strokes behind Wayan, surprised by the coolness of the water, hoping his ribs had healed enough for the task ahead. Swimming wasn't his favorite way of getting from A to B. Over a mile in open sea would be a challenge, though Wayan assured him of resting opportunities on buoys anchored to reefs closer to the shore.

They hadn't told Bec and Mike the whole truth about what the Kelarahu gang was up to in Pemuteran. Wayan's contacts in the town reported armed thugs were patrolling the beaches from the Pulaki Temple in the east to Burung Point in the west.

Ocean swimming in the dark without headlamps was a new experience for Jay. Fragments of moonlight helped him follow

Wayan, but the thought of night-hunters lurking on the fringes kept the adrenalin levels honest. His suspicions were confirmed half-way to shore when they struck a band of phosphorescent plankton and were treated to a magical ballet by more than a dozen giant manta rays pirouetting and gliding through millions of tiny spheres of light.

Jay's shoulders were throbbing by the time they reached a small wooden platform floating above Deep Reef, less than 600 feet from the shore. Wayan took the binoculars from his backpack, scanned the coastline. The welcoming party were in two pairs – one at the end of the jetty in front of the Glass House Hotel, the other near the Leon Beach Bistro in front of the Beachcomber Resort. Between the two was a point jutting out in front of a temple. Doable, but they'd need clouds to dim the moonlight.

While they waited, Jay outlined the plan he'd been devising during the swim. The aim was to draw the thugs away from the beach long enough to bring Bec and Mike in on the boat, then get them to the airfield to the west of the town where Wayan kept the Cessna he used for whale-watching flights.

'I'll get you to lay low in the temple while I work out a way to give these lowlifes and their brothers-in-arms a reason to head east.'

Wayan started to protest. Jay stopped him.

'No offence, mate. What I've got in mind requires a different set of skills. Horses for courses. I'll need you to collect Bec and Mike, get them to the airfield.'

Jay looked up at the sky. A cloud the shape of a frog would reach the moon by the time they got to the shore.

'How long do you reckon we've got before dawn?'

'Four hours.'

'Right. Let's do it. I'll aim to meet you back at the temple inside two.'

*****

The manager of the Beachcomber didn't appreciate being summoned from his bed so early but became more accommodating when he recognized the tattoos on the necks of the three preman accompanying the man in the sunglasses.

Montoya was tired, hungry and in no mood to wait for the scheduled opening of the restaurant. The chef and kitchen staff were summoned immediately.

As he waited for his breakfast, Montoya got updates from Agung and his lieutenants in other parts of the town. A second fisherman returning from a night on the water had confirmed an earlier tip that the boat stolen from the Muslim village was headed for Pemuteran. It was only a question of time.

*****

Vulnerable. Exposed. Defenseless. Abandoned. Take your pick. Bec had tried every self-managing and calming technique known to mankind. S-T-O-P. Breathing her lungs dry. Squeezing beyond pain. Splashing water nowhere near cold enough over her face. Dashing wasn't an option in this floating wooden casket.

Nor was darkness an ally, as Aristotle coerced her to *imagine* the faded orange of the rope holding the anchor, the orange of the buoys Wayan said floated above the reef, even clown fish jeering at her from the depths in some Stephen King-inspired underwater horror. Mike had tried to pull her back towards yellow but given up after his second spell of vomiting. Now she was cocooned in the folds of the sail, stupefied by the orange lights witching her from the coast.

She heard the slopping of oars before she saw the canoe. Closed her eyes, withdrew deeper into the salty fabric of the sail, chasing invisibility, until a familiar voice punctured the delusion.

It was Wayan.

Alone.

Aristotle, ever the fickle accomplice, mutated instantly from the yellow hull of the dugout to the red of Wayan's backpack.

'What happened to Jay? Where is he? The gangsters, they've got him, haven't they? Is he…'

'Give him a chance Bec,' said Mike, steadying the canoe against the fishing boat so Wayan could climb aboard.

She sunk back within the asylum of the sail, willing the lapping of the water to drown out the inevitable news.

Twenty minutes – or was it ten, thirty – passed in a brain fog. The boat was moving. Oars splashing. Waves slurping. Voices whispering. Words hovering. *Diversion… signal… Cessna.*

Then Mike's volume broke through.

'How the hell is the guy going to signal us? He doesn't use a phone?'

'Shhh. You look. Or listen.'

*****

The second preman put up even less resistance than the first. The Kaluraha mob's operating manual obviously didn't extend much beyond nightclub security, pimping, mindless intimidation. And substance abuse.

The first guy, who Jay found having a piss against the back wall of a laundry on the main road, reeked of Balinese moonshine. Jay left him gagged and zip-tied round the wrists and ankles, relieved of his cellphone, Kaluraha headscarf and revolver – probably a knock-off of a Smith and Wesson.

After returning to give the phone and instructions to Wayan, Jay made his way east as far as another temple, where he'd found thug number two, gazing out to sea through the smoke of a joint, his firearm leaning against the trunk of a coconut palm. He was now trussed up under a pile of leaves behind the restrooms.

The M1 carbine was so ancient some of the notches probably dated from the Vietnam War, but it had a full 15-round magazine so might do the job Jay had in mind.

He found what he was looking for on the other side of the road, behind a parking lot used for the nearby Pulaki Temple. Two sides of the large open area were taken up by stores and cafes which during the day would peddle souvenirs and food to busloads of visiting worshippers and tourists. Most of the signage on stores on the eastern side of the lot was in Indonesian, but pictures of concrete pipes, temple statues, rattan furniture gave clues to their offerings.

Jay was drawn to a store with faded photos of marlin and tuna. The windows were barred, but the lock on the rear door gave way to two paper clips he found in a garbage can.

Inside, once his eyes adjusted to the darkness, he found a 275-yard big game fishing line, selection of screws and a driver, islets, compression spring, lengths of half-inch ply. The 10-gallon container of gasoline and cigarette lighter were unexpected bonuses.

By the time he'd completed the set-up, he figured there were about 30 minutes of darkness left. He moved into position, fired two rounds from the M1 into the air.

*****

Mike jumped at the shots, almost falling over the side of the boat. Not one of the scenarios he'd been considering since Wayan returned without Jay involved gunfire.

Bec's reaction was to sink deeper into the sail.

Mike looked back to Wayan, who was smiling.

He took out a cellphone – different to the one he'd been using up till now, touched the screen.

'Mereka datang ke pantai dekat Pura Pabean.'

Then he took up the oars, started rowing towards the shore.

'What was that about Wayan? Who were you talking to?'

'Man called Agung.'

'One of your friends?'

'No. I think he with Kaluraha. Agung means *big*. Maybe he boss of gang.'

'What the hell's going on Wayan? What did you tell this guy?'

'Mereka dating ke pantai dekat Pura Pabean. *They go to beach near trader temple.*'

*****

Montoya dismissed the first sound as thunder and continued mopping up the egg yolk with a piece of toast. When a second boom lit up the sky to the east, followed by the cracking of automatic gunfire, he reached for his phone.

Agung told him the trio had come ashore about a mile to the east of the resort. His men had them pinned down in a compound beside a temple parking lot. All the other gang members were racing there like bees to a honeypot.

'Is that wise?' Montoya asked, as another fireball exploded above the temple.

'I cannot stop them. Five million rupiah can do that.'

'Where are you?'

'I watch from house after Pura Pabean. On left side, opposite parking lot.'

Montoya saw the small house as they passed the temple and another explosion lit up a communication tower a quarter mile away. He ordered his driver to pull over and joined Agung on the veranda.

Three trucks were parked beside a billboard near the entrance to the parking lot. Most of Agung's men were sheltering behind the trucks. Others cowered in a stone-walled drainage canal parallel to the road.

A single shot came from the area of the tower and was answered with deafening volleys of automatic fire from the men in the canal. Most of the return fire went up into the air. Montoya had no military experience, but even he could see the only people *pinned down* were Agung's men.

'Why don't your hombres attack?'

'Mortars. Two already hit ground. There and there,' he said, pointing to trees in the parking lot.

Montoya grabbed Agung's binoculars. Smoke drifted up from the burnt-out remains of a garbage can beside the nearest tree. It was too dark to make out the second. He looked across to a third tree, not far from a fishing tackle store. A wire can at its base was stuffed with paper and cardboard.

Another single shot drew more aimless fire from the canal, until an explosion sent them ducking for cover. Montoya trained the binoculars on the tree by the store. The can had been obliterated.

Two trees could have been a coincidence. Three was absurd.

He handed the binoculars back, started walking towards the parking lot.

'What you doing?'

Montoya ignored him and crossed the road.

'Hold your fire,' he yelled as he strode past the men behind the truck. He walked over to the remains of the third can. He jumped at the sound of another single shot, which hit the back of the sign above the roof of the tackle store.

Duggan was either a poor shot, or…

Montoya ran up the side of the store, across the gravel driveway at the back, and sheltered behind the trunk of a tree.

Another shot hit the sign above the store. It had been fired from somewhere near the foot of the communication tower.

He ran from tree to tree until he was about eighty feet from the tower. He slowly leaned his head out from the trunk, just in time to see the shudder of the barrel as another round thunked into the sign.

The rifle was tied to one of the steel legs of the tower, at the same height as the sign it was aimed at. As Montoya got closer, he saw a spring-loaded mechanism attached to the trigger, a taut fishing line running down the side of the leg and across to the trunk of a tree about fifty feet away. He followed the line to where it passed through an islet screwed into the trunk about three feet from the ground.

Montoya took out his penknife, cut the line, called Agung.

They traced the line to a dirt track at the base of the hill overlooking the parking lot.

Montoya's phone sounded. It was Arief, who had been asking questions about Duggan's Balinese friend from Lovina.

'He owns a Cessna, which he keeps at the Lieutenant Colonel Wisnu Airfield.'

'Which is where exactly?'

'About three miles from where you're standing.'

*****

The airfield was a private one-runway affair used by the Bali International Flight Academy to train pilots for Garuda and a bunch of smaller airlines and charter companies. Wayan was allowed to keep his Cessna there, in return for helping with advanced mountain flying instruction one week a month.

The matter-of-fact manner Wayan got them ashore and into a waiting friend's SUV, his indifference to the explosions, gunfire, and sirens, had tugged Bec back from the abyss. Calm could be just as contagious as panic.

Dawn was breaking as they'd merged with the waking canines of Pemuteran, snaking westward along backstreets between the sea and main road.

Aristotle's scattergun shots at holding Bec's attention on the red of a bridge railing, a cigarette billboard, gas station, Honda flags, were missing the mark as she locked onto the oranges of a tarpaulin, a truck cab, the exposed wood of a tree stripped of bark, a row of painted iron fence stakes.

He had one last attempt with the red Indonesian flags flapping at the entrance to the airfield, but Bec kept her eyes riveted to the terracotta brick of the traditional Balinese split gateway.

A small single-propeller plane was being towed from an open-fronted hanger as they drove onto the apron. Its three tiny wheels reminded Bec of stabilizers on a kid's bike.

As they walked from the SUV across the tarmac towards their flimsy escape capsule, she glanced over her shoulder for the umpteenth time.

'He will come,' Wayan whispered, reading her thoughts.

*****

Montoya ordered his driver to ignore the cop trying to wave them down as they sped along the highway towards the airfield.

The Lexus had left Agung and his truckloads of incompetents in its wake.

Only the hombre on the dirt bike, who had joined the chase from a side road, could keep up.

And he had a pistol, which he was waving in the air. It would add to the firepower of the two men in the back seat.

*****

To take her mind off the empty seat in front of her, and their rapidly diminishing window of opportunity, Bec got Wayan to talk her through the dials on the dash as they waited – rattling – at the end of the alarmingly short runway.

He pointed to and explained the function of various indicators: altitude… airspeed… heading… vertical speed… but lost her at *turn coordinator*.

Bec's gaze drifted from the spinning propeller back over her shoulder, toward the road from Pemuteran. A black sedan appeared in the distance, followed closely by a guy on a motorbike. Bec's heart sank as she recognized the scarf around the rider's head. Yellow.

'We've got to go *now*,' Mike was shouting.

The car was getting closer.

'He's right, Wayan. Jay's not gonna make it.'

Wayan pulled the steering column in and out, looking at the wings on each side.

The car was within three hundred feet of the corner when the gangster on the bike accelerated up the inside. Bec saw him hold out a pistol and fire *towards* the tires.

The sedan wobbled as the driver fought for control, slid in gravel at the side of the road and flipped, smashing through a flimsy wooden fence, and rolling two, three times.

Bec screamed as the motorbike came flying round the corner and skidded to a stop in the grass beside the low stone fence of the airfield. The gangster, still brandishing the pistol, dropped the bike, scaled the fence, sprinted for the plane.

Wayan leaned over and opened the passenger door.

What the fricken hell was he playing at?

'Five Charlie Lima Bravo ready go,' he said into his microphone, as if he was heading off on a routine flight to watch whales.

Bec froze as the gangster pulled himself into the seat, tossed the pistol onto the runway, closed the door, pulled off the headscarf.

It was Jay.

'Copy that Five Charlie Lima Bravo,' came the voice from the control tower. 'Wind speed is two five zero one four knots. Runway three two cleared for take-off.'

*****

Montoya extracted himself from the window of the Lexus as Agung pulled up in the first truck. Just in time to see the Cessna lift off, head out to sea, bank left and set a course south. Toward Denpasar. Ngurah Rai Airport.

Montoya looked at his watch. Duggan and the two journalists would make their flight to New Zealand. There was not a thing he could do about it.

He slammed his fist into the already dented door of the Lexus.

When his heart rate subsided, he phoned his travel agent to book the next available flight to New Zealand.

Then he punched in the number for Carlos.

23. Eating from the palm

The entourage pulled up in the parking lot of the Lancaster Seed Company outside of Helena, Montana. Lines of stainless-steel bulk bins gleamed in the afternoon sun, beneath a blue sky that was impressive, though no bigger than the one in Georgia.

Carl had arrived before them. He pulled Ped aside before he reached the office.

'Good news and bad.'

'Give us the bad first. I'd rather face the workers on the back of something positive.'

'The issue I mentioned in Bali. Couple of American journalists have been snooping around, asking questions about cocaine. Rodrigo thought he had things contained, but they've slipped through his net. He thinks they're heading to New Zealand.'

Ped sniffed, looking around to check nobody could hear them.

'What do they know?'

'We think they're onto the limousines.'

'Fuck. And you say they're going to New Zealand?'

'Looks that way. So is Rodrigo. He's confident he and Mauricio can take care of it.'

'So why are you smiling?'

'The good news. Congresswoman Hunter got knocked up in her last year in high school. Her parents arranged for the abortion at a clinic in a place called Cochrane, near Calgary. False name, false passport, the works.'

'We have proof?'

Carl tapped his jacket pocket.

'An affidavit signed by the anesthesiologist. Identified Hunter from her high school yearbook.'

Ped's press secretary was marching toward them, holding a bunch of cards.

'Good work Carl. Let's keep this to ourselves. Hopefully we won't even need it.'

Amanda handed Ped the cards, started briefing him about *the message*.

'Relax, I've got this,' he said, tucking the cards in his pocket.

'You did see the polling summary I sent you last night? Showing you behind here *and* in New Jersey? Hunter only needs fifty-point-one percent to take all 78 dele…'

'I understand the math Amanda, and how winner-take-all primaries operate. Those polls were outliers. And even if they're accurate, I'm gonna get more than I need from New Mexico and South Dakota. Relax.'

Other than a few negative comments on the death penalty during the Q&A, Ped left the meeting with staff even more convinced the polls showing him behind in the Big Sky state were way off the mark. Amanda cornered him as he left the cafeteria.

'You didn't use any of the five points. Not one!'

'I thought it went real fine.'

'Not only were you off-message, you…'

'Which meeting were you at woman? I had 'em eatin' right outta my palm.'

'That's not how the press saw it. *Sleepwalking to power, arrogant, unfocused* is how they're going to report this one. Precisely the wrong message to send ahead of Tuesday.'

*****

Excitement buzzed through the cabin, but Jay was watching the jet's shadow as it passed over the houses of South Auckland, the iron industrial roofs of Wiri, across open fields, a gray tidal estuary, the airport perimeter fence, then rushed closer and closer to converge as the wheels hit the tarmac.

Jay didn't buy into the flag-waving lines about New Zealand being some pristine paradise sheltered from the turmoil of the planet. If there had ever been truth to the claim, it was blown apart the day France's foreign intelligence agency bombed the Greenpeace protest ship *Rainbow Warrior* in Auckland Harbor. Jay was just a kid at the time, and that single act of state-sponsored terrorism set him off on a life of activism against the power and abuse of vested interests.

Memories of the *Rainbow Warrior* bombing had faded in the minds of most New Zealanders, who gullibly feasted on the Garden of Eden evangelism of the tourist industry.

The clean green mantra had also anaesthetized them to the environmental vandalism of the country's burgeoning dairy herd and its insidious contribution to global warming. Five million cows releasing tons and tons of methane into the atmosphere, one fart or burp at a time.

A sinister underbelly had been callously exposed when a white supremacist entered two mosques in Christchurch and slaughtered 51 Muslim New Zealanders during Friday prayers, but Jay sensed the significance of that atrocity, streamed live on social media, was already being swept beneath the carpet of utopian rhetoric.

Still, there was always something reassuring, revitalizing about returning to your country of birth after an absence. Jay was also conscious it was Bec and Mike's first visit down under, didn't want to spoil the moment for them.

After clearing immigration and customs, he led them out into the late afternoon chill to get an Uber. Jay had arranged for them to stay in Epsom with the Pearses – friends from way back. Tony was an environmental lawyer, Julie a King's Counsel specializing in criminal law.

As they cruised along George Bolt Memorial Drive towards the city, Jay kept his eye on the side mirror. He suspected a tail as they crossed the Mangere Bridge. His fears grew when they left the highway and the white Peugeot swung in three cars behind them.

Jay sized up their driver, a young Indian with a black turban, probably the son of one of the thousands of Sikhs from the Punjab who settled in New Zealand after changes to immigration rules in the 1980s. His name was on the ID badge on the dash.

'Listen up Vinu, I want you to turn into the parking lot beside The Warehouse up there.'

Through the mirror, Jay watched the Peugeot slow, then continue along Queenstown Road.

'What's going on Jay?'

'We may have company. I'm just checking.'

He directed Vinu through the lot to a rear exit. As they waited for traffic to allow them to cross, Jay noticed the tail turn the corner, pull into the curb. He told Vinu to head east, then left into another parking lot in front of the Royal Oak Shopping Mall.

Again, the Peugeot slowed at the entrance before driving past. Jay got Vinu to drop them beside a dry cleaner. Once inside the mall, he asked Bec for her phone. Her open arms and raised eyebrows deserved an explanation.

'We were followed from the airport. Which confirms the link between Bali and New Zealand's as tight as a fish's...'

'What now then?'

'Tony and Julie's place is out. Too risky for them and their kids.'

Jay called the Pearses to explain the change of plans, then got Bec to search for somewhere to stay near the travel agency.

*****

The Airbnb was a multi-chimneyed wooden villa overlooking Devonport. Sunshine after a heavy downpour gave everything a fresh feel, exaggerated the sharpness of colors as Bec and Jay walked down the hill to the seaside village.

Bec was edging into yellow, with Aristotle sparkling in the yellow road markings, flowers on the wall of the restaurant in the Bank of New Zealand building, the pastel façade of the old Post Office which was now a French café. *Quaint* would about sum up Devonport, with its impressive palms nodding in the wind, the Māori carving over the entrance to the public library on prime real estate opposite the beach.

The boutique Aventura travel agency was tucked between a fruit and veggie store offering *broccoli two for $2 and firewood at $8.99 a bag*, and an emporium with rusted shopping trolleys of junk.

Bec paused beside a yellow-topped wheelie bin to check the glasses were recording before they entered. Rule-bound former colleagues at the *New York Times* would be shocked she'd resorted to covert filming, but Bec no longer felt conflicted with the direction her moral compass had spun. The ends definitely justified the means. Guilt had given way to determination, empowerment. And fear of being discovered was swamped by the rush of adrenalin.

Two women sat at glass-topped tables with laptops and bowls of frangipani petals that had to be fake. Aventura promoted travel to a range of destinations, but Bali was clearly its specialty. Half the pamphlets in the display shelf were for accommodation or activities on the island. Bali guidebooks –

the same brand Jay found at the mansion on the south coast – had been placed in the most eye-catching positions.

As Jay chatted to one of the women, Bec rotated her head smoothly to take in two large prints on the wall – showing the spa at the Nyalahutan near Ubud and the Tanah Lot sea temple near Denpasar – then took a few paces forward to get a close-up of a poster advertising free limousine transfers, *conditions apply*.

She walked over to stand behind Jay and film over his shoulder as the woman explained the limousine offer.

'The deal applies to anyone booking accommodation at one of the four Nyalahutan resorts. We arrange for the limousine to collect you from your home and take you to the airport for your flight. Then from Denpasar another limousine will take you to your resort.'

'Sounds like an amazing deal,' said Jay. 'What's the hook?'

'No hooks. The limousine transfers are complimentary, as long as you book through us. The arrangement is exclusive to Aventura.'

Bec smiled. Mission accomplished.

*****

It looked like a perfume bottle, but if someone tried to push or unscrew the spray head, they'd probably break the camera and Mike would be $79.99 out of pocket.

He leafed through the user manual. *Wake up upon motion in 0.7 seconds… 1080P high-definition video quality… 940 Black LED night vision up to 26ft…*

He prized open the bottom plate, pushed the reset button, inserted an SD memory card, switched it on, then pushed the magnetic plate back into place.

After pairing it with his phone, he looked around the living room of the Airbnb. The top shelf of the bookcase seemed a good option.

24. Gut instinct and chemistry

Ped slammed the phone down on the sofa.

'Amanda will have to go. She's driving me crazy.'

'There's no need to pitch a fit, Ped. How can you even think of dumping Amanda when she's helped you get this far, so close?'

'The woman's givin' me an earful about being here instead of Newark – and the message it's sending. She's always harpin' on about the fuckin' message.'

'Language Ped! What's got into you? And you've barely touched your breakfast.'

'I'm not hungry.'

'You'd want to pink slip a press secretary if she wasn't focusing on the message. That's her job.'

'Jin would do the job much better.'

'Who's Jin?'

The backroom operation had been so discreet, even his wife didn't know about Jin and the Ciph.

'Just someone who's been helping us with messaging for social media.'

'Male or female?'

'What?'

'This Jin. Is he or she a man or woman?'

'Woman. Jin Ly. A very smart, astute woman who doesn't rub me up the wrong way.'

'Is she good looking?'

'What? No. Yes. I don't know. Jin's not my type. Cut me

some slack, Patricia, for goodness' sake.'

Ped had elected to remain in Atlanta to meet privately with prospective running mates, forgoing last-minute campaigning in New Jersey. He was flying up to Newark that afternoon to announce his choice at the party to celebrate winning the nomination.

The three candidates shortlisted for interviewing ticked all the boxes for what he needed in a Veep, to balance the ticket. A white woman from inside the Beltway with experience in national government. All three hailed from northern states, had strong DC credentials, were younger than Ped, and better looking.

Each interview lasted more than an hour. They all presented well, any of the three could do the job, so it came down in the end to gut instinct and chemistry. Madeline Walters just felt right.

The plan had been for her to accompany Ped to Newark, but they decided to delay her public unveiling when exit polls showed he might fall tantalizingly short.

It was the right call. Hunter swept the winner-take-all states of New Jersey and Montana, as well as South Dakota and the Virgin Islands. Ped squeaked home in New Mexico, but ended the day two delegates short of the 1237 needed to claim the nomination.

Which meant he would have to go to Puerto Rico.

*****

'Welcome to Auckland Mr. Montoya.'

The immigration officer handed back his passport and Rodrigo went through the *nothing to declare* lane.

He ignored the crowds in the arrival hall, cursed himself for not bringing warmer clothing as he strode over the zebra crossing to the Novotel Hotel. His brother Mauricio was waiting in the lobby, sitting in a chair by the window with a phone to his ear.

He finished the call and they embraced.

'Hola.'

'Hola.'

'¿Qué mas pues?'

'Los he encontrado. But it is better to speak English here. It will arouse less suspicion. I've tracked them to a villa in Devonport.'

'Perfect.'

*****

Jay chose a Toyota Rav4 four-wheel-drive, and waited while the rental service guy gave Mike tips on driving on the left.

'The thing most Americans have trouble with, sir, is looking to the right. When you're at home, you're used to watching left for traffic. Here it's the opposite. The danger will be on the right. Remember that and you'll be sweet.'

Mike assured the man he got it, then followed him out to the yard and tried to get in the wrong side.

Jay shook his head. 'You'll have more luck reaching the steering wheel from the other side mate.'

Mike palmed his forehead, mumbling some lame excuse about jetlag, then swapped sides. They drove through the village, approaching a roundabout from different directions until Mike got used to the traffic flow.

Jay took over before the highway. At the airport, he checked out a filling station, cargo inspection depot and logistics warehouse, before deciding the short-stay parking lot over the road from the international terminal was the best location.

Aventura gave clients three options for flights to Bali – direct with Air New Zealand, or via Australia with Jetstar or Qantas. The Qantas flight was leaving in just over three hours. Jay dropped Mike off at a cab rank, then settled in for the first shift.

25. The packages

San Juan, capital of Puerto Rico and oldest city under the Stars and Stripes, was known more for its fabulously restored sixteenth and seventeenth century buildings and El Morro Fort than for the role it played in choosing American Presidents.

Residents of the laid-back Caribbean Island didn't get to vote in Presidential elections, but they did have a say in primaries, sending 23 delegates to the Republican convention.

The island's winner-take-all election was normally held earlier in the cycle, but this year had been shifted to the penultimate spot to give the territory more time to recover from a hurricane. Which thrust San Juan front and center of a political maelstrom.

Ped was squinting out over the Atlantic from the backroom of his suite in the Intercontinental, wondering if any of the people on the beach below were eligible to vote. And how they'd react to what he was about to unleash.

If and how he used the information on Hunter's abortion was arguably the most important call of the entire campaign, given the context of the race.

He was desperate to nail Puerto Rico to avoid going to the final primary in DC where Hunter, a Beltway insider, would have home advantage.

Which is why he'd brought Jin and Amanda together for the first time. He knew they'd have differing views on how the information should be used. Ped could taste the tension in the room behind him, the stakes were so high.

In the blue corner, Amanda was thinking long-game, arguing

caution. News of Hunter's abortion might work for Ped in Catholic-dominated Puerto Rico, not in DC.

In the red corner, Jin was gung-ho. Play the abortion card for all it was worth to lock up Puerto Rico's delegates. Then if DC was still in play the following week, shift the messaging away from the termination and a woman's right to choose to Hunter's hypocrisy.

On one matter the two women agreed. Ped I-don't-run-negative-ads Garland had to stay a million miles from whatever was released.

Ped sniffed, turned to face the two women.

'Y'all both got some valid points. Let me mull it over for a spell.'

Once they'd left, Ped grabbed a tissue, blew his nose, sat on the sofa opposite Carl.

'Couldn't have picked a worse time to catch a cold, huh?'

'You sure that's all it is?'

'What do you mean?'

'Running nose, sensitive eyes... this would also be a terrible time to start using again, Ped.'

'Don't be absurd. Probably just the weather shift down here.'

'I hope so, my friend.'

Ped changed the subject.

'You heard what those two message-crafters had to say. What's your take on it, Carl?'

'Always been one for takin' care of what's in front of me. Worry about other bridges when and if you must cross 'em.'

'How we goin' on the other matters in front of us?'

'Stable on both fronts. Rodrigo's in Auckland, taking care of business. The Archbishop and the Commissioner have both received the packages, so we'll hear from them soon enough.'

*****

Mike fingered the receipt card in one hand as he scrolled through his social feed with the other. He was leaning against the pay station, ready for a quick exit.

He'd dropped Bec and Jay off at a Vietnamese restaurant in a heritage warehouse near the downtown ferry terminal, offering to stake-out the airport for the Air New Zealand and Jetstar flights – to give them some time to themselves.

Mike had mixed feelings – lurching between hope and dread – about Bec's deepening relationship with Jay. There was a lot to like about the Kiwi, who obviously cared for Bec as much as she did for him. But her growing reliance on a guy who attracted danger like a moth to a flame had alarm bells ringing. The intensity of Bec's borderline emotions, her fear of abandonment, meant the risk of heartbreak – or worse – was forever lurking just below the surface. The higher the mountain, the greater the depth and darkness of the valley.

Mike checked his phone. The departure window for Air New Zealand had come and gone with no sign of a limo. He was beginning to wonder if they needed to change their approach when he saw a black Lincoln town car pull up outside the main arrivals door.

The license plate was AVENT3.

He stuck the receipt card into the slot, paid with his credit card, then ran over to the rental, keeping one eye on the limo. It swept past him as he waited for the barrier arm to rise, but he caught up with it before leaving the airport precinct.

Driving on the left was easier at night, with fewer distractions, traffic lighter. Mike kept two places behind the limo as it merged onto the highway. It took the first exit after the Mangere Bridge, looping the ramp onto a road the navigation app identified as Onehunga Mall.

He had to run a red to stay behind the limo when it turned into a road lined with wheelie bins, blue and red tops glowing under the streetlamps.

Mike lost contact when he was held up behind a truck and trailer, then caught sight of the limo again as it crossed an intersection on a yellow. Fortunately, the road it entered – Beasley Avenue – showed up on the app as a dead end.

Up ahead Mike saw the limo's turn signal blink. He waited for the green, then shot through the intersection and parked opposite a business called Charteris Woodturners. He got out and walked up to the where the limo had gone – just in time to spot the tail-lamps before the roller door reached the ground.

The building was towards the rear of a flood-lit yard surrounded by a high wire fence. Mike noted four security cameras, signs warning of guard dogs.

He returned to the car, noted the location on his phone, then went on TripAdvisor to choose somewhere to eat.

*****

They'd given themselves the night off, and Bec was thinking about making love. It had been more than three weeks since Jay's rib was broken in Ubud. When he made it clear over dinner at Café Hanoi he was *good to go*, they skipped dessert and virtually jogged the short distance back to the terminal on Quay Street.

Aristotle was sashaying in the undulating blue neon of The Cloud function center as the ferry left the dock, cast in a honeycomb of lights from a cruise ship berthed at Princes Wharf.

The late fall evening in Auckland was a world away from the swelter of Bali. Bec spooned into Jay's embrace as they stood on the deck, taking in the floodlit cranes and containers at the port, the distant arc of the harbor bridge. By the time the ferry neared Devonport, the glitter of downtown, the chatter of passengers, thrum of the engines, had receded into a soft fuzz, pierced by a single blue beam from the Skytower shimmering across the water.

Green had become such a rare sensation for Bec, she would have missed the faint glimmer from the beside clock if Jay, undoing his belt, hadn't pointed out most people associated the color with the word *go*.

She crossed her arms, pulled her top over her head.

Three cracks like gunshots torpedoed the desire, an instant before the front door to the Airbnb exploded inwards. Shouts of *Police, put your hands in the air* ushered dazzling white-hot lights as the bedroom convulsed with dark shapes in helmets, goggles, yelling, pointing rifles, prying...

Before she could begin to process the intrusion, Bec was snatched and whipped onto her stomach, face planted into the duvet, arms pulled behind her back, wrists cuffed.

She was pulled into the living room, behind Jay who was being dragged, unable to walk because his trousers were around his ankles.

Bec focused on the yellow stripes on the tie of the smug asshole standing over her.

'What the fricken hell is this about?'

'We have reason to believe there are drugs on the property.'

'That's absurd. Who the hell are you anyway?'

'Your worst nightmare lady.'

'I need a name asshole. You picked the wrong... I'm gonna splash your name...'

'Detective Robinson. Max Robinson. Friends call me Robbo. You can call me sir.'

'Let's see some ID. For all we know you could...'

'Just shut the fuck up. This isn't an episode of *CSI*, Corelli.'

'You got a warrant to show us Robbo?' It was Jay, who could have been sharing vacation snaps at a party instead of surrounded by cops, his hands cuffed behind his back, trousers round his feet.

'Don't need a warrant lover boy. Reasonable grounds for believing there's controlled drugs. S'all we need.'

The cops were searching the room, opening cupboards, drawers. Bec screamed when one of them reached for her bag.

'Take them outside. Search them as well.'

A beefcake in Kevlar shoved her into the porch, pushed her up against a wall. He started patting her down. She shuddered when his gloved fingers lingered on her breasts.

He leaned in closer, the bristles of his goatee scratching her neck, the aftershave all masculine wood and hay.

'What's the matter bitch, didn't your boyfriend have time to get it up?'

'Don't let him goad you, Bec.'

The cop's hands moved from her breasts down her sides and squeezed the cheeks of her butt. Bec tensed. When his hand reached around her stomach and he slid a finger inside her panties, she snapped.

She wriggled free of his grip and spun round, aiming her knee at his groin. He anticipated the move, twisted, took the strike harmlessly on his padded thigh.

The cop laughed as Bec was thrown off balance. Infuriated, she turned to lunge again. The blast of pepper spray lashed her flush in the face, like the juice of a million lemons. Her eyeballs convulsed, bursting to explode from their sockets, as suffocating, choking gunk cascaded from her nose.

Laughter nearby made her to refocus, rationalize. She'd written about this. The mucus and tears were her body's defenses kicking in, flushing out the contamination.

She tried to focus on sounds, a voice…

'…arresting you for possession of a class A…'

Bec forced her eyes open. The detective was holding a plastic bag the size of a brick, containing white powder...

'... right to stay silent... talk to a lawyer... noted down and used as evidence against you...'

She opened her mouth to protest, but the words were lost in a fit of gasping, coughing, wheezing, until she succumbed to the pain – to Aristotle dancing in the fires of hell – and collapsed to the ground.

*****

Corelli's screams reached the ears of Rodrigo Montoya and his brother, even though the windows of Mauricio's Peugeot were closed. They were watching the arrest from the parking lot of a school, across the road from the Airbnb.

The street was ablaze with the flashing lights of four cars with yellow and blue police markings, beside a black Holden, presumably belonging to a detective.

Rodrigo couldn't understand why the cops were so restrained.

'Things are different here. Most of the cops follow the rules. It's nothing like in Bali or back home.'

'So how much did this pequeño truco cost us?'

'Enough coke to put them away for a long time.'

Rodrigo watched as Duggan was led to one of the police cars.

'I've only seen two of them brought out. What about the other American, Bullard?'

'Relax. If he's not there, I'll find him.'

26. Changes of heart

Forty-eight hours can be a dog's age in politics.

Two days after the humiliating defeats in New Jersey and Montana, Ped was enjoying quesitos at a breakfast function at La Concha resort hosted by the Resident Commissioner of Puerto Rico, who had just announced she was endorsing him for President.

The turnaround from the Commissioner, who until the previous night had been signaling she would be backing her friend Kate Hunter, followed the front page story in *El Nuevo Dia*, largest newspaper on the island, about the leader of the Roman Catholic Church also switching his endorsement from Hunter to Garland.

The changes of heart were based on the contents of packages delivered the day before.

The Archbishop received a copy of an affidavit from an anesthesiologist in Canada, stating he was present at the termination of a pregnancy of a woman he now knew to be Congresswoman Katherine Margaret Hunter of Maryland. There was also a page from the yearbook of a high school in Olney, Maryland, with red circles drawn around two heads in a senior class photo. From the names below, the Archbishop could see the students identified were a young Kate Hunter and the vice-captain of the boys' basketball team. His Excellency shared the package with his inner circle at the Archdiocese and consulted with them before making his decision.

The package that arrived anonymously at the office of the

Resident Commissioner contained two black and white photos and a sheet of paper with a single type-written sentence. The photos showed the Commissioner in compromising positions with two different men, neither of whom was her husband of thirty-four years. The typed sentence said: *Withdraw your endorsement for Hunter and these will never see the light of day*. The Commissioner elected not to share the package with her inner circle or husband before deciding Ped Garland would make a fine President.

Ped's phone vibrated in his jacket pocket. He picked up a napkin to dab his mouth, subtly wipe his nose, then put the phone to his ear.

It was Carl, reporting that one of the American muck slingers and an accomplice from New Zealand had been arrested in Auckland, in possession of a large quantity of cocaine.

Ped put the phone back in his pocket, drained his coffee, reached for a guava turnover.

*****

'I think it's best you wait in the car and let me handle this, Michael.'

'But they'll need me to verify…'

'No, they won't. Not at this stage. And if things go badly, they'll want to arrest you too.'

This wasn't going as Mike expected. He'd been making headway with an enchanting accountant at a nightclub when he got the call from Jay's lawyer friend to say Bec and Jay had been arrested and cocaine found at the Airbnb. He'd rushed back to the rental car, decided he'd drunk too much to drive in a foreign city, grabbed his bag with laptop and jumped in an Uber. On the way to the lawyer's house in Epsom, he'd reviewed footage from the camera in the perfume bottle.

Now they were parked half a block from Auckland Central Police Station, and Julie, the lawyer, was trying to deny him a seat at the show-and-tell.

'What if they confiscate the phone?'

'I assume you've backed it up.'

He had. And it made sense to let her do her job.

He watched her disappear through the station's main doors, then fired up his laptop.

*****

'How does a dropkick drug dealer like you hook up with a lawyer like Julie Pearse? What am I missing here Duggan?'

Jay had refused to answer any questions since he was arrested, and wasn't about to start now.

Detective Robinson, slouching on the other side of the table, was still talking tough, but Jay could tell doubts were creeping in.

'Five hundred grams Duggan. We're talking ten years minimum for you and your girlfriend.'

Jay yawned.

The atmosphere in the room changed the moment Julie Pearse KC appeared. Robinson sat up straight, like a student caught off guard by the principal. Julie took control, glaring at the detective.

'Where's Rebecca Corelli? The arrangement was that both my clients...'

'She's on her way Mrs. Pearse. Corelli has cooperation issues, if you know what I mean.'

'And who are you?'

'Detective Maxwell Robinson, CIB.'

'What unit?

'Organized Crime and Drugs.'

'Figures. I suggest you *organize* for Rebecca Corelli to get here quick-smart detective.'

'If she…'

'And we'll need a monitor I can connect an iPhone to.'

'You don't…'

'I'll need a moment with Mr. Duggan. Alone.'

'I don't…'

'Now.'

Robinson remained seated long enough to satisfy his male ego, then stood as slowly as he could and left the room.

Jay was impressed. He was aware of Julie's reputation, but had never seen her in action professionally. She got straight to the point.

'What have you said to the police, Jay?'

'Nothing. I'm familiar with the drill.'

'What about…'

'It was planted Julie. We're being set up.'

'I know. And fortunately, we have compelling evidence. Let's hope Bec hasn't… overcomplicated what should be a straight-forward outcome. Initially at least.'

'What evidence?'

She didn't get to answer. Bec's voice thundered from the hall.

'Get your fricken hands off me, you moron. I'm familiar with the concept of one foot in front of the other.'

Jay grinned. He and Bec had been separated soon after arriving at the station. He feared for her mental state, particularly after the pepper spray. The sarcasm in her voice suggested she had a measure of control. She strode into the room, red-eyed, but defiant, followed by Robinson.

A policewoman wheeled in a monitor. Robinson launched into the formal preamble. Julie cut him short.

'I suggest, detective, before we go any further it would be in your interest to watch this video.'

She ignored his protest and, after getting the constable to set up the wireless connection, began the clip.

'As you can see from the time stamp, this footage begins at 8.21pm. The camera was concealed in a perfume bottle on the bookshelf in the Airbnb, set up to begin recording when it detected motion. For the record detective, the maître d' at Café Hanoi has electronic confirmation my clients checked in to the restaurant at 7.56pm, and I have the booking details from a roomful of witnesses who will confirm Mr. Duggan and Ms. Corelli were seated at a table until at least 9.15pm, enjoying their meal.'

Jay couldn't resist: 'The stir-fried asparagus was delicious Robbo. You should try it.'

Julie, who had paused the clip, pressed *play*, and the door to the Airbnb slowly opened. A figure dressed in black with gloved hands, face covered with a ski mask, walked in carrying a small backpack. He looked around the room, then disappeared off-screen for a few seconds, presumably to check the bedrooms. When he came back into shot, he put the backpack on the table, took out a plastic bag containing a white substance. He walked to the kitchen section, opened the drawer beneath the basin, raised the bag to his lips, appeared to kiss it, then tucked it behind the garbage can. He collected the backpack and headed for the door.

Julie hit pause, freezing the man's body in the door frame.

'How tall are you, Jay?'

'Six-two.'

'And how tall would you say the person in the picture is, detective?'

'Five-eight, five-nine. About Corelli's height.'

Julie sighed, as if she was indeed dealing with a moron. She turned to Bec.

'Are you right or left-handed Ms. Corelli?'

'Right.'

Julie rewound and replayed the video. The planter was a leftie.

Robinson wasn't looking so smug, all of a sudden.

'Let's not beat around the bush detective. We have evidence the drugs were planted in the Airbnb by a person you acknowledge couldn't have been Mr. Duggan, and is unlikely to have been Ms. Corelli, at a precise time when both Mr. Duggan and Ms. Corelli had a rock-solid alibi.'

'I'd have to…'

'Let's not waste each other's time detective, not when you have an actual criminal to catch. I'm even prepared to provide you with a copy of the video to kickstart your investigation.'

'You're dreaming lady. There was half a kilo of coke in that bag, which qualifies as large commercial quantity. Your asparagus-munching clients are looking at eight to eleven years for sale or supply. You expect me to let them just walk on the strength of a video that could have been doctored by AI or created in any high school media lab? Even if it's for real, this third party could be an accomplice.'

'Be that as it may, detective, both my clients have alibis.'

'Which will have to be thoroughly checked out, *counsellor*.'

'Where were the drugs found?'

'What?'

'This bag of cocaine. Where exactly in the Airbnb did your team find it?'

'Under the basin, but…'

'And what made you raid this particular Airbnb, detective?'

'We got a tip.'

'Let me guess; it was anonymous.'

'I don't have to…'

'Oh, come on detective. You know as well as I, my clients

have been set up. At the very least, if you insist on pursuing these ridiculous charges against them, this evidence justifies their release on bail.'

The door to the interview room opened, and in walked a welcome blast from Jay's past: Chris Hansen. She'd put on a little weight since Jay last saw her, but was still wearing the same greenstone hei matau pendant in the shape of a fishhook round her neck.

Her arrival clearly surprised and unsettled Robinson.

'Detective Superintendent Hansen. Is there something I can help you with?'

'I doubt it detective. You're probably the one in most need of assistance.'

'But… what… why are *you* here?'

'I was asked to come. By Mrs. Pearse, on behalf of Mr. Duggan. There are few people on this earth who could drag me from my bed this time of night. And have my private number. Mr. Duggan just happens to be one of them.'

'This is… most irregular.'

'In my experience detective, anything involving Jay Duggan falls into that category.'

'But this is a drugs matter, nothing to do with…'

'Humor me detective. What have we got here?'

Robinson told her about the discovery of the cocaine at the Airbnb leading to the raid and arrests, Bec *attacking* one of the officers and having to be OC-sprayed, then the lawyer turning up with a video purportedly showing an unidentified person placing the drugs in the Airbnb.

Julie's phone beeped. She left the room to take the call.

'You forgot about our alibi, Robbo. Stir-fried asparagus.'

Robinson glared across the table.

'Duggan and Corelli claim to have been having dinner at the Café Hanoi at the time the drugs were… the video was taken, but we have yet to verify this. On the strength of that, their lawyer had the nerve to suggest we let them walk.'

Hansen turned to Jay, a puzzled look on her face.

'I thought you'd given this game away, Jay. If I remember correctly from our last meeting, you were putting your previous life behind you, planting a forest.'

'Old habits die hard. And trees take a while to grow. There's a fair bit of down time.'

'We missed you at the Prime Minister's ceremony.'

Jay and Hansen, along with an American biologist and English IT expert, had been nominated for New Zealand Bravery Awards for their roles in exposing an international conspiracy over the release of a genetically modified seed coating. Jay turned it down.

'Not my thing,' he said.

Julie came back into the room, shaking her head.

'Before we go any further, Detective Superintendent, I think you're going to want to see this.'

She put her phone on the table, tapped a few keys.

'It's a video, taken from the same camera that captured the drugs being planted at the Airbnb. This shows the raid, led by Detective Robinson, and how your officers behaved while arresting my clients.'

They watched in silence. By the end Robinson was shifting uncomfortably in his seat. Hansen was pinching the bridge of her nose.

Julie stood and walked behind Jay and Bec.

'Here's what I'm seeing detective, in no particular order. One: You failed to tell my clients under what section of what Act the entry and search was being made, as you are required to do under the Misuse of Drugs Act. Two: You failed to produce evidence you were a member of the Police when specifically asked by Ms. Corelli. Three: You denied my clients the right to watch your officers search the property. Four: The officer searching Ms. Corelli's person was not of the same gender, as is required under the Act. Five: Ms. Corelli was searched in a location that could clearly be viewed by the public. Six: The officer searching my client deliberately touched the bare skin of her breasts, genitals and buttocks, a clear breach of...'

'I think we get the point Mrs. Pearse.'

Detective Superintendent Hansen turned to Robinson.

'I'd like a few moments alone with Mr. Duggan, Ms. Corelli and their lawyer please, detective.'

Her tone left no room for dissent.

'And remove the cuffs please.'

'Corelli has been extremely un...'

'*Now* detective.'

Robinson obliged. When he'd left the room, Hansen faced Bec.

'Firstly Ms. Corelli. You have my apology on behalf of the New Zealand Police for the way you were treated during that search. It was unacceptable, on a number of levels. How are your eyes? Do you require medical treatment?'

'I've been seen by a doctor, thank you.'

Hansen turned to Jay.

'What the fuck is really going on here?'

'Is this being recorded?'

'Not yet.'

Julie started to caution Jay, but he held up his hand.

'It's OK Julie. I trust her. The Superintendent and I have history.'

He outlined their investigation into Charlie Scott's death, giving as much detail as necessary, but not so much that would blow their chances of completing the project. Hansen listened poker-faced, conceding nothing. When Jay finished, she looked at the ceiling, shaking her head.

'Why does none of this surprise me? And the video?'

'Mike, the third member of our team, must have set up the camera at the Airbnb.'

'There's more of you? Who's this Mike? We're going to need a full name.'

'I thought this was off the record.'

'Get real Jay. Half a kilo of cocaine's been found in your room, whether it belongs to you or not. Let's assume for a moment it was planted, as you say. We're still going to have to talk to everyone involved.'

'Bullard,' said Bec. 'His name's Mike Bullard.'

'Where have I heard that name before?'

'Mike Bullard, formerly with the Wooster blog in New York.'

Hansen's eyes widened.

'Wasn't he the journalist who broke the Cabo virus story in India?'

'Mike worked the story from the States. Jay and I were in India.'

Hansen looked at Jay, then Bec, then back to Jay.

'You guys were this, whatya call it, Aristotle team?'

Jay nodded.

'And what we're talking about here is a little bigger than one bag of coke planted in an Airbnb in Devonport, New Zealand. Lock us up and you'll be blowing our chances of getting to the bottom...'

'Not to mention,' Bec butted in, 'the humiliation your police department will suffer if Mike releases that video to his social media followers.'

Hansen leaned back in her chair, folded her arms.

'That sounds like a threat Ms. Corelli. Perhaps you don't understand the seriousness of your position. You and Mr. Duggan have been found in possession of a large quantity of drugs, for which you must answer in a court of law. Your claim the drugs were planted, along with this suggestion there is a connection between the drugs in New Zealand and Bali, will of course be investigated. *By the proper authorities.*'

'But...'

'The only reason I'm even entertaining the idea of giving you any benefit of the doubt is because of your association with the gentleman sitting beside you, with whom, as he so succinctly puts it, I have a certain *history*.'

She leaned forward, placing her hands together on the table, looked at Jay.

'Given what I have just said, Jay, what exactly do you expect me to do here?'

'Give us seven days.'

'To do what?'

'Complete our investigation.'

'You're dreaming.'

Julie cleared her throat. 'Come now Superintendent. You have discretion in these matters...'

'Very little.'

'... so, I have a proposal. Continue with these ridiculous charges if you must, but release my clients on bail while you investigate who planted the drugs.'

'That's asking a lot, Mrs. Pearse.'

'For which you and your department will be amply rewarded, and lauded internationally, when you get to land a much bigger fish.'

'There's a lot of *ifs* involved here, Mrs. Pearse.'

'Allow me to remove a few of your doubts, Superintendent. Release my clients on bail, to be reviewed in seven days or sooner if they conclude their investigation. They can live at my house, which should satisfy your requirements for residence.'

'They'd need to surrender their passports.'

Julie looked at Jay, who nodded.

'Done.'

'And report in every twenty-four hours...'

'I'm sure that won't be a problem.'

'... and share any information pertinent to our investigation.'

'My clients could agree to that condition Superintendent, but you and I both know the word *pertinent* is open to interpretation.'

Hansen smiled. 'They'll need to turn over the video.'

'Of course.'

'And all copies.'

Julie looked at Jay again, but it was Bec who answered.

'No way. We may decide to use some of that footage in the package we produce at the end of our investigation.'

Jay sensed the real issue, that if Hansen was to go out on a limb for them, she'd need something in return.

'How about we agree not to use the second part of the footage, showing the police raid?'

Julie started to protest. Jay cut her off again.

Hansen twirled the fishhook pendant in her fingers. 'I'd be sticking my neck out a long way for you here, Jay.'

'I know,' he said, offering his hand across the table.

Hansen leaned across and shook it to seal the arrangement.

'One more thing,' Jay said as they stood. 'Can you tell the media an American woman and New Zealand man have been arrested after a drug bust in Devonport, in possession of however much cocaine was in that packet?'

'Why?'

'Firstly, because it's the truth. Secondly, it might buy us time.'

*****

The guest wing of the Pearse's home in Epsom was a haven from the hell of the twenty-four hours it took Bec's eyes to recover from the pepper spray, her breathing to return to normal, and for Aristotle's grip to slacken from red through orange to shades of yellow.

She welcomed the color downgrade in the bananas in a bowl on the breakfast bar, the stylized yellow palm tree on the mango and passionfruit yoghurt cup, even the faded sticky note with the phone number for Detective Robinson, to whom they had to report as part of their bail conditions.

Mike came into the kitchen, scratching his head.

'Is it worth trying the SwordPhish?'

'I thought he, or she, could only be used as a last resort.'

'*He's* a guy, according to Jay. Canadian. How did Jay describe him? *Had a ponytail, but I can assure you the bloke has balls. In more ways than one.* Quote, unquote.'

SwordPhish was the moniker for a mysterious hacker Jay had come across during a mission involving a genetically modified seed coating.

Mike had communicated with him briefly by email during their investigation into the Cabo virus.

Bec considered the suggestion. They were out on bail with the clock ticking, and hitting brick walls – physically and emotionally. Not to mention legally.

Their investigation into the source of the cocaine that killed Charlie Scott had compounded into a personal mission to prove their innocence, maintain their freedom. Jay would almost certainly not consider their position last resort, but he wasn't here, couldn't be contacted.

'Have you still got the email for the hacker?'

Mike showed Bec how to work out the email address using a calculation based on the date and a word on a website that changed every ten minutes.

She sent a message asking the SwordPhish to investigate links between the limousine companies in Bali and New

Zealand, the resorts, the travel company in Auckland and the property in southern Bali, signing off with an identifier code Jay had been given for use *in the last resort.*

*****

Jay bought a Kiwiburger and fries to go from a Mickey D's, and walked round the corner into Beasley Avenue, pulling the hoodie tighter around his face as he sauntered along the sidewalk toward the place Mike said the limo went.

Beasley ran down the east side of Mt Smart Stadium, one of Auckland's larger outdoor events venues in the middle of an industrial area. The limo building was a few doors down from the headquarters of the New Zealand Rugby League, between a gearbox manufacturer and woodturning factory.

Jay crossed the street, climbed onto a grass verge behind a low retaining wall made from volcanic basalt rock common throughout the city. He sat, casual as you like, dangling the imitation hobnail boots he'd bought at a Number One Shoe Warehouse, and attacked the burger.

The ledge gave him a good view of the front of the limo building. Unfortunately, Mike hadn't been exaggerating when he likened the security arrangements to Fort Knox. The only potential vulnerability Jay had found during two laps of the block was the iron roof of a plumbing supplies store backing onto the property, but it would be high risk. Bec was right. Better to play the percentages by following limos leaving the building, hoping for a break. For the time being at least.

27. The folded sheet

The brutality and manipulation of the capos and teniente of drug cartels was well documented, but Ped had been surprised to find figures in the upper echelons of politics just as ruthless, premeditated.

The difference was that if something went down in the alleys of Bogota or Cali, there was usually a corpse or life sentence to gloat over. In politics, the convention was to be gracious to the vanquished.

Ped was sitting alone at the piano in the backroom at the Intercontinental in San Juan, conjuring up nice things to say about Kate Hunter, as he waited for her to appear on the screen of a laptop perched on the music shelf.

The Congresswoman had called the press conference after cancelling campaign gigs in Ponce and Arecibo two days out from the Puerto Rico primary, and flying back to Baltimore. Speculation among muck slingers was that Hunter was withdrawing from the contest. *Fox* was reporting she was *devastated* by the abortion revelations and switch of allegiance by the Catholic Church, and the *betrayal* of her long-time friend, the Commissioner. A poll by Radio WAPA in San Juan showing Garland with an *unassailable* lead piled on the misery.

The choice of venue for the announcement – the library of Hunter's grand stone and slate home overlooking Lake Roland – confirmed to Ped she was throwing in the towel.

He looked at the way the room had been set up for the press conference streaming onto his laptop. A long mahogany and partridge wood table with four chairs, the Stars and Stripes and state flag of Maryland behind the central microphone, flanked by three smaller mics presumably for the husband and two sons Ped had met at debates.

Hunter walked in, followed by a woman Ped didn't recognize. He could tell from the way she wore the conservative jacket, blouse, and skirt, they were not her normal attire.

But it was the folded sheet of paper in her hand that sent Ped's heart racing and made the tiny muscles at the base of the hairs on his arms contract.

The woman was introduced by Hunter as a hotel housekeeper from Helena. Reading nervously from an affidavit, she said she had cleaned the suite occupied by Mr. Garland during his recent visit in Montana, and found traces of cocaine in the bathroom of an adjoining room.

Ped slumped back into the sofa. There were still two empty seats at Hunter's table. This was going to be a drip-feed.

Witness number two for the prosecution was a clean-cut young man, the kind you'd expect to see sippin' tea on a porch swing. He worked as a scheduler on Hunter's campaign until he was fired after the New York primary for leaking information to the opposition. He admitted he'd been encouraged – and paid handsomely – by a man called Carl Tyler, who ran Garland's off-book backroom operation. He said Garland used a two-team system – public front office and private backroom team that called all the shots and engaged in the dirty tricks Garland swore he'd never use, including negative advertising through third parties, push-polling and robo-calling.

Witness number three sauntered into the room pushing a squeaky hand truck loaded with dozens of books, which he stacked up on the table beside Hunter, spines facing the camera like characters in a courtroom drama. He didn't need introducing to Ped.

Simon Heath, head librarian at Hays State Prison in Georgia.

He explained how Ped Garland had worked in the library for the last five years of his sentence, had been a model prisoner.

'Much like that Andy Dufresne character from *Shawshank Redemption*. Ped helped lots of inmates with their legal affairs, badgered organizations all over the state to donate books, set up an inter-library loan program.

'In his last year at Hays, after he'd outlined the business plan for his drug foundation to the warden, Ped was given special dispensation to order eBooks online and have a Kindle in his cell – for research purposes.

'As I said, Ped was a model prisoner and frankly his plans for the drug foundation were so impressive, we wanted to give him all the help we could. We didn't pay much attention to his reading list.

'It was only when I was re-ordering copies of his book *Straight Up* for the prison library, I thought to look up what he'd been reading.'

Hunter took over, pointing to the stack of books beside her.

'What we have here is a selection of hard copies of just some of the books Mr. Ped Straight Up Garland read on his Kindle in that cell.'

She started reading out the titles, as the camera zoomed in on the tower of spines.

Trust Me, I'm Lying: A Playbook for the Dark Arts of Exploiting the Media… The Cheat Code: Secret Tweaks, Hacks and Tips to Get Noticed and Get Ahead… How to Lie with Statistics…The Science of Likability: 27 Studies to Master Charisma, Attract Friends, Captivate People, and Take Advantage of Human Psychology… And my personal favorite: *Faking It: How to Seem Like a Better Person Without Actually Improving Yourself.*'

Ped threw the laptop across the room, tramped into the bathroom, dragged the briefcase down from the shelf. He punched in the combination, snatched one of the small resealable bags.

*****

The Pearse's house backed onto One Tree Hill, one of more than fifty volcanic cones in Auckland. After her morning stabilizing routine of breathing and squeezing, Bec decided to add splash and dash by having a cold shower and jogging to the summit before breakfast.

A gate in the back fence opened onto the domain, not far from the road to the lookout point. Other joggers were out, along with a man walking a poodle dressed in a tartan thermal coat, and a woman being led by a Bichon Frise furball.

Sheep grazed beneath limbs of pohutukawa trees reaching across the road like the fingers of giants. Yellowing leaves clinging to the branches of massive English Oaks rustled in a breeze laden with the smell of damp wool.

Bec half-jogged, half-walked up the winding road toward the obelisk, dodging sheep shit and Chinese tourists posing for innocuous photos. It was refreshingly cool after Bali and India. Like Manhattan in October, minus the mayhem.

She didn't make it to the summit.

Her phone beeped, indicating an incoming email. The domain name *dea.govt* threw her for a moment, until she remembered the sample of NuNu they'd sent from Lovina to the forensic drugs lab in Chicago.

The cocaine was the highest quality the lab had seen in more than twenty years. The analyst was ninety-eight percent sure it was produced from coca grown in the Nariño region in south-western Colombia between 1993 and 1995.

*****

The decision on who would go to Colombia had been made by the New Zealand Police, when they confiscated Jay and Bec's passports.

Auckland to Bogota was not a well-trodden path. The quickest route was via Santiago on the Chilean airline Latam. Mike did as much research online as he could before the flight, downloaded more to read on the plane.

The latest State Department travel advisory rated Colombia a level-two risk, meaning visitors should *exercise increased caution*. Five districts were listed in the *Do Not Travel to* section, including Nariño. *Violent crime such a homicide, assault and armed robbery is common. Organized criminal activities such as extortion, robbery and kidnapping for ransom are widespread.*

The website of the New York-based Committee to Protect Journalists put things in even sharper perspective. More than 90 reporters had been killed in Colombia since the early 1990s, the latest a community radio journalist in a town called Samaniego. In Nariño.

Mike was going to need local help. He made several calls to buddies in the media and government back home, and was eventually given the name of a guy who'd spent time at the US Embassy in Bogota as an intelligence analyst for the DEA. He put Mike onto a Colombian journalist-turned-academic, Duvan Delgado, who he said *wrote the book on the narcos of Nariño.*

Mike was in luck. Delgado was on leave from his part-time lecturing role at a university in the capital. He arranged to meet Mike when he landed in Bogota.

CNN was screening on one of the monitors in the departures lounge at Auckland Airport. Mike caught the tail end of a report on the Puerto Rico primary, just before he boarded. Kate Hunter won 51 percent of the vote, but because of the island territory's winner-take-all system, she claimed all 23 delegates, denying Ped Garland the two he needed to take the nomination.

A political correspondent was speculating that an attack on Hunter for having a child out of wedlock hadn't worked for Garland, whose *Straight Up* honesty line was being questioned.

*****

The New Zealand Warriors were playing the Canberra Raiders from Australia and the noise suggested the home team had scored another try. Jay, lying prone on the roof of the plumbing store at the back of the limo building, watched the two Rottweilers rush back to the front fence to howl at the stadium.

Tries in rugby league were followed by conversion attempts. Jay was hoping the Warriors goalkicker would add the two points and set off another eruption to keep the dogs distracted.

He tugged the rope to check it was anchored to the bracket holding an air-conditioning unit. Tailing limos from the building to the homes of travelers, then to the airport and back to the building had revealed nothing. Yawn. It was time to take the direct route, high-risk or not.

The kick went over, the crowd – and dogs – went ape-shit. Jay slipped over the edge, abseiled into the yard.

He'd only taken two steps before the din from the stadium was overwhelmed by the piercing shrill of an alarm. Followed immediately by barking. Of the blood-curdling variety.

*****

The name of Bogota's airport wouldn't win any prizes for brevity, but El Dorado Luis Carlos Galan Sarmiento International was ranked the best in Latin America, comfortably ahead of LaGuardia and LAX.

Best didn't mean safest. Mike had read the headlines, heard the horror stories about Colombia. He gripped his passport, seeking reassurance from its cool, smooth surface, as he entered the terminal.

The immigration officer scrutinized the passport, his eyes lingering on Mike's face longer than necessary.

'Purpose of your visit?'

Mike forced a smile, tried to keep his voice steady.

'Vacation.'

'And where are you staying in Bogota, senor?'

Mike hadn't thought that far ahead.

'The Hilton.'

He'd read somewhere the chain had hotels in more than eighty countries. Colombia was obviously one of them, because the officer waved him through.

The most striking feature of Duvan Delgado – other than eyes that conveyed silent acknowledgement of the risks they were both taking – was his hair. Thick white tufts flowed over his tanned forehead and tops of his ears like drifts of snow.

'Welcome to Colombia, Mr. Bullard. I'm afraid we need to move quickly. I have made some inquiries since you called, and I've located a man I believe you should meet. He is willing to talk to you on the condition of remaining anonymous.'

'Great. Is he here at the airport?'

'No sir. He is in Pasto, the capital city of Nariño. There's a flight departing in 40 minutes. I went ahead and reserved two tickets.'

On the satellite bus to Terminal 2, Mike tightened the grip on his bag, and joked that the State Department should update its travel advisory for Colombia.

'They make it sound like there could be terrorists, kidnappers behind every column, bombs in every suitcase. I feel safer here than I do at airports in the States.'

'That might be true, sir. This airport is indeed safe. Some would argue it is the *only* safe place in Colombia.'

The flight to Pasto took a little over an hour. By the time they began their descent, Mike realized he'd struck gold teaming up with Delgado.

The guy was like an encyclopedia. He'd worked as a reporter for the Cali regional edition of *El Tiempo*, Colombia's largest newspaper, during the 1990s and 2000s, before swapping the newsroom for the lecture theater.

When the former DEA analyst said Delgado had written the book on the narcos of Nariño, Mike hadn't taken it literally. But he had! Unfortunately, it had been published only in Spanish.

Which made Mike think of Ped Garland's book. He asked Delgado if he'd read it.

'Yes, I have read it. Hijo de puta. The book is nothing more than a publicity stunt. Full of mierda. Bullshit. Cover to cover. Most of it is made up, fabricated. A convenient rewriting of history. Pedro Garland's name is barro... mud in this country Mr. Bullard. The man made a lot of enemies. People, dangerous people with long memories. I wouldn't mention his name out loud in Colombia, if I were you.'

'Thanks for the tip. But I'm not here to dig up Garland's past. My sole interest is in a particular batch of cocaine produced in Nariño between 1993 and 1995. And why it is now being sold on the streets of Bali.'

Antonio Nariño Airport was perched on a plateau six thousand feet above sea level, twenty miles from Pasto. As the plane banked left over folding hills, backbone ridges, gaping chasms, to line up for its approach, Mike got a view of the runway. It was impossibly short, like a tiny strip of band aid on the shoulder of a green giant.

His fingers dug into the armrest, and for the first time in his life, he had to close his eyes for a landing.

*****

Bec hadn't been able to sleep, after coaxing an admission from Jay he'd tried unsuccessfully to break into the limo base. He claimed he left nothing behind to link him to what he was sure would be seen as an attempted burglary. That was beside the point, and no help.

Her thoughts were flooded with fear – of abandonment, danger, failure, a prison cell – trapping her in a state of high alert, unable to slow her heart, unwind her muscles, relax.

After editing video from their visit to the travel agency, and the drugs being planted at the Airbnb, Bec began researching cocaine production in Colombia in the early 1990s until exhaustion finally set in around 2am.

She was woken an hour later by her phone. It was an unknown caller with a 44 country code, which Bec recognized as the United Kingdom. Intrigued, she tapped *Accept.*

'Hello?'

'Is this JFK-Governor?' The accent sounded like the woman worked for the BBC.

'Who?'

'Are you the person who sent me a message using the string JFK-Governor?'

Bec rubbed her eyes, shook her head to focus. That was the code she'd used in the email to Jay's hacker contact. But *he* was supposed to be a guy.

'Is this… SwordPhish?'

'I prefer not to use names.'

'Jay said… I expected you to be a male.'

'I prefer to use voice transformation. How is our mutual friend?'

'Asleep, with his tail between his legs.' This was weird. Talking to an English woman who was probably a Canadian man. With the name of a fish.

The hacker had answers to some of her questions. The

owners of the limousine company and Nyalahutan resorts in Bali, and the property in Uluwatu had gone to great lengths to mask their identities through layers of anonymous LLCs.

'But I've tracked all three to one dude: Rodrigo Montoya.'

The name meant nothing to Bec.

'What about the travel agency in Auckland. Aventura. Any luck there?'

'Similar arrangement. The dudes used the same layers to avoid identification.'

Dudes sounded just plain wrong in a British accent.

'Don't tell me. The travel agency is also owned by this Rodrigo Montoya.'

'Close, but not quite. It's owned by a Mauricio Montoya.'

Bec thanked her... him... for the information, was about to end the call when she had an idea.

'I don't suppose you could ha... get... into the Aventura computer system from... wherever you are?'

'Depends. If they went to the same lengths setting up their IT system as they did to hide their identities, it could take a while. Let me get back to you.'

Bec had been asleep less than an hour before she was woken again, this time by a call from country code 27.

'We're in,' said a voice resembling the late Nelson Mandela.

Bec got the SwordPhish to navigate to the limo booking system, where they quickly identified a rogue vehicle with a registration number different to the ones Jay and Mike saw leaving the building in Penrose. It was scheduled to make two pick-ups the next day, in Mission Bay and Remuera. Bec wrote down the names, addresses and contact details of the couples to be collected, then thought of one more question.

'Can you tell whether the bookings were handled by any particular staffer at Aventura.'

'Let's see. Yes. Both were logged by a Kirsty.'

28. Bare knuckles

Hunter came at Ped from the opening bell. The debate in the ballroom of the Ronald Reagan and International Trade Center in downtown DC, just days out from the final primary, had been promoted like a world championship bout. Bare knuckles.

With so much at stake, staggering revelations pummeling both sides, no reason for either candidate to hold anything back, the gloves were seriously off. The live television and streaming audience were sure to set a record for a primary debate.

Candidates would normally use an opening statement in the final debate to eloquently outline their platform and the attributes they would bring to the presidency. Hunter used the entire sixty seconds trashing her opponent's credentials for office.

Ped was caught off guard, with no teleprompter to help him. Squinting uncomfortably in the glare of the floodlights, he fell back on his pre-prepared spiel, which even he realized was flat in comparison to Hunter's opening barrage.

He tried to come out swinging about Hunter's teenage pregnancy and the lengths she went to cover up the abortion, but could tell from the huffy faces in the front row that DC was a completely different beast to Puerto Rico.

The congresswoman parried with a line about *doing things when we were young we now regret,* and somehow twisted the argument to trap Ped into admitting his staff tracked down the anesthesiologist and were behind a series of attack ads – after promising he wouldn't go negative.

Hunter was relentless, accusing him of making up this, fabricating that, exaggerating or distorting this comment or that fact, faking a smile or grimace or look of confusion, engineering numbers, goading him whether his answers were from the public team or the backroom? She even teased him about what she'd find if she stumbled across his Kindle account from the last few months.

After two hours of pummeling without let-up, Ped was dazed, slurring his speech, hanging out for someone – anyone – to throw in the towel.

Hunter even managed to land a late shot after the bell: 'Are you high, Mr. Garland?'

*****

'I visit Pasto every January, sir. For the Carnaval de Negros y Blancos. A six-day celebration of culture. Very vibrant. Colorful. It has been recognized as a Masterpiece of the Oral and Intangible Heritage of Humanity.'

Mike recalled the name of Bogota's airport.

'You guys sure like your long names. Signwriting must be a lucrative occupation in Colombia.'

Delgado chuckled.

'This one is not a Colombian title sir. The carnaval was so named by UNESCO. There is an excellent museum in the city, Museo del Carnaval. Perhaps you will have time to visit?'

'Not this trip, I'm afraid.'

The cab wound its way through the city, past buildings in vibrant ochre, cobalt, and emerald defying the region's dark reputation. Some stood tall, proud. Others, tired from the weight of time and challenge, leaned precariously.

As they got closer to their destination, the streets narrowed. Facades dimmed to faded hues of red, blue, yellow. A mishmash of peeling concrete, crumbling brick, and DIY lean-to, iron security bars the common architectural feature. Lines of laundry crisscrossed between windows, swaying gently in the breeze that carried the sounds of vendors peddling their wares, children laughing.

Despite the liveliness, Mike could almost taste the undercurrent of tension. The wary glances of residents, their eyes assessing him with a mixture of curiosity and suspicion.

Walls of graffiti marking territories of rival factions or spouting political slogans were visual reminders of the complex layers defining the neighborhood, where resilience clashed with adversity.

The cab dropped them outside a non-descript apartment block. Delgado explained that Hugo – he insisted on using his first name only – had been a cop in the Grupo de Operaciones Especiales back in the nineties.

'He was my primary contact within the Nariño Police Department. He would provide me with information about drug busts, activities of the cartels. He was especially helpful with a story that exposed corruption in the Seccional de Investigación Criminal. Hugo operated anonymously back then, and it's crucial we maintain that anonymity, sir.'

'Even though he's retired?'

'Absolutamente. Dangerous people. Long memories.'

The elevator wasn't working, so they took the staircase. Their footsteps echoed off the concrete, interrupted occasionally by muffled conversations behind closed doors, the clinking of utensils, a baby's cry.

When they finally reached the top floor, Mike wiped sweat from his brow as Delgado rapped a gentle pattern on the wooden door of the apartment.

It creaked open, revealing a man in his late sixties, early seventies.

Hugo apologized about the elevator.

'I turned it off. There's a security camera. Can't be too cautious.'

'No problem. I understand.'

Mike got his phone out, placed it on the coffee table.

'Mind if I record...?'

'Yes. I do mind. This conversation is not happening.'

'Of course. Sorry.'

Over the next half-hour the former cop captivated Mike with war stories, bringing to life – and death – many of the accounts he'd read during his research, filling in some of the blanks.

The top-end cocaine being manufactured by the Rosario cartel in the 1990s was considered by many the finest ever to come out of Colombia. Batches were custom-made to order for extremely wealthy clients in the United States, Europe, the Middle East. Because of its value, production and distribution was tightly controlled by the Lopez brothers. Very few people were allowed close to the operation. Hugo knew of at least seven who took their knowledge to the grave.

'No-one was caught?'

'Many were caught, faced justice. Eventually. But we never uncovered the truth about those prima batches.'

'Any suggestions where I should look... where I might find this *truth*?'

Hugo leaned forward, resting his elbows on his knees, steepling his hands together as if to pray, but pointing them at Mike.

'There is one man. He used to be Felipe Lopez's driver. He might talk. If you get him on one of his good days.'

*****

Bec was thinking of two passages in the *New York Times*

handbook of values and practices for ethical journalism as she waited for the phone call to be answered: *Staff members should disclose their identity to the people they cover…* and *may not pose as anyone else.*

'Good morning. Dee speaking.'

'Hello Mrs. Wiggs. My name is Cate Bachelor. From Pacific Media Solutions. I'm sorry to trouble you at such short notice. I was given your name by Kirsty at the Aventura travel agency. We're doing a promo video for the agency's flights to Bali. You're going to Denpasar tomorrow, right? Is it your first time?'

'No dear. We go every year.'

Bec negotiated through a few minutes of small talk before popping the question.

'Part of the promo will show the limo pick-up. As I said earlier, I realize its short notice, but would you mind if we filmed you and your husband getting picked up tomorrow?'

'I'm not really the filming type, dear.'

'I promise you Dee, it will only take a few minutes, and you and your husband will get to veto any footage we use.'

'I guess that will be OK.'

'Thank you so much. Kirsty has given me the limo pick-up time. How about I pop round, say, thirty minutes before?'

'Very well. Do you know where we are?'

'Yes, thank you Dee. Kirsty has given me all the details.'

*****

They found him in a slum on the outskirts of Tumaco, a coastal town near the border with Ecuador, far from Mike's comfort zone. Delgado's commentary wasn't helping: The city had a murder rate four times the national average, and the largest concentration of coca plantations in the country.

The locals – mostly Afro-Colombian with pockets of indigenous – had counted on the 2016 peace deal between the government and Revolutionary Armed Forces of Colombia ending half a century of violence. They were still counting – the cost, the bodies, the displaced. Caught in the crossfire between mobs of *dissidents* with sinister names like las Guerrillas Unidas del Pacifico and Clan del Golfo fighting over the FARC's cocaine-trafficking network. One mob was even called the Oliver Sinisterra Front.

The slum was a sprawling dump of salvaged wood and corrugated metal sheets held down by bricks. Clotheslines hung across dirt paths dotted by puddles of murky water. The air stunk of saltwater mingled with waste and decay. Stray dogs, ribs visible through patchy fur, roamed the maze of narrow alleyways scavenging for food amongst the filth. The only color was in the shirts of the barefoot kids who bee-lined for Mike's white face, demanding to have their pictures taken.

Spanish rap was spewing from someplace nearby, a music style called *narcocorrido,* according to Delgado. The source of the sound was mysterious in a dump with no obvious electricity supply. Or running water.

Santos, which Mike didn't believe for a minute was the former cartel driver's real name, was sprawled across a piss-stained mattress surrounded by discarded syringes, crumpled aluminum foil, torn pieces of paper. The overpowering stench of unwashed bodies tussled for airtime with the acrid smell of burnt plastic.

The roadmap of track marks on the man's arms, blanched clammy skin, the itching, fidgeting, the black mucus, said it all.

But Santos wasn't saying anything. He just wheezed, eyes darting around the room for an escape as Mike pleaded with him on his hands and knees. The only reaction he got was a widening of the pupils when he mentioned the *prima* batches.

Mike decided to change tack.

'Senor Delgado, how much would you say addicts round here pay for a shot of coke? Ballpark.'

'I've heard you can get a gram for the price of a Big Mac. Twelve thousand pesos.'

'Which is, what, three dollars-seventy?'

'Something like that.'

Mike took out his wallet, counted off five Jacksons. Flapped them above Santos, just out of reach.

The pupils pulsed again.

'A hundred American my man. Good enough for at least thirty grams, I'm thinkin.'

Santos snatched for the bills, but Mike raised them out of reach.

Five minutes later they had a name (Danilo), a location (Tio Jairo on Carrera 19 near the docks), and a curious phrase: *Envio Fantasma.*

29. Country code 57

Ped only found out about the violence after the rally.

While he was inside the Walter E. Washington Convention Center preaching to the choir, hundreds of demonstrators wearing masks – each with two faces of Garland – sat down and blocked the intersection of L Street and Seventh.

A group of Garland supporters had started taunting the protesters as Hunter ass-kissers, and the cameramen filming them as fake news muck slingers. There was pushing, shoving. Suddenly it was all on. Rocks were hurled, police barriers upended, punches thrown, car windows smashed.

Ped had left the rally through a back entrance and was returned safely to his hotel room, where he was now watching an interview on Fox with a body language expert analyzing the DC debate.

His phone vibrated. An unlisted number beginning with 57, the country code for Colombia.

Ped hesitated, then took the call.

It was Emmanuel Lopez, son of Felipe, current lord of the Rosario cartel.

The last time Ped had seen or spoken to Emmanuel was the day before he flew to Miami to hand himself in to the DEA. The boy had squirted him with a water pistol beside the pool at the Lopez mansion in Tumaco.

'Como obtuviste esto… *How did you get this…*'

'Shut the fuck up, Garland. One of your gringo journalists, Mike Bullard, has shown up in Tumaco asking very specific questions about a batch of blow produced here. I don't give two fucks about you Garland, or your wife, daughter, or your *adorable* grandson. I hope you púdrete en el infierno for what you did to mi familia. I'm only telling you this because I am still deciding if whatever this journalist is seeking could reflect badly on la organización. Deal with it.'

The line went dead before Ped could answer.

*****

Dee and Nigel Wiggs lived in a dramatic apartment block on Tamaki Drive with circular verandas stacked out front like giant petri dishes. Dee was a recently retired arts therapist, Nigel a hematologist. They were all packed and ready when Bec arrived, but were happy to open their suitcases and pretend to finish packing so she could film them.

There was an awkward moment when Nigel asked why she wasn't using a *proper* camera, but he seemed satisfied with Bec's explanation about the picture quality of her iPhone and stability achieved with the gimbal.

She focused on the Bali guidebook, which Dee said had arrived by courier the night before, courtesy of the travel agency. Bec got her to leaf through the pages while she filmed.

After explaining that her colleague, Jay, would film them arriving at the airport, Bec wished them a safe trip and great vacation.

*****

Envio Fantasma translated as *ghost shipment*. A Google search showed Tio Jairo was a fast-food joint in Buenaventura, a mile or so from the port city's container terminal. That, and the obvious reference to *aventura*, was the good news.

The bad was that Buenaventura was 500 miles by road, and Google Maps was showing the current fastest route a tick under 16 hours.

The only commercial flight available was in five hours via Bogota, but he'd have to add eight hours for the stopover.

Delgado had the solution: private chopper. An outfit called Air Charter Tumaco had a three-seater available.

While they were waiting at La Florida heliport for the Robinson R44 to be refueled, Mike scrolled through a couple of news articles on their destination.

One was a piece about drug traffickers moving record amounts of cocaine through the port on shipping containers, fewer than three percent of which were checked by anti-narcotics police.

The second, titled *Once Colombia's Deadliest City, Buenaventura is Coming Back*, was about how the place had become a member of UNESCO's Creative Cities Network, based on its gastronomy.

Mike didn't see much evidence of the union of fine food and culture when their cab pulled up outside the fast-food joint. He asked the driver to wait.

They were greeted by the smell of sizzling meat and fried potatoes. Fluorescent lights flickered overhead, casting a sterile glow over plastic tables, mismatched chairs. Specialty of the house was hamburguesa de chicharonnes. Fried pork belly burger. The meat was like flavorless plastic, the cheese *could* have been mozzarella. The only ingredient marginally cultural was the Colombian beans.

Uncle Jairo either didn't speak English or wasn't prepared to, so the conversation was with Delgado in Spanish. Other than *Envio Fantasma* and *Danilo*, Mike didn't understand a word. The shaking head and shrugging shoulders required little translation.

Out on the street, Delgado summed up: Danilo was a reasonably common name in Colombia, but not the name of any of his current customers. *Envio Fantasma* meant nothing to him.

'You believe him?'

'Not entirely. Did you notice when I mentioned *Envio Fantasma*, he glanced across at you, then to the hombres by the window?'

'Not really.'

'It was delicado... how do you say in English? Subtle. I believe he knew more than he was telling me, but was temeroso. Afraid.'

'Dangerous people, long memories, right?'

'Exactamente.'

'So where to from here?'

'Tio Jairo said many of his customers are sailors, dock workers, who eat here one night, move to other restaurants around here on other nights.'

After the hamburguesa de chicharonnes, Mike could see why.

They worked their way along the road and into nearby calles and callejones, trying restaurants and food vendors hawking empanadas, arepas, churros, and something called salchipapa, which Delgado explained was a cross between a hot dog and potato.

The alleys were bustling mosaics of sight, sound, smell. Fishermen in rubber boots, weathered hats. Colorful storefronts with hand-painted signs, murals. Glimpses through doorways of families gathered around tables, sharing meals. Street vendors hawking handmade jewelry, traditional Colombian sweets. Women haggling over the price of plantains. Salsa and reggaeton floating from open windows. The distant clanging of metal, low hum of engines from the port. All overlaid with diesel exhaust, the tang of saltwater, scents of fish and damp earth.

Any mention of *Envio Fantasma*, however discreet, drew a

blank. The only Danilos they came across were ankle-biters. Mike was dejected. He had nothing tangible to add to their investigation. Coming to Colombia had been a waste of time.

They decided to take one last shot at Uncle Jairo, hoping to catch him with an empty restaurant. No witnesses.

It was empty all right. The door was locked, windows shuttered. A handwritten sign said *Cerrado hasta nuevo aviso*.

'Closed until further notice. I'm sorry, sir.'

They got back into the cab.

'¿A donde?' said the driver, holding up piece of paper.

'Que es esto?' said Delgado. He opened it and passed it to Mike.

Eight words: *Danilo Rojas. Centro Paliativo Ezequiel Moreno y Diaz.*

Delgado asked the driver where the message came from.

'Niño en una patineta.'

'Kid on a skateboard.'

'Mean anything to you?'

'Saint Ezequiel Moreno y Diaz was a former Bishop of Pasto.'

'And the other words?'

'Palliative Center.'

*****

Jay was parked on a wooden bench outside International Departures, sipping a flat white from the Retro Express trailer shaped like a silver bullet.

He saw the limo approach, so slunk behind the trailer to film it pulling in behind a shuttle van, the couple getting out, the driver getting a trolley for their suitcases. Then he slipped into the terminal, turning to capture them pushing the trolley through the doors, past a parking warden in yellow hi-vis, walking over to look at the large electronic departures screen. Jay zoomed in on the flight to Denpasar, then introduced himself.

'I'm afraid I've got some good news and bad news, Mr. and Mrs. Wiggs.'

'Don't tell me the flight's delayed.'

'No. Not at all. And that's the good news. You're on your way to Bali.'

Mr. Wiggs looked at him suspiciously.

'Bad news is that I, that is me and Bec, are not really filming a promo for Aventura. We're part of an investigative team working on a story about drug trafficking.'

'What's that got to do with us?'

Jay looked at the suitcases on the trolley.

'Don't worry. You've done nothing wrong, and the video Bec shot of you packing your bags will prove that. Not that I expect it will come…

'I don't understand.'

'Sorry Mrs. Wiggs. Can I ask, have you got a guidebook to Bali in your luggage?'

'Yes, as a matter of fact. Your friend, accomplice, partner in crime, whatever you want to call it, filmed me looking through it.'

'Perfect.'

'You better explain yourself young man, or I'm calling the police.'

'Relax Mr. Wiggs. We could be completely mistaken, and if so, I apologize. I'm pretty sure, though, if we go into that restroom over there, look in your suitcase, we'll find a quantity of drugs has been inserted, planted, into the guidebook.'

'Oh my God, Nigel! This can't be happening.'

'There's no need to worry Mrs. Wiggs. I suggest your husband and I quietly and calmly go into the restroom. If I'm right, I'll take the drugs off your hands and you both can forget all about this, go catch your plane.'

The old guy was too stunned to speak, as he nudged the trolley into the parent changing room and allowed Jay to film him opening the suitcase, sifting through clothing, picking up the guidebook.

He turned to face Jay and opened the cover, revealing a block wrapped in latex.

*****

Centro Paliativo Ezequiel Moreno y Diaz was a cancer care home in Cali, a two-and-a-half-hour cab ride from Buenaventura.

The lobby, in contrast to the chaotic energy of Colombia's third-largest city, exuded serenity, compassion. Soothing colors, soft music, staff in cheerful uniforms, walls adorned with uplifting quotes, tasteful artwork.

Danilo Rojas was sitting with his eyes closed, propped up on pillows in a private room cluttered with photographs of container ships. One showed him standing on the bridge in a white cap with an embroidered gold anchor; another in healthier days with his wife and two children. Faded prints of Catholic saints looked down sternly from the walls. There was a cross above his head. A bible lay open on the bedside table.

A nurse was reading to him from a newspaper when Mike and Delgado arrived.

'Tienes visitas,' she said, smiling and folding the newspaper, before placing it on a sideboard.

They'd been warned by the manager that *el Capitán* was in his final weeks, and having difficulty concentrating and talking. His eyes remained closed as Delgado introduced Mike, explained the purpose of the visit.

Until he mentioned *Envio Fantasma.*

The eyelids shot up. Cracked lips formed into a smile.

'Déjanos por favor, Antonella.'

The nurse nodded.

'Y Cierra la Puerta si no te importa.'

She left the room, closing the door behind her.

'El senor Bullard esperaba…'

'English please man,' said Danilo, his hands trembling as he held onto the railing of his bed. The skin was mottled dusky blue, like molded cheese.

'What day is it?'

'Friday, Capitán.'

Danilo crossed himself.

'Of course it would be. The Divine Mercy.'

He closed his eyes.

'For the sake of His Sorrowful Passion, have mercy on us and on the whole world.'

The old guy's breathing slowed, though the fluids continued to rattle in his throat.

Mike wondered if he had gone to sleep.

'Captain Rojas?'

The hand rose again, slowly. The eyes remained shut.

'Patience Mr. Bullard. I have waited many years for this moment. I have few words left inside me. Must pick them carefully.'

Between bouts of coughing, in and out of sleep or consciousness, lurching from lucid to fog, he told his story.

Danilo Rojas had been the captain of a container ship plying the route from Buenaventura to ports in East Asia. Yokohama, Busan, Shanghai, Singapore. Occasionally as far south as Sydney. And once to Auckland.

Before the voyage to New Zealand, in February of 1995, he was visited at his home by two men. It was a Monday. Angels

Day. One of the men identified himself as a senior member of the Rosario cartel.

'He told me to set up a trade – one coffee container exchanged for another that looked the same from the outside.'

'Told you, Captain?'

'It was a request. However, during those times, you did not dispute with tenientes of Filipe and Àngel Lopez.'

Danilo was paid well, by the second man – an American lawyer – for his cooperation and silence. It was only later, after the Lopez brothers were arrested and rumors began circulating that a large quantity of premium cocaine had mysteriously disappeared on an *Envio Fantasma*, a ghost shipment, that Danilo realized the two men who visited him had been working alone.

Mike was also joining the dots.

'And the names of these two men, Captain?'

'Pensé que nunca preguntarias. I thought you'd never ask, senor.'

One was the cartel's head of security, Carlos Jiménez. The other, the lawyer, was…

'Ped Garland.'

'The malparido was known as Pedro back then, but yes.'

Mike gulped.

'Jiménez was the guy who ratted on the cartel, right?'

'Si.'

'We know Garland is running for President. What about this Jiménez. You know what happened to him?'

'No-one knows, senor.'

Mike covered his face in his hands, exhaled. This was incredible. He had to focus.

'Can I get you saying this on video, Mr… Captain Rojas?'

'I would like that very much.'

Mike quickly set up his phone on the tripod, attached the

microphone, arranged it on a bedside table, which he rolled into position.

Danilo was a star, willingly summing up the key points in juicy soundbites like a pro. And there was more.

'Pedro Garland was in Auckland to greet the ship when we arrived. He was on vacation with Sara and their twins.'

The old man raised his hand slowly, pointing to a framed photograph on the wall behind Mike. The image showed Danilo, in his captain's cap, flanked by two young boys.

Mike was missing something here.

'Hang on a minute. I've just read Garland's book. His wife's name is Patricia. Who the hell is Sara?'

'Sara Montoya. She was Garland's Colombian lover. She had twins with him in 1990. Rodrigo and Mauricio.'

'Fucking hell.'

'Which makes me want to... how you Americans say?... puke.'

'I don't follow.'

Danilo pointed to the sideboard.

'There, the front page.'

Mike grabbed the newspaper. The masthead said *El País*, the language was Spanish, but the photo needed no translation. It showed a fired-up Ped Garland pointing an accusatory finger at Kate Hunter during the debate in DC. Mike had read how he'd attacked the Congresswoman for covering up a teenage pregnancy, then admitted it was his team that tracked down an anesthesiologist in Canada to prove it.

'I have endured a lot in my life,' Danilo coughed. 'One thing I cannot tolerate is hipocresia.'

The old captain's head slumped back against the pillows. Mike sensed a glimmer of catharsis in his eyes, as if the act of confessing had released a burden that had weighed him down for years.

Mike also realized his day was just beginning.

He thanked Danilo, took a still shot of the framed photo of the captain with the two boys, and left.

In the lobby, he posted a teaser to his social media accounts: *I have evidence linking a prominent American politician to an active international drug trafficking ring and a ghost shipment of cocaine from Colombia in the 1990s. Watch this space.*

*****

Mike Bullard's post reached the journalist's online followers, including Rodrigo Montoya, who until that moment had been enjoying breakfast at his brother's house north of Auckland.

Word that Bullard had turned up in Colombia and was asking *incómodo* questions had filtered back to the brothers, who had been assured by their contacts in Nariño the American was under surveillance and would be dealt with if he stumbled across anything *incriminatorio*.

Problem was, with the names Montoya and Garland persona non grata with anyone connected to the Rosario cartel, Rodrigo had to rely on contacts in a criminal gang that had been at war with the cartel on and off for more than a decade.

When Rodrigo called to find out what was going on and was told the journalist had been tracked by the gang to Buenaventura, Rodrigo exploded.

'He's in fucking Cali now. Find the asshole. Silence him.'

The contact agreed, for the right price, to double the gang's presence on roads to Cali Airport, and guaranteed the journalist would not leave Colombia alive.

*****

Bec and Jay were sitting in the rental car at a scenic lookout a mile or so from Auckland Airport, between a people mover full of Asian tourists and a low-hanging Japanese import with fogged up windows and a boom box thumping out Metallica.

Scenic lookout was a joke. The wipers were struggling to cope with the deluge obliterating any view of the runways. Aristotle was oscillating yellow in the blurred headlights of passing cars, thanks to the block of cocaine Jay had perched on the dash.

'How much you reckon is there?'

Jay picked it up, balanced it on his palm.

'Kilo maybe. Two pounds.'

'What would it be worth?'

'Here? On the streets of Auckland? I read somewhere Kiwis pay more than anyone in the world for this stuff. Four times what it goes for in the States. Something like $350 a gram. And that's for run-of-the mill-blow. If this stuff's as good as your analyst reckons, it could be worth two, three times that.'

'Fricken hell Jay. That's a million bucks. I don't want to be caught with this stuff.

Jay smiled.

'Didn't seem to worry you in Bali. You sat on that packet of NuNu two days before sending it offshore.

'That was only a couple of grams.'

'True, but Bali has the death penalty. Here you'll only get life in a comfortable cell, protected by human rights laws for Africa, be out in ten years. Assuming you behave yourself, which could be a stretch.'

She punched him on the arm, knocking the cocaine to the floor.

'So what's our next move, wise guy? No way I'm sitting on *that* for two days.'

Jay picked up the block, tossed it from hand to hand.

'There's gotta be a stash of this stuff stored somewhere nearby. That limo wasn't one of the ones from the building we were watching, must have come from someplace else. We're close to cracking this Bec, I can smell it.'

She glanced at her phone, noting the date and time: 'Our bail deadline was up two hours ago.'

There was a text message from Mike. She read it out: '*Have discovered link between PED GARLAND and shipment of cocaine to Auckland from Buenaventura port in the 90s. Rodrigo and Mauricio Montoya are Garland's ILLEGITIMATE children.*'

'Fricken hell.'

Bec tried to call Mike. It went to voicemail. The phone beeped again.

Jay put his hand on her arm.

'Who is it?'

'The detective.'

'Hansen or Robinson?'

'Robinson.'

'Ignore it.'

'Fricken hell Jay. If Garland's involved, this is… huge.'

'Correct. And well outside the bandwidth of a bottom feeder like Robinson. Forget about him. Let's keep our eye on the prize. Where are the Republicans at with their primaries?'

'Haven't been following it that closely.'

'Can you check? The timing might be important.'

Bec entered the keywords *Garland* and *delegates,* scanned the top few results.

'They're up to the last primary. DC. He only needs two of the nineteen delegates to seal the nomination. Fricken hell.'

They sat in silence, digesting the news, the challenge.

The rain had stopped. Colors indistinguishable during the downpour were taking form.

Jay broke the silence.

'Wasn't the limo booked to pick up a second couple?'

'Yes. At a place called Remuera. Why?'

'I could follow it after it drops them off at the airport. Might lead us to the stash. Last piece of the puzzle.'

Bec scrolled through the notes on her phone.

'Here we are. They're leaving on the Jetstar flight.'

He looked at his watch.

'She'll be tight. What say I drop you back at the Pearses to work on the video, hopefully hook up with Mike and get his info? Then I'll come back to the airport to tail the limo.'

'You're forgetting something.'

'What?'

'The million dollars of cocaine at your feet.'

Jay tucked the block inside his shirt, got out, climbed over the wire fence between signs saying *Alcohol Ban Area* and *No Fishing Permitted in Pukaki Creek*.

He disappeared for a couple of minutes before returning, pretending to zip up his fly for the benefit of their fellow sightseers.

*****

Mike was clenching his muscles to stop him wetting himself.

He was slumped as low as possible in the back seat, beads of sweat trickling down his temple, tracking the cab's movement through the streets of Cali on his phone.

Alone.

Delgado had messaged him half an hour earlier to say he'd gone into hiding, advising Mike to leave the country. The former cop in Pasto and the drug addict in Tumaco were dead. Uncle Jairo's burger joint in Buenaventura had gone up in smoke.

Mike was too rattled to look out the window. He locked his eyes on the pulsing blue dot on the phone, willing it to slide faster along the road toward the airport.

It inched along Via Cali Palmira, dawdled through a clover-shaped interchange, then finally swung north onto Via Aeropuerto De Palmira.

Two miles to go.

Two inches on his screen.

He clutched the bag holding his laptop, bracing for a quick exit.

One inch.

Half an inch.

The first bullet detonated the windshield, sending shards of glass flying and Mike sinking lower to the floor.

Automatic gunfire exploded around the cab, which had come to a stop under a tree. Mike had no idea if the driver was still alive. The gunfire intensified, bullets whizzing like angry hornets, the road outside transformed into a war zone.

It took Mike a while to realize the car wasn't being hit.

One hand was instinctively shielding his head, the other still clutching the phone. He tapped the camera icon, hit record, then lifted the screen and rotated it quickly through three-sixty. He brought it back down, hit play. The shots seemed to be coming from two groups – one sheltering behind a corrugated metal shack on the other side of the road, the other from behind trees to the east. Instead of targeting the cab, they were blasting away at each other.

Heart racing, adrenalin surging, his mind a whirlwind of fear, Mike's world narrowed to a single, desperate desire – escape.

As the survival instinct kicked in, he reached up, opened the door, rolled onto the grass, took a deep breath, sprinted for the airport gates.

*****

The photo on the screen of Rodrigo's phone hit him like a

haymaker to the throat, but the post beneath was the sucker punch: Meet the twins Rodrigo and Mauricio Montoya, illegitimate sons of Republican Presidential candidate Pedro Garland. More to follow that will BLOW your mind.

The photo could only have come from Danilo Rojas, which meant...

The phone sounded.

It was Cali.

Los bastardos from the Rosario cartel had intervened to let the journalist reach the airport.

He had got away.

30. No longer in service

'How 'bout we go back to *vein for a vein*. Worked before.'

Ped was in the backroom of the Washington DC hotel suite with Jin, putting the finishing touches to the victory speech to launch the national campaign.

Polls continued to show DC would be a close race, but with Ped needing only two of the 19 delegates on offer, the nomination was a done deal.

Jin shook her head.

'Don't think so. It's a new ballgame. You've got to appeal...'

The door burst open. Patricia blustered into the room holding up her iPad like it was radioactive. She brushed past Jin, marched up to Ped, slapped him hard on the face.

'What?'

She thrust the iPad into his chest, spun on her heels, stormed out, slamming the door.

Ped looked at the screen. There was a post from the journalist Bullard with an old photo of the twins. The phrase *BLOW your mind* hit him between the eyes. Then he saw the word *illegitimate*.

'Give me a minute will you, Jin?'

She left through the back door.

Garland walked over to the piano, sat on the bench, willing himself to keep calm.

He placed the iPad on the music rack.

Took out his phone, tried Carl again. His right-hand man and former partner in crime had been AWOL since being outed in

Hunter's show-and-tell press conference.

The dial tone sounded once, followed by a faint click, then an automated message: *The number you are calling has been disconnected and is no longer in service.*

*****

The appropriately named Fern Avenue was a narrow private lane, and Jay saw the rear of the police car just in time. Parked at the end of the cul-de-sac, beside a black Holden, same license plate as the one Detective Robinson was driving the night of the raid on the Airbnb.

Jay reversed and drove into the empty garage of one of the Pearse's neighbors.

'Fricken hell Jay. My laptop's in there.'

'Give Julie a call. Put her on speaker.'

The lawyer picked up after two rings.

'The police are here to arrest you and Jay for breaching the conditions of your bail.'

Jay answered: 'Where are they, Julie?'

'Here, at the house.'

'Where specifically? No, don't answer that. Are they in the living room, yes or no?'

'Yes and no.'

'OK, there's more than one of them. Are they close enough to hear your answers to my questions?'

'Yes.'

'Are any of them near the guest wing, yes or no?'

'No.'

'Do they have a warrant?'

'Yes.'

'For our arrest, or to search the property?'

'The former.'

'So, you can keep them away from the guest wing, yes or no?'

'Absolutely.'

Jay smiled. 'OK Julie. Thanks for that. What do you suggest we do?'

'As your lawyer, my advice is to hand yourselves in?'

'Can't do that I'm afraid, Julie. I'm sorry if this puts you in an awkward position as our guarantor. Can you put Robbo on the line please?'

'How did you…? Just a minute, he's all yours.'

'Tick tock tick tock Duggan. Time's up.'

'We need just a few more hours, Detective. We're close to breaking...'

'Save your breath for the judge, Duggan. Only thing being broken here is your bail. As well as your lawyer's reputation. And whatever trust you conned out of Superintendent Hansen.'

'Three hours Robbo, that's all I'm asking.'

'You're in no position to ask for...'

'Listen you moron. What we're dealing with here is far bigger than one packet of blow planted in an Airbnb. We're talking about a global trafficking operation linking Bali and Colombia and New Zealand and…

'I don't give a…'

'… the guy likely to be the next President of…'

'… rat's ass. Tick tock tick tock. Hear that Duggan? Rant all you want about conspiracy theories. You and your girlfriend have broken bail on serious drug charges. Time's up. Your number's up. Do as your lawyer suggests, before you dig the hole even deeper.'

Bec raised the phone to her mouth.

'That's not happening Detective. You've got no idea what you're interfering with here. Our investigation…'

'Tick tock tick tock Corelli. You might do things differently in the States, but I'll let you in on a little secret. This isn't

Hollywood or the pages of some Lee Child thriller. In this country the *police* do the investigating. Whatever game you think you're playing almost certainly constitutes obstruction of justice.'

Jay had an idea.

'How's your investigation going into the guy who planted the drugs in the Airbnb, Robbo?'

'He's on the other end of this call.'

'You're full of shit, Robbo. But I'm prepared to cut you some slack.'

'Just tell me where you are Duggan?'

'You know the scenic lookout point a mile or two east of the airport, where you can see planes landing and taking off?'

'I do.'

'There's a kanuka tree about fifty paces on from the *Alcohol Ban* sign at the back of the parking lot. Ten feet further on, towards the creek, there's a rock shaped like a turtle. Under it you'll find a bag containing about a kilo of cocaine we, ah, intercepted from a mule.'

'Last chance Duggan. Before I call in the cavalry.'

'Haven't got time for this bullshit, Robinson.'

He ended the call. They slumped down in the seats to wait. The marked police car left after a few minutes, but not Robinson's Holden.

Jay reversed onto the lane, drove round the corner, parked beside a back entrance to the domain. He put on a New Zealand Breakers cap, pulling the brim to cover half his face, then walked through the gate and along the path at the back of the houses.

A guy approached on a mountain bike with chunky tires. After he passed, Jay slipped through the gate behind the Pearses, entered the guest wing through the bathroom window they'd left open. He returned to the car with Bec's laptop and a backpack, into which he'd stuffed a couple of toys Mike had left behind and other kit that might come in useful.

Bec was looking… defiant. A good sign.

'Any word from Mike?'

'No. I'll keep trying him.'

'OK, what do you need?'

'A place to work. With Wi-Fi.'

'I'll find somewhere on the way to the airport.'

He dropped her at Greenwoods Corner, where there was a selection of cafés to choose from, gave her the number for Superintendent Hansen in case the shit hit the fan, then sped out to the airport.

The fuel gauge was getting low. He approached the Z Service Station on George Bolt Memorial, considering whether to risk stopping to top up, when he saw the limo sail by in the opposite direction.

Shit. He cut across the front of an Airport Express bus, drove up onto the median strip, then swung right and ran the red back onto George Bolt Memorial.

He caught up with the limo just before an exit, slipped in a few cars back. The limo slowed to the required speed limit through the Waterview Tunnel, obviously keen not to attract attention, which suited Jay fine.

They stuck to the highway through downtown, across the harbor bridge and through the North Shore. Jay smiled at the irony of the *Keep a Safe Following Distance* sign soon after passing beneath wire mesh stanchions holding toll cameras. The smile went west when the fuel indicator light began flashing in the Johnstones Hill Tunnel.

He began riding the accelerator to conserve fuel. He lost sight of the limo for a while, but caught up when it was forced to stop for roadworks near the offramp to Puhoi. Jay gave the thumbs-up to the exaggerated arm movements of a Māori guy holding a stop-go sign.

The limo finally left the highway near Warkworth, turned into the road to Matakana, then right towards Sandspit. With no vehicles between them, Jay let the gap widen as they passed through rolling green farmland with tall roadside trees denuded of leaves. The arrow on the fuel gauge had nowhere left to go. He was on borrowed time.

He got his first glimpse of the ocean at Snells Beach, a village of down-market houses, holiday homes, a park with dual soccer and rugby posts, a Bottle-O liquor store. Not the sort of place you'd expect to see a limo.

The engine started sputtering as Jay limped through Algies Bay, past a guy mowing his lawn in a beanie and gumboots, a sign advertising horse poo for sale. The engine finally died on a downhill bend. He was able to coast long enough to see the limo turn right onto Ridge Road, before the rental came to a rest beneath a sign saying *Winding Road 2km*.

'Not good.'

*****

Mike had been pinballing on adrenalin and coffee for the entire four-hour flight from Cali. He'd edited the Danilo interview, selected other background footage and images, including the photo of the smiling Montoya boys. He'd made a start on the voiceover text when the seatbelt sign came on and he had to stow the laptop for landing.

As soon as he got into the transit lounge at Miami, he phoned Bec, told her what he had and was about to send. He was distracted by familiar images on a TV screen on the wall.

'Just a minute, Bec.'

An NBC affiliate was running a story on a shootout near the airport in Cali. There were shaky pictures recorded by cellphones of passing motorists, clearer footage taken from a drone shooting promotional video for the airport company.

A banner across the top of the screen said *Five dead in shootout between rival gangs*. There was no mention of the part played by the gringo at the bottom of the picture, half-crouching, half-running from a white cab like a war correspondent leaving a chopper.

'You still there, Mike? You OK?'

'Yeah. Never better. What can I do? I've got Wi-Fi and about ninety minutes here in Miami before I board for DC.'

Bec asked if he had access to any footage of Garland they could use.

'I should have some material from the visit to his drug foundation center in Harlem. I'll check my phone.'

They divided up the tasks, got to work.

Mike did a search on Garland's movements, and the time the polls opened. He did a quick calculation, placed a call to DC.

Then he fired off messages to the network of influencers he'd been grooming for this moment, giving them a confidential heads-up on what the Aristotle team was about to publish, urging them to share the video when it went live.

*****

Rodrigo Montoya's day had gone from terrible to catastrófico.

He'd just heard from Bali the first package did not arrive, and whoever took it left a smart-ass note inside the guidebook. Had to be Duggan. Which meant they knew how the coke was transported.

He checked the time. The second shipment, if it got away, would already be in the air.

Rodrigo had heard from a source at American Airways in Cali that Bullard was heading to DC. He had arranged – at great expense – for the journalist to be *intercepted* after he left the airport.

Mauricio wanted to warn the old man.

Rodrigo looked out over the inlet, past the boats moored in the channel to the jetties poking into the gray water from the opposite shore. He was weighing the pros and cons when an alarm sounded.

'What the fuck is that?'

'The drone detector.'

*****

Jay adjusted the forward pitch, applied the rudder and fin to make the drone bank left for another sweep.

He'd wasted fifteen minutes finding a bucket and hose at the back of a farmhouse, siphoning enough fuel from a paddock car to bring the rental back to life.

Ridge Road snaked along the top of the Mahurangi East peninsula towards a restored nineteenth century homestead. Driveways headed off both sides of the road to dozens of secluded properties where a limousine would not look out of place. If you could find it.

Jay had driven with growing frustration past tourists on e-bikes, a woman walking a dog, a carpenter working a skill saw outside a garage being extended. He slowed at an intersection with a Little Library and Neighborhood Support sign, wondering if the readers realized they had an international drug trafficker for a neighbor. Jay had almost given up finding the limo when the road narrowed and he came across a high stone wall with razor wire, iron grill gate with keypad, camera, spotlight. A level of security over-the-top and out-of-place for rural New Zealand. The sign declaring *Private Property, No Public Access* was hardly necessary.

He'd reversed and parked under a large mahoe tree, then scrambled up the embankment to launch the drone. The large property, ringed entirely by an electrified fence, extended from Ridge Road down to the water's edge, with stands of mature bush to the north and south. Jay recognized pohutukawa, cabbage trees, kauri, manuka. The main house was a multi-level affair set into the hillside, with a deck along the front and a sunken hot tub. There were several outbuildings, a large shipping container, tennis court, impressive orchard. When he lowered the drone to hover closer to the ground, the camera was good enough to pick up tui feeding on the juice of mandarins that had fallen to the ground – and the license plate of the limo parked beside a white Peugeot in the open garage under the house.

Jay pushed the throttle to gain altitude, flew the drone towards the water to look more closely at the place he'd identified as the most promising penetration point.

*****

The walls of the Coffee & Tea Lovers Café at Greenwoods Corner were crowded with teacups, coffee mugs, tea pots, coffee presses and machines, an aroma center, burlap bags stenciled with exotic names.

Bec had commandeered a table for six and, surrounded by yellow sticky notes, edited the footage of the Wiggs couple being picked up by the limo, dropped at the airport, finding the cocaine block inside the guidebook.

With a detailed storyboard in her mind, she knew instinctively which images and segments of video best conveyed the key messages, how to manage the transitions, and to keep the content compelling, viewers engaged.

She was trying to script a voice-over connecting Ped

Garland's twin sons to the Bali resorts, the property in Uluwatu where Jay found the lab, the limo companies in Denpasar and Auckland. The words weren't flowing.

There had been plenty of free tables when Bec arrived, but the café was filling now with customers in puffer jackets and scarves. Rising volume from the chatter, and traffic through the open door, was becoming a distraction. When people began eyeing up the empty seats at her table and the sound system started playing *I Want To Break Free*, Bec took it as a cue.

She'd noticed a group of women having what looked like a business meeting through the window of another café across the road. Time to move.

*****

Jay had to backtrack half a mile along the road to a find a path down through the bush. He emerged onto a pebbly beach. The trunk of an ancient pohutukawa grew horizontally over the water. Seagulls wheeled above white-hulled boats moored in the channel. Half a dozen dinghies were stacked on their sterns against a rock wall. Jay chose the lightest, dragged it across the mud, rowed out around the headland.

He was aiming for an old man pine he'd noticed with branches hanging across the electrified fence at the north-eastern end of the property. Once ashore, he tightened the straps on his backpack, climbed the tree. The only limb reaching over the fence that would hold his weight was higher than he'd anticipated, so he cut a length of supplejack vine, tied it to the end of his rope.

He was confident he couldn't be seen from the house, so shimmied quickly down, dropping the last eight feet to the ground.

A siren blared, followed by the baying of maddened dogs.

Jay looked around for an escape route. The vine was out of reach. The fence electrified. The dogs seconds away. Options limited. Chances of reaching the house under his own steam: zero.

There was a raised water tank with a rusted ladder about fifty feet away. He sprinted for it, reaching temporary safety just in time. As the Rottweilers salivated beneath him, he took the drone out of the backpack, set the mode to *transmit*, launched it to hover above the tank. He used tape to stick the settings in place and attach the controller to the side of the tank.

Then waited for his escort to arrive.

31. The red room

Ped splayed his hand over the soft leather where Patricia would normally be sitting.

He was riding solo in the back of an SUV, cruising along Constitution Avenue, the Lincoln Memorial to the right. Honest Abe. Another lawyer-turned-President. Ditto more than half of those to have held the office.

They glided through 17th Street on a green, then stopped to let a couple of pedestrians cross in the shadow of the Washington Monument. John and Jane Doe. Would they bother voting in a few hours? Or were they residents of one of the pro-Hunter neighborhoods who would get a text alert warning of a security issue at their local voting center?

Ped gazed to his left, over the expanse of lawn to the White House. It was so close. He visualized the Oval Office, Situation Room, the Red Room he'd turn back into a music space for the baby grand, as in the days of Honest Abe and Unconditional Surrender Grant. He wondered what nickname he'd be given. Hard to beat *Straight Up*. He'd speak to Jin about how to engineer it.

Patricia had refused to accompany him to the function, but she'd come round. *First Lady* would be too much to resist.

Ped was more concerned about Carl, who he now realized was gone for good. The muck slingers and Dems would be hunting him, smelling blood, but they'd never find him. Carlos Jiménez would have dumped the name Tyler, and would surface some time some place with a new face, new name, new past –

just as he did when he gave witness protection the slip and showed up in the visitors' room at Hays State six months into Garland's stint inside. As planned.

They turned right onto Pennsylvania Ave. Up ahead was the Capitol, where Ped would deliver his State of the Union address in January.

His phone beeped. It was Rodrigo. They'd caught the New Zealander Duggan. Bullard would be stopped soon after landing at Reagan National.

The SUV had reached First Street, was passing the Supreme Court building. Further along the road Ped could see the media spotlights set up outside the club – venue for the election-eve dinner with the party hierarchy and captains of industry.

Lights flashed, questions flew the instant his foot hit the red carpet, but the candidate was guided safely through the bedlam. The Republican establishment was closing ranks around their man.

*****

One hundred dollars each had been enough to convince the four women using the meeting room of Café Kākāriki to conclude their business and turn the space over to Bec. The soundproof room helped her regain focus, make progress, until her phone interrupted her thoughts.

Country code 46. Sweden.

In female Swenglish, with *Jay* pronounced *Yay* and *three* sounding like *tree*, the SwordPhish said he'd picked up Mike's post about the Montoya twins and decided to dig deeper. He'd managed to hack into Garland's public donation website, found regular transfers of large sums of money from an account he'd traced to Rodrigo Montoya in Bali.

'They then used bypass software to move the money in small

quantities into the accounts of hundreds of thousands of voters in different states – almost certainly without their knowledge – then into Garland's campaign account.'

The SwordPhish had also found evidence of payments to three accounts in Canada he thought might be of interest. Fifty thousand dollars to Chase Morton, Garland's old cellmate now living in Alberta; twenty thousand to the anesthesiologist at the abortion clinic in Calgary who identified Kate Hunter from her high school yearbook, eight thousand to a graphics company in Montreal for the design of the NuNu branding.

Bec wasn't sure how much of this would, or should, make it to the final video package, but realized its value for follow-ups.

'Can you send me any visual proof of this stuff?'

'Will screenshots do?'

'Sure.'

The new information, added to the deadline pressure, sent Aristotle pivoting from yellow to orange in the phrases she'd highlighted on scraps of paper purloined from the printer, sticky notes she'd plastered to the wall, in the funky plates and matching aprons of the waitresses through the glass wall dividing the meeting room from the rest of the café.

And in the shirt of a man knocking on the glass door at the same time an email arrived from Mike, who had just landed in DC. She ignored the shirt, who was tapping his watch, and opened Mike's attachments. There was edited footage of his interview with Danilo Rojas and clips from the gunfight outside Cali Airport, as well as voiceover text summarizing the discoveries from Colombia.

The knocking on the glass became more insistent. The shirt had been joined by two others.

Bec yanked the door open.

'Can't you see I'm busy, you imbeciles. What the fricken hell do you want?'

'This room lady. We've had it booked for a week.'

'Well go find someplace else. I'm in the middle of something.'

Bec slammed the door in their faces, turned the lever to lock it, returned to the table.

She loaded Mike's video clips into the appropriate places in the sequence, incorporated his text into the master script, making one or two edits. She then recorded the missing voiceover sections, thankful for the room's soundproofing. The businessmen at the door were getting agitated, had been joined by three or four other customers.

Bec gave them a filthy look, then noticed an icon pulsing on her desktop. She'd been so consumed by the main story she'd missed notification that the drone had been activated.

She double-clicked the icon. The image screen was blank, but she could see from the progress bar along the bottom there were just under two minutes of footage. She dragged the dot back all the way left, hit the *play* arrow.

It took her a few moments to orient her view to the drone, hovering above the ground. Jay was perched on a ladder on the side of some sort of tank, two ferocious dogs snapping at his feet. He had his arms folded, like he was bored. A man entered the frame, pointing a rifle towards Jay. He said something Bec couldn't pick up over the barking of the dogs, then turned, aimed the rifle up at... Bec... the camera... the drone. His arm and shoulder jerked. The screen went black.

*****

Mike walked into the arrival hall at Reagan National on high alert, scanning the crowd for potential threats, faces out of place. Every casual glance felt like surveillance, until his eyes locked on Neil Scott. Would have been hard to miss him in the black suit and bow tie standing beside a chauffeur holding a suit bag.

He looked as if he'd aged five years since their meeting back in New York, when Mike had interviewed his son's three surfing buddies.

They shook hands.

'Thanks for meeting me, Mr. Scott.'

'Please, call me Neil. We haven't got much time. You'll need to change into these. I hope they fit.'

Mike relieved the chauffeur of the suit bag and went to the restroom. It was the first time he'd worn a tux. The guy in the mirror scrubbed up surprisingly well for someone who'd hardly slept in forty-eight hours.

Their ride was a glistening black Cadillac Escalade with all the bells and whistles. They took the George Washington Memorial, turning off the parkway to take the 395 across the Potomac. Mike was showing Mr. Scott the edited Danilo interview on his laptop when a motorcycle screamed up alongside them.

Mike swiveled just in time to see the pillion passenger yank a semi-automatic from his jacket and unleash directly at him. A staccato of bullets pummeled the window, but didn't break the glass. Before Mike knew what was happening, tires were screeching as the driver swerved across the path of the motorcyclist. There was a thump. Mike looked back to see the bike smashing into the side of the bridge, the rider and pillion cartwheeling over the railing.

'Nice driving Don. You OK, Mike?'

'What the… how did…?'

'Bullet-resistant glass. You kind of need the protection in my line of work.'

'Holy fuck. Seriously?'

Mike's heart was racing as they left the bridge and swung

right, between the Thomas Jefferson Memorial and a sign saying *Report Disabled Vehicles*. He was about to make a wisecrack, when he heard another motorcycle revving from behind.

He picked up his phone just in time to film the second volley of gunfire. The result was the same, except this time the bike ploughed through road cones, depositing the riders in a pile of gravel.

The driver looked at his passengers through the rearview mirror.

'Do we continue to the club, sir?'

Mr. Scott turned to Mike.

'Your call Mr. Bullard.'

Mike exhaled.

'My vote's yes. Let's confront this sucker.'

*****

The drone footage of Jay being captured – or worse – had catapulted Bec to the fringes of red. The appearance of Detective Robinson on the other side of the glass carried her over the precipice.

The video package was almost complete, but Aristotle was sneering at her feeble efforts like a red editor's pencil slashing through the candy apple lightshades, the burgundy doors of the stationery cupboard, the scarlet headscarf of the manager approaching the door with a set of keys.

Bec detonated, sending the chair crashing into the wall. She yanked open the stationery cupboard, her eyes seizing on a container of glue. She grabbed it, dashed for the door, arriving just before Robinson and the manager. She snapped off the lid and used both hands to squeeze the clear liquid all over the lock mechanism.

She marched back to the table, turning her back on the

throng behind the glass, which had had doubled in size and anger.

Her phone sounded. Country code 64. She hit *Accept.*

'I'm not sure I can take any more at the moment.'

'Am I speaking to Rebecca Corelli?'

It couldn't be the SwordPhish. There was a hint of Latin America in the voice.

'Yes. What do you want? I'm kind of busy at...'

'My name is Rodrigo Montoya.'

Bec was too stunned to speak.

'I have a message from your boyfriend. Publish one word of what you have, you will never see him again.'

The call ended.

Her phone chimed.

A message this time, with photo attached.

A macabre throwback to the days of the ISIS beheadings.

The image showed Jay kneeling on a concrete floor, gagged, hands behind his back. Standing over him was a man in a black balaclava holding a large machete.

The only difference was the logo on the wall behind Jay's head. The black and white Arabic scrawl of the Islamic State had been replaced by the black and yellow circle of the Kaluraha gang.

*****

Jay heard the siren just before Montoya's brother entered the cellar.

'Los tombos?'

The brothers had been talking mostly in English. Every now and then, Spanish words slipped into their conversations. Jay figured *tombos* was a Colombian phrase for police.

Not that Mauricio appeared concerned.

'Just the one patrol car.'

'How do you know?'

'Webcam. Above the Little Library.'

'Why now? How did they...?'

'The gunshot. You shouldn't have taken down that drone Rodrigo. People don't fire guns around here. One of the neighbors must have reported the shot.'

A bell sounded.

'That'll be the cops at the gate.'

'What's the plan?'

'Relax. I'll let them in. Tell them I was shooting a possum. The animals are public enemy number one with all the greenies. I've got a license for the rifle. It was on private property. Won't be a problem.'

'What if they search the place?'

Mauricio tilted his head toward Jay. 'Take him through to the vault, just in case.'

Jay was pulled to his feet, frog-marched up the stairs into the kitchen. Latin jazz music he'd been hearing dimly from the cellar spilled from a speaker beside the range hood. Rodrigo slid open the door to a walk-in pantry, reached under a shelf to push a button behind the toaster. The back wall of the pantry, stocked with cans of mango and guava and packets of achiote seeds, swung silently inwards.

Once through, Rodrigo pushed another button. The wall swung back into place.

They were in a white-tiled air-conditioned room Jay figured must be set into the hillside. Two walls were lined with glass-fronted commercial refrigerators, their shelves stacked with sealed bags of cocaine. The back wall resembled the *lab* in Uluwatu. A measuring scale, powder trays, rolls of latex, mixing blade, cartons of gloves and face masks. Shelves loaded with Bali guidebooks. And a wall-mounted screen, split to show live video from other rooms in the house, the gate, front door.

Mauricio was showing the two uniformed cops through the living room like a real estate agent.

There was no camera in the vault. Jay realized the jazz music had disappeared. The walls must be sound-proofed. Ideal place for an execution.

His eyes settled on the red-handled blade on one of the powder trays. He'd sensed a subtle change in Rodrigo's demeanor since the cops showed up. The bravado he'd flaunted after finding Jay up the water tank had slackened, ever so slightly.

'On your knees, over there with your back to the table.'

Jay guessed the cord binding his hands was going to be secured to the table leg, which was bolted to the floor. His window of opportunity was closing.

As he bent to kneel, the two cops appeared on the screen showing the front door. Mauricio had obviously convinced them they'd wasted their time. Rodrigo exhaled audibly. His grip on Jay's arm relaxed a fraction.

Jay shifted his weight to his right foot and mushroomed up from the crouch, jerking his shoulder into Rodrigo's chin, then spun to this right and drove his elbow into the arm holding the gun. It flew across the room, smashing through the door of one of the refrigerators.

Before Rodrigo could recover, Jay leapt forward, driving a knee into his groin, slamming his forehead onto the bridge of the nose. The Colombian slumped to the floor, screaming, clutching his balls.

Jay charged to the table, reached for the blade.

Rodrigo was groaning, trying to stand.

Jay maneuvered the blade to cut the cord binding his wrists.

Rodrigo had regained his feet. Blood streamed from his nose. He looked over at Jay, realized what he was doing. He hesitated, unsure whether to go for Jay or the gun.

He chose the latter.

Wrong decision.

As he reached through the broken door of the refrigerator for the gun, Jay launched at him, slamming his shoulder into Rodrigo's hunched back, and the guy's face through the glass.

By the time Rodrigo extricated himself, Jay had cut through the cord, removed two zip ties from the hem of his shirt. He used one to bind the dazed man's hands behind his back, the other to attach him to the table leg.

Jay stuffed a wad of bubble wrap into his mouth, was looking for some tape when he noticed movement on the monitor. Mauricio was in the kitchen, approaching the pantry.

*****

The National Republican Club was a five-level townhouse opposite the Capitol South Metro Station.

Mr. Scott's fortress on wheels pulled up outside. The initial shock on the valet's face was quickly – and comically – replaced by dead pan, as if greeting guests arriving in bullet-riddled vehicles was standard operating procedure.

'This is an invite-only function Mike, so you're my assistant tonight, alright?'

Mike hit *send* to email an update to Bec, with attached video of the attack on the Caddy, adjusted his bow tie, followed Mr. Scott through the green awning into the citadel of schmooze.

The doorman greeted the businessman like the billionaire he was. Ignored Mike like he didn't exist.

*****

Seeing Jay with the machete poised over his head had pushed

Bec across the line beyond red, beyond Aristotle, to a state where anxiety and thoughts and her worldview crystalized into hyperfocus like a futuristic television screen where the resolution was outside the scope of gigapixels. Editing dilemmas that moments earlier appeared insurmountable melted away as solutions materialized, the path ahead became obvious. Blindingly.

Her fingers waltzed over the keyboard, troubleshooting on the fly, re-ordering scenes, adding visual metaphors, tweaking transitions, cropping for impact, spontaneously choosing music to build or maintain the drama.

Even receiving Mike's jolting footage of the attack on Scott's car didn't faze her. Bec knew intuitively how to trim, where to slot it into the timeline, the perfect words to make it fit seamlessly into the video.

The momentum was pulverized by her phone's ringtone.

Country code 64. New Zealand.

Montoya.

She reached over, picked up the phone, gently, as if it was primed to explode.

Her thumb hovered over the *Accept* icon.

She closed her eyes, took a couple of deep breaths, tapped the screen.

It was Jay. He'd discovered the stash of cocaine.

'You should see it. Must be hundreds of millions worth.'

'But… are you… what about… where are you?'

'The Montoya's. Place called Mahurangi.'

The sound of shattering glass made her spin around.

Detective Robinson had used a chair to smash through the door of the meeting room.

Bec still had the phone in her hand.

'Can you film the stash?'

'Already have.'

'And email it to me?'

'Sure. Didn't know if you'd want a shot of the Montoya boys as well. One of them's not looking too…'

Jay's words trailed off as the phone was snatched from Bec's hand. She was hoisted from the chair, her hands pulled behind her back. The cuffs clicked closed, drowning the pinging sound of the incoming email icon on her laptop.

'I want this room cleared. Anyone not in here on police business, make yourself scarce. Immediately.'

The voice was deep, but female. Bec turned to see Detective Superintendent Hansen pushing through the crowd.

Her relief was short-lived.

'Have you read her rights, Detective Robinson? Let's do it by the book this time please.'

'Was just about to.'

Robinson began the blurb.

Bec wasn't sure whether to laugh, cry or scream.

'You've got to be fricken kidding me. We've just…'

'Save it for the judge, Corelli. Where was I? Anything you say will be recorded and may be given in evidence…'

'Shut the fuck up, Robinson.'

Bec looked across at Superintendent Hansen.

'Jay has just sent me footage… proof… evidence… call it what you want… of a massive stash of cocaine at the Montoya's place. Mahurangi.'

Hansen's brow furrowed.

'We know about Mahurangi, Ms. Corelli. We used the navigation app in the rental car to track Jay's… Mr. Duggan's movements to the peninsula. Officers found the car abandoned on Ridge Road and were searching the area for him when they heard a rifle shot nearby. They investigated, but were assured by the landowner he was using it for pest control.'

'But…'

Hansen put up her hand.

'I haven't finished. Because the officers were aware of Mr. Duggan's... background, they asked to search the house. The owner had no objection, was fully cooperative. There was no sign of Mr. Duggan. They are still searching the penin...'

'We haven't got time for this bullshit, Hansen. You want evidence, look at my laptop. Double click that drone icon.'

*****

Mike tailed Mr. Scott into the Presidential dining room. Chandeliers dripping crystals, candlelight flickering off polished mahogany, the hum of privilege and influence. Speeches had just wound up. Waiters were bringing out the desserts. The contrast between the ethnic, gender and age diversity of staff and the geriatric white males they were serving was striking.

Mr. Scott got several greetings from fellow squillionaires, as they were directed to a table near the rear. Mike spotted Garland backslapping at the top table, wedged between the party chairman and house minority leader.

The chairman rose, tapped his wine glass for silence, thanked the guest of honor for his *thought-provoking* speech.

'Mr. Garland has indicated he is happy to take questions.'

Mr. Scott was on his feet in a flash. He took a small, framed photo from his pocket, started weaving through tables towards the front of the room.

Necks turned.

Mike started discretely filming.

'I have something to show you, Mr. Garland.'

Murmurs grew.

Mike adjusted the zoom on his phone camera.

Mr. Scott reached the top table, handed the photo to Garland.

'That, sir, is my son, Charlie.'

Garland shifted a little in his chair.

'Fine looking boy. Looks like he's got his daddy's... sense of occasion.'

Mr. Scott's voice quivered.

'Charlie's dead, Mr. Garland. Killed in a surfing accident after snorting cocaine…

'I'm sorry for your…'

'… in Bali. Premium-quality cocaine produced in Colombia around 1995, shipped to Auckland, New Zealand for storage, smuggled into Bali in tourist guidebooks, packaged and sold under the brand NuNu – Cloud Nine – to unsuspecting people like my son. Any of this ringing bells for you, sir?'

The room fell silent.

Mike zoomed in on Garland's face. He swallowed, pinched the top of his nose.

Mr. Scott pounced.

'I'd like to introduce you to Mr. Mike Bullard, who has just flown in from Colombia. Stand up, Mike.'

Every head turned toward him.

'Mike is part of a special team that has been investigating the death of my son, following the trail of cocaine from Bali all the way to its source. All the way to you, Mr. Garland. The story is going to be published when, Mike?'

'It's pretty much ready to go live…'

'So, let's have it, Pedro. Straight up.'

32. Saddlebags

The phrases *fake news* and *sue your ass to hell and half of Georgia* spilling from his mouth were nothing more than default sounds. Reflex. The overwhelming thought pounding inside Ped Garland's head was *saddlebags*.

If Kate Hunter had been less selective regarding his reading list in Hays State, she would have discovered the book he borrowed – and read – the most was a novel by Tom Wolfe called A *Man in Full*. There was this scene, Wolfe called it a *workout session*. The main character – another larger-than-life self-made man from Atlanta – was so humiliated by loan officers from the bank that sweat spread from under his arms to join up at the sternum. Like saddlebags on a horse.

Ped looked past Mr. Scott, past the dumbstruck faces of the fair weathers who minutes earlier had been groveling to circle the wagons around their man but were now throwing him under the bus, to the journalist Bullard. The *workout artiste,* humiliating him not with debt columns, demands to sell the Gulfstream, but with the camera of a fucking iPhone.

The saddlebags were forming.

*****

Bec Corelli was not one for clichés, but if Jay's video of the stash at Mahurangi was the final piece of the puzzle, his shot of the Montoya brothers bound, gagged, and surrounded by mountains of cocaine was *the cherry on the top*.

Superintendent Hansen had cleared the meeting room, was ordering officers back to Mahurangi, as Bec put the finishing touches to the package.

Wide-eyed café customers were pressed three-deep against the glass.

Bec trimmed the last clip, adjusted the fade-to-black to match the end music, then clicked the video connection to full-screen mode.

Mike hadn't stopped smiling.

'We done?'

'We're done.'

'Let's do this.'

Epilogue: Calling it

The video, uploaded to the Aristotle YouTube channel, ended as it began. With Charlie Scott. From the GoPro footage in Bali to his framed photo in the hands of Pedro Garland.

Within seconds, the exposé was being shared across multiple platforms by Mike's network of influencers, unleashing an avalanche of views, comments, outrage.

But what propelled the video into a viral frenzy were the unexpected contributions of two young women – one who used to ditch school with her bestie and daydream about rockin' out together at the Garden; the other a teenager with half her head shaved and rods of steel through her nose.

From her parent's home in Milwaukee, Natalie Zhang, AKA the singer-songwriter known as NatZ, shared the video to her 150 million followers, laced with tags like UsedAndAbused, NotYourPuppet, RegretAndRedemption.

With a few keystrokes on her laptop, Nadia Zapora, AKA the Ciph, ordered a squad of bots to share, like and comment on the video, using fake profiles she'd created with pictures, bios, history of social media activity. After programing some of the bots to engage with unrelated content to throw-off YouTube's moderation algorithms. As the volume of shares exploded, the bot squad adapted and grew – as designed – to continue the momentum.

Other metrics were moving. The volume of donations to the Aristotle channel – and comments and suggestions for the team's next project – were threatening to crash the system.

As polling booths opened across the District of Colombia, the video had been viewed by every man and his dog.

Garland followed the exit polls from a cell in the basement of the Metropolitan Police headquarters less than a mile from the White House. The networks, even Fox, were calling it a 19-0 slam-dunk for Kate Hunter before midday. She had the numbers to become the Republican Party's candidate for President.

Acknowledgements

Researching, writing, and publishing a novel is a team effort. Thanks to everyone who gave helpful advice during several trips to Bali; especially Wayan, and some of the drivers who must have wondered why I wanted them to take me to places on the island few tourists visit. To former colleagues whose knowledge and shared experiences during my years in journalism and politics were invaluable as I crafted the thoughts and actions of Bec, Mike, Jay, and Pedru Garland. Thanks also to friends who kindly allowed their names to be used for characters. Most of all to my wife Sue for her unwavering support, advice, patience, and love.

Any errors are my own.

If you enjoyed the adventure, tell a friend, rate or review the book on Goodreads, or check out my other novels at:

www.geoffreyrobert.com

**Want to know what Bec, Jay and Mike got up to before
The Ghost Shipment?
Check out Geoffrey Robert's pulsating thriller...**

FINDING FABI

When brilliant but emotionally-tortured New York journalist Bec Corelli learns her father has died mysteriously on vacation in India, she walks out on her job and heads to Delhi.

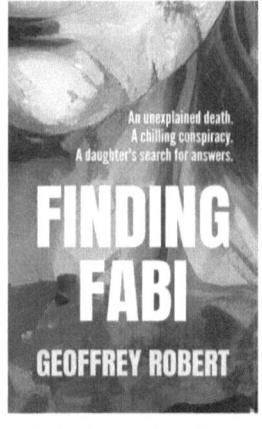

Pharmaceutical CEO Ernst Reiniger, facing ruin over a failed drug, has hatched a chilling plan to save his 300-year-old family company. With a lethal virus decimating the Mexican resort city of Cabo San Lucas and threatening a global pandemic more deadly than Covid, Reiniger has the inside running on producing a vaccine.

As Bec chases leads across India, supported by blogger Mike Duggan and New Zealand eco-warrior Jay Duggan, she is confronted by powerful forces determined to stop her discovering the truth about her father.

For more details, go to:

www.geoffreyrobert.com

Intrigued to learn more
about the backstory of **Jay Duggan**?
Check out Geoffrey Robert's debut thriller...

THE ALO RELEASE

Nine days before the global release
of a genetically-modified seed coating
set to make starvation history, the IT
advisor for an environmental group
receives a cryptic email from an old
friend working for the seed
corporation. The email triggers a frantic
manhunt from the glass towers of Los
Angeles to the towering rainforests of
New Zealand as the corporation's
security chief tries to track down and
silence the English IT advisor and his colleagues – an
American biologist and Kiwi eco-warrior, **Jay Duggan**.

As the clock ticks down to the much-anticipated and highly
stage-managed release of the coated seeds, the trio are pitched
against ruthless corporate thugs, law enforcement agencies,
politicians, journalists and bloggers... and the overwhelming
weight of world opinion as they race to unravel the truth
behind the email.

For more details, go to:
www.geoffreyrobert.com